How we buried Puso

How we buried Puso

MORABO MOROJELE

First published in 2006 by Jacana Media (Pty) Ltd.
10 Orange Street
Sunnyside, 2092
Johannesburg
South Africa

ISBN 1-77009-098-3
    978-1-77009-098-9

Cover design by Michiel Botha
Set in Sabon 11/14
Printed by Paarl Print

See a complete list of Jacana titles at www.jacana.co.za

This book is dedicated to the memory of my late mother, Lindiwe Caroline Nkepile Morojele (nee Ngakane), artist, intellectual, humanist, freedom activist, mother and friend, with whom I shared books until her last days.

For my children Naleli Mpho Soledad and Djibraeel Pako Lionel.

Thanks to Kgotso Schoeman, Thulani Grenville-Gray,
Tim Mc Donald, the Voice boys, Hlaks Mokoteli,
Michael Lewis (for the music), Lungile Ngakane,
Gael Reagon, Thandi "Bling Bling" Mphahlele, Angela C
and all my siblings, who remained despite...

*The language of the present
will not undo our memories
of the future.*

One

My brother's death has been the only thing to bring me home in seven years. His coffin stands in the front room, its polished handles bronzed and gleaming in the mid-morning sun. Tomorrow, we will put him to earth.

Since I arrived by taxi in the early hours of the morning, I have met too many half remembered aunts, uncles, gleaming children of shining cousins, and not knowing their names, or who saved me, or who even I saved from a quick and intimate moment of despair, it has been easier to remain here at the relatively quiet front of this house.

In the dusty yard at the back of the house, the men and women have divided themselves into work groups. The men cluster around a carcass, shouting instructions to each other on the finer details of its disembowelment. Women stand around them holding enamel vessels to carry away the stomach, tripe and other choice offal, which after duly cleaning they will prepare and serve later to the people come to prepare for tomorrow's funeral. The carcass will be hung to dry overnight. The women will wake up early tomorrow morning to carve it and cook it and prepare to serve it to those returned from the funeral.

Others work at preparing the vegetables and starch to go with the meat in huge black three-legged pots rested on wood fires. An asthmatic woman in a florid green dress starts the refrain of a well-worn hymn. She is interrupted by the bolder voice of a dark and broad woman of about thirty-five years who walks up and down amongst the women busy at their tasks. In the manner the woman commands the others to work faster or to fetch things from the house, she is clearly no stranger to this homestead.

The four-room home I shared with my brother, Grandmother and the woman firmly in charge of preparations for the funeral is situated at the centre of one of the oldest townships of our capital city. It stands not far from the arterial road that runs through the township and served for us almost as rivers might do for other villages in other far away places, carrying goods, people, news and sometimes, even the detritus of war.

An early childhood pastime those many years ago was to identify the names and models of approaching vehicles as they belched their way up the corrugated road that ran up the spine of our township. There were few cars in our township so that, after a while, the game lost its appeal. But at Christmas or on the occasion of other extended holidays, we would gather excited along its length to spot the sometimes new and gleaming, but usually old but well-spruced second-hand, vehicles of clearly successful neighbours returned from the country neighbouring ours.

Located at the firm centre of a large yard, our house was guarded on the one side by a line of five single rooms standing shoulder to shoulder and rented out by Grandmother to supplement her late husband's teacher's pension and what remained of our parents' will. A pit latrine and tap serviced the transient occupants of these rooms, mainly single working men new to town, young nurses and teachers, and once, for a short time, a loud woman who had too many visitors for Grandmother's liking.

A tall hedge that was more symbolic than real protection against anyone or anything that might have wanted to come in marked the rest of the yard. We used to throw stones at the large rats that would run along its length. At the bottom of the yard, a rusty wire gate I never remember being closed hung open to the street.

Like every other yard in the neighbourhood, ours had proud peach trees that would shout the arrival of spring in bright pink and white blossoms. Plucked and consumed fresh from the top of the trees, or dried or processed into jam or pureed and preserved in large syrupy containers to be opened by Grandmother for our Sunday meal, peaches were then always part of our diet. Between the peach trees, Grandmother tended leafy cabbages, patches of sweet carrots, bright-red tomatoes and maize that grew tall and swished in the wind.

I remember the first time the woman who was now managing preparations for my brother's funeral arrived to live with us. I was woken one night by the bark of our dogs and the slow approach of a car. Grandmother had shuffled to the door that leads on to the stoep and responded in a quiet "Who is that?" to the quick rap on the door. She unlocked the door and I heard the scuffle of shoes on the wooden floor as the visitors entered the room.

"Puso, Puso," I whispered to my brother sleeping above me in the top bed of the double bunk we shared. No response forthcoming, I slipped out of bed and walked to the door that separated our room from the kitchen, choosing my way carefully to avoid the floorboards that would squeak and give me away. Yellow slivers of light shot through the thin gaps between the panels of the door as Grandmother lit the paraffin lamp on the table in the next room. I could feel heat from the old coal stove in the kitchen slowly spread across my chest as I approached the door. Through the panels of the door, I saw Grandmother with her back to me standing at the near end of the kitchen table. Opposite her and partially obscured by her broad back was a young girl sitting on a chair, a blanket drawn close around her against the cold of winter and the unknown perils of nocturnal travel. I could barely make out her dark face hidden in the shadows of the room, but when she quietly began to sob, I saw a fast glisten of tears sliding down her face.

I peered at the faces of the two men in the room. Tall and black in the shadows of their jackets, there was nothing familiar about them. They pulled chairs from the table and sat down. As one of them began to speak, swallowing and biting his words with the hardness of a stranger speaking an unfamiliar language, I knew they were not from these parts.

"We had trouble with the car. We should have arrived here a long time ago," he offered.

The other man chipped in, "I hope you received the letter from her father who is my brother. Thank you for keeping her." Groping inside his heavy coat he continued, "Here is a little money for her until he can send more. This is for her keep and to pay for a school for her."

Grandmother reached across to take the folded bills. "How old are you?" she asked the girl, in our language. The girl lifted her head and answered barely audibly, "I have fifteen years." Her voice had the same lilting accent as the men.

"She will sleep on one of the boys' beds tonight," Grandmother said, turning and pointing to the door I stood shivering behind. "Tomorrow, I'll see what I can make up for her."

I quietly bolted and made my way to my bed, sure that Grandmother would burst in at any time. Ears straining, I made out snatches of their conversation, Grandmother offering tea which was declined, the men promising to carry greetings to the girl's family and then final salutations between the whistle of the wind as the front door opened, the men shuffled out, and the door closed quickly behind them.

Our dogs began to bark again and others in neighbouring yards replied as the car started. In the next room, I could hear the faint convulsions of the girl left behind and Grandmother's voice, softened from a harsh interrogator of men sent by what I assumed to be distant relatives, to Grandmother, as I knew her, entreating and placating as she consoled the girl.

Grandmother quietly opened the door to our room and shook me to wake me. "Come 'Lefe," she whispered using the diminutive to my name Molefe, "wake up and join your brother. There's someone to use your bed."

Feigning half-sleep, I asked who would be sleeping in my bed, which she promised to tell me the following day. I climbed into my brother's bed and used knees and elbows to force a space for myself. I was tempted to wake him, but then thought of how tomorrow he would envy my solitary witness of the night's unusual goings on.

Eyes half closed, I peered at the now silent girl in the faint light as she looked around the room, removed the blanket from her shoulders and slipped into the still warm bed below. Grandmother whispered a few last words to her and shuffled out of the room, her familiar musty smell lingering behind her. The girl turned a few times but was quickly asleep. Once, much later, I heard the door leading from our room to the yard open and saw her squat quickly in the sand to relieve herself.

By the time I woke, little refreshed from hollow dreams and an eventful night, I could see from the light soaking through the white sack of maize meal Grandmother had fashioned into a curtain that it was well into the morning. Running my eyes around the room, I saw it orderly and tidy the way Grandmother insisted and Puso's bed below stern and made up. Outside I could hear the dogs barking as they ran around my brother who was throwing a ball against a wall.

He stopped his game and turned towards me as I walked out into the yard. "Did you see the girl who came last night? Why didn't you wake me? Grandma says she is our relative and will be staying for a long time. I've told her I'm not sharing my bed with you, and Grandmother said we have to get a new bed." He pushed at the dogs climbing at his chest.

I stared at him through half-open eyes, acutely aware of how it must feel to be a nocturnal animal stranded in the glare of the midday sun.

"She's fifteen years old, and she'll be going to school here. She's at the front of the house. Let's go and talk to her."

We found the girl hanging out washing on a line stretched between two peach trees. At first she did not notice us but continued to bend to the bright red bucket at her feet, to lift out a piece of wet clothing and drape it on the line, hooking a peg at each end. She was singing a soft song in a vaguely familiar language, but my brother and I stood there silent and enchanted by the simple rhythm of this act.

She suddenly noticed us and looked up and smiled a nervous smile. "My name is Thembi," she said in a shy voice. My brother, always fast to everything, had already told her his name, how old he was, what grade he was in school. "You can call him by his nickname, 'Lefe if you want," he said pointing at me and skipping away to a tree.

"You, how old are you?" Thembi asked, her eyes wide and shimmering in the light. I lowered my gaze unable to speak, and Thembi's soft laugh chasing behind me, turned and ran to the house and Grandmother, hoping she could explain this delightful new intrusion into our lives.

In all the years Thembi lived with us, she only ever once returned to where she came from, a letter the reason for her departure. I had gone as usual at the end of the month to collect mail from 'Me Thuso's trading store that also served as our post office. Collecting the mail was a ritual I keenly relished.

'Me Thuso's shop was a general dealership with a more expansive array of goods than available in the many cafés in our township. The shop was a square well-organised room with a large door framed by unchanging displays that looked onto the street on one side, blankets, hats and clothes draped in plastics at the back, a hardware section of nails and pockets of cement and a few bicycles opposite the door and a large counter behind which 'Me Thuso sat. On shelves behind her were items of grocery, candles, boxes of matches, tins of pilchards and corn beef, bars of soap neatly stacked and plastics with sweets and little packets of peanuts. To one side of the counter was a large steel trolley of bread delivered every day and beside it, bottles and hand pumps for the paraffin that flowed into the room through a pipe linked to the large container outside. An old man in a grey dustcoat who was not her husband roamed about the shop, mainly to prevent pilfering, but also to sometimes show items of clothing, bicycle tyre repair kits and the other hardy goods to the few who ever wanted them. The old man also poured paraffin and wrote out receipts to be handed to the men in the coal yard at the back of the shop. These were two soot-blackened men who spent their whole day shovelling coal into burlap sacks.

Arriving at the shop, 'Me Thuso would first hand me four brittle sweets, two for myself and two for Puso for the cents I would give her and then hand over the shoe box in which the mail was kept.

I would perch myself on the shaded stoep at the front of the store, unwrap a sweet and pop it into my mouth and then begin to go through the mail.

Two or three letters always stood out because they had colourful stamps from countries like Helvetica and UAE that I had never been able to find on the map of the world hung crookedly in the staff room at school. These letters boasted clear, square handwriting almost like in books. They were all addressed to J. Mosala who would always collect them long after I would have told him there was mail for him at the store.

J. Mosala, who was more commonly known as Abuti Jefti, had been overseas to study and I, like all the kids in the neighbourhood, had been enthralled by the stories he used to tell when he first arrived, about aeroplanes, and large cities full of white people who also cleaned streets and collected garbage and were poor. Grandmother didn't like us talking to Abuti Jefti. He was a drunk and a no good she said. But we continued to because he would sometimes let us keep the change when we returned from buying him long cold beers from the little house where they were kept in a paraffin fridge, where the loud music never ever seemed to stop. Abuti Jefti was a teacher at a secondary school belonging to one of the denominations, but he always seemed to have more money than the other teachers. Nobody knew where Abuti Jefti got his extra money from, but someone once said he had married a rich white woman overseas.

At the shop, 'Me Thuso never threw the old mail away and the shoebox usually held numerous letters I would have seen many times in my many mail runs. The old letters in brown or cheap pastel-coloured envelopes, sat smudged and dog-eared at the one end the box. The oldest letter I ever saw was more than a year old, but after months of sitting there unclaimed, it was one day simply gone.

I always wondered whom the old letters were for and why they had not been collected. Many were addressed in barely legible writing that sloped across them, or with lettering that had obviously required great effort and concentration in scripting. I wondered what news they carried, whether they brought news of marriages and children, death and desertion, or the simple greetings of people whose lives proceeded without too much mishap. I mused that even if these letters were not collected, the weddings and funerals and births happened anyway, and those who were supposed to know, now knew whatever was to be known through some other means. Or maybe it was somehow a good thing that they did not know, because perhaps in not knowing they were saved from knowing something terrible.

These thoughts were the body and the blood of my ritual visits to the store, and I would return home chastened, the shuffle of my walk more tenuous, resolved to be kinder to friends and neighbours whose fathers, mothers or siblings were across, over there, in the country neighbouring ours, from where these many letters arrived.

Once, out of a hotter than usual curiosity to know what kind of news these unclaimed letters held, I stole an old, forgotten missive under my sleeve and, guilty like a thief, hid away to read it. To this day, I recollect it like a well-remembered photograph.

It was dated 7 August 1972 and started...

Dear Adelina,

I greet you my sister with all my love. I trust that you and the children are all well, and that you remain at the warm breast of God. Here, I am well, though the news contained in this letter is not good.

The letter continued, now more illegible as if frightened by the calamity of the message it conveyed...

I regret to inform you about the grave illness of your husband. Over the past few months, your husband's health has deteriorated to the point that he is now in hospital. The doctors say he does not have long to live. When he first fell ill, we took him to a traditional doctor as is our custom, but he continued to get worse despite the large amounts of money we gave to the big Nyasa doctor.

We eventually had no choice but to take him to the hospital where he remains. His condition is very bad. He has lost a lot of weight, coughs much and passes blood in his water. His body is covered all over in sores that cause him much irritation and pain.

Dear sister, by this letter I am imploring you to rush here quickly to see your husband who I am afraid does not have much longer to live. He also urgently wants to see you and to talk about the children and what to do with the things at home.

The letter ended quickly...

Please try to come as soon as possible. I am still living at the old place, so you should have no problem finding me. If you have trouble with money, show this letter to 'Me Thuso at the store there and ask for her help. She has always been a true friend of the family.

With all my love to the family,

Your sister,

'Ma Paseka

The message in the letter staggered me as if I had been hit a blow in the chest, and I had ran blindly through the back streets of our township. Eventually, tired of eyes that seemed to stare in alarm at my stumbling retreat, I had found a hidden path near the stream that winds its way to the lake at the bottom of our township, where I collapsed exhausted, my legs sore, my face a muddy canvas of dirt and tears.

I had read the letter over and over again, as if in doing so I could undo the shame of this reckless act, or perhaps even undo the death it spoke of. Addressed without a surname, I scoured my memory to remember who was called Adelina in our township and remembered a proud woman who lived some distance from us. She did have two children, and her man, like many others did work in the country neighbouring ours. But there was no way I could be certain this letter was meant for her. Adelina was a common enough name. As I already knew, white people here were too deceitful to learn people's local names, and insisted that they use what they termed Christian names. Where they did not have Christian names, they were simply and randomly allocated them, names like Columbus and Abednigo for the boys and Francina and Chrisentia for the girls. There could well have been many Adelinas in our township.

I had not know what to do, whether to take the letter to woman called Adelina I knew, or to acknowledge my guilt and return it to 'Me Thuso and bear whatever might be the consequences of the act. I had looked at the date on the letter again. Seven months had passed since it had been written. Surely another message must have come to Adelina since then, I thought. If not, what would taking this letter to her now do to her and whatever was her life? Her husband must surely have died by now, and if she did not know this, somehow it seemed terribly wrong that I, a half-remembered young boy from the neighbourhood, should be the bearer of such tragic news. If she still did not know, perhaps there was some comfort in that, and until she did eventually find out, maybe Adelina would be happy, or happy to the extent that a woman can be who awaits even a simple message that just says, "I am alive, and trust my children are well."

In the end, I threw the letter into a small fire burning waste from a nearby house.

Of course Grandmother never understood why I volunteered my brother for the next mail collection. She had insisted that I go, and it was with heavy legs that I had walked that reluctant half-mile to the store. 'Me Thuso had looked her normal self and had duly and cheerfully handed me the four sweets of the ritual and the box containing old letters at the one end and the new at the other. This time I did not commence my search at the old end of the box. Instead I started where the clean, recently arrived letters were kept, picked out envelopes addressed to Thembi and to Grandmother, and stopped abruptly at the first old letter I remembered from the previous time. 'Me Thuso was a little surprised at how quickly I had finished, and said as if to save me from myself, "Ah, the years are flying and you are growing up. Soon you won't be collecting letters but sending them, eh?"

I ran home and placed Thembi's letter in the cupboard in the kitchen where she kept her private things, a few pictures of her family, her clothes and blankets and a basket of straw with her few vanities, a deep-red lipstick, a plastic comb, a toothbrush and toothpaste, some body lotion, and a few necklaces and bits of fake jewellery.

I had not been at home when Thembi returned from school, thanks to another errand to the shops for Grandmother. Grandmother truly believed that being named after her late husband bestowed on me the dubious honour of being the first and sometimes only one between my brother and I to do her bidding. I hated the way she always called me to go to the shops, to fetch this or that from some far-flung corner of the yard, to accompany her to hospital on the days of her check-ups, and always with a perfect timing, when I would be in the middle of an enthralling play time activity with friends or alone at a secret and favourite pursuit. It seemed her voice could cut through any sound, travel any distance to find me.

But in all fairness, running for Grandmother sometimes had its compensation, for I remember also the sweet privilege of the first taste of her peaches lovingly dried in the sun, or the change I would sometimes get to keep on returning from the shops, or the hot vinegar-soaked bag of chips she would buy me from the Portuguese café on our trips into town.

"Did you get your letter," I stammered to Thembi, rushing

into the kitchen. Still in her school uniform, she had looked at me as if without seeing me and stalked out of the room into the yard. I heard my brother's half-broken voice call from the kitchen, "Molefe, come here and leave Thembi alone."

"What's the matter with Thembi?" I had asked, walking into the kitchen.

"Thembi is leaving tomorrow."

"Why? Where to?" I stammered, "When will she be back?"

Grandmother stood up and shuffled towards me. "Thembi will be back. There are things she has to do where she is from." I was only to learn the reason for Thembi's departure many years later.

Those years rush back at me now, as I look at Thembi, the centre of preparations for the rituals for my brother's interment. Dismissing a woman asking for money for more provisions, she calls me, "Come my brother, let's talk you and I." She approached me wiping the palms of her hands against the towel fastened firmly around her broad hips.

"It's been a long time hasn't it? Come, let me make you some tea and we can talk a while." She grabbed my hand and gently pulled me towards the house. We entered the front room, which was curtained against the glare of the midday sun. The furniture was pushed back against itself to give space for my brother's coffin on a low table against a wall. Thembi shouted to someone in the kitchen, "Hey you in there, please make some tea for us. And call my daughter so that Molefe can know her."

Apart from the slight rearrangement of the furniture to accommodate a few of Thembi's things and the coffin, the front room was exactly as I remembered it. Against a corner was a heavy imbuia sideboard with sliding glass, behind which fragile porcelain figurines, miniature cups and saucers, ornaments of copper and the odd photograph were displayed. Three heavy ball and claw armchairs stood gathered around a low table on which was a light blue vase with faded plastic flowers, on top of a pink crocheted tablecloth. At one corner of the room stood a kist in which Grandmother used to store her best linen and bedclothes that were only ever taken out when we had important visitors. In an opposite corner sat a gramophone, still and firmly shut as it almost always was, except on those odd occasions when Grandmother would dust off her few records and sit tearfully to the plaintive melodies of Jim Reeves or Brook Benton.

I new Thembi was going to hint at difficult things, like why I hadn't made it home when Grandmother passed away or why I come to write so rarely, except to send cards with pictures of snow at Christmas. She caught me staring at the wooden-framed black and white photograph of Grandmother and her husband, then freshly married, hanging at a tilt on the wall above the coffin.

"Your Grandmother asked for you when she died. You know you were always her favourite. Still, her heart would have been broken if she were here now. Your brother was much too young to leave us."

I looked at the coffin. Inside it was my brother who I had not seen for seven years. Later tonight, it would be opened and the old people would gather around it to sing hymns and pray before, tomorrow, it was finally put into the ground. I did not know if I wanted to see my brother's broken face or to see how the years might have changed him. Maybe it would be better if I remembered him as I had last seen him, however vague and faded that memory might be.

Thembi glanced at the clock near the picture of my grandparents. "Look 'Lefe," she said, "I know you must be tired, but you must go to your brother's wife's place. It is not far from the border. My little one will show you where it is."

"Please try and convince her she must be here for the wake tonight. She only wants to come tomorrow. You can use your uncle's van. It's the white one, parked outside the gate."

I was aware my brother's parting from his wife had been acrimonious, but never imagined it had come to this, especially because, in all his letters, he had always been at pains to explain how she was not like other foreigners here. He had always referred to her by the name she was given on their wedding, 'MaTsepo, mother of their son Tsepo.

A young girl holding a tray of tea entered the room. She put the tray down between us and stared demurely at the floor, one dusty leg coiled around the other.

"This is my daughter, Molefe. Thandeka, greet Uncle Molefe."

The girl greeted me in the plural used in addressing an elder or to show respect. She had her mother's dark complexion and strong legs.

"Thandeka, please go with your Uncle Molefe and show him Palesa and Tsepo's house." Still staring at the floor, the girl left the room to fetch her shoes.

We sat silent and self-conscious as we sipped our tea. This was probably one of the few times we would have alone together for the next few days and though we might have talked about my brother, Grandmother and Thembi and her child and their life here at home, or my long absence, somehow we both knew that, for now, the unsaid would speak so much more for the years that had passed.

Thembi handed me the van keys as I stood up. With a heavy sigh, she led me out of the room in to the yard. "What can we say, my brother? Life is sad, not so?"

For a brief moment I stared at the squat mountains across the valley where we stood, and remembered how, the sun lowering between them in the late afternoon, this spot on the front porch had been a favourite place to end the day. Grandmother and Thembi would be busy with the coal stove and preparations for the evening meal. My gregarious brother would be out on the streets somewhere at some last entertainment. I would watch neighbours alight from buses at the end of our road and greet our tenants as they trafficked from the gate to their rooms at the back of the house.

As if on cue, as the bats would flit out from between the ceiling and the corrugated-iron roof of our house, Grandmother would call to send me to the café or butchery to buy salt or meat or paraffin for the night.

Later, my brother dusty and home from the streets, we

would quickly wash. Grandmother would then remind me to call our tenants in for the evening prayer. Though they complained, evening prayer in the main house was as obligatory as the weekly rent. Fetching them, I took great pleasure in rudely entering their rooms with barely a knock, where I would inevitably catch them in some state of undress, or embarrassed at the opened beer bottles gathered on the floor around their legs, which Grandmother did not allow.

One tenant, an irritated middle-aged single man would always come slightly inebriated, and my brother and I would battle to contain our giggles at his resolute but sometimes unsuccessful attempts to remain upright through Grandmother's long and sombre petitions to God.

Thembi would then warm our evening meal, which would overpower our tenants' various odours and we would sit down at the kitchen table to eat. Afterwards, we would help Thembi dry the dishes she would wash in a round bowl on the kitchen table. We would then all of us quietly sit around the table, Thembi, Puso and I doing our homework and Grandmother peering at her well-thumbed bible.

Grandmother finally withdrawn to her room, Thembi would often then regale us with vaguely ribald stories about her schoolmates or one or the other of our various neighbours. Every now and then, she would burst into a jig as the radio perched precariously on the windowsill scratched out a favourite song. Over the years, she developed a cast of characters she would always talk about, either in envy at their adolescent charisma or in feigned disgust at their various scandals. As for our tenants, they were her greatest victims, and Grandmother would shout to us from her bedroom to be quiet and go to bed as my brother and I would burst out in laughter at Thembi's perfect mimicry of how they walked or talked.

Alone at last, Thembi would pour herself steaming water from the big kettle on the coal stove and wash for the night. Once, after a particularly descriptive story about the woman tenant of the high heels, torn stockings and too many visitors, and curious to see what Thembi looked like underneath her clothes, I treaded my way to the door that separated our room from the kitchen to peer at her as she washed.

She was standing naked in a bucket of steaming water, her back to me. A cloth in hand, she bent to scoop water from the bucket and her abundant black buttocks tautened behind her like two separate beasts. Her breasts stretched and hung below the curve of her armpits. As she rose to lather herself the bar of soap slipped from her hand and slid across the floor behind her. With a quick shrug of her broad shoulders, she turned and lifted a foot out of the bucket to retrieve it. As she turned, I saw the hair of the dark cleft between her legs, thick and wild and glistening with beads of water and not at all like the hair on her head.

Now almost directly facing me, she proceeded to apply more soap and water, first in between her legs, and then onto her strong legs and ankles. She then began to rinse herself, whispering a song as she did so and then dried herself with an old towel. Finished she reached for petroleum jelly in a red and white jar, which she liberally applied to her body until she gleamed in the yellow light of the paraffin lamp on the table. Finally, dressed in a faded sleeping thing, her hair quickly combed and a scarf tightly fastened around her head, she opened the front door, lifted the bucket of water and walked out to spill it into the yard.

From that day on, my image of Thembi was never the same again. From a slightly older adopted sister, overnight she became the bright light of my awakening sexuality and the shadow of its fear of things only guessed at. I came to measure everything by her. When friends at school pressed a girlfriend on me, selected for me on what basis I did not know, perhaps her height, or perhaps because she, like me, always remained at the periphery of the group and needed to be reigned in, or perhaps simply because she was friend to their girlfriends, the image of Thembi's nakedness would confront their choice, and I would only half-heartedly agree. When with others I would sneak to our break-time refuge behind the school toilets, and arms wrapped around the new incumbent would extend my tongue to wrestle with hers in a pit of saliva, it was the idea of Thembi's tongue, her breath, the roundness of her breasts, the imagination of the rising odour of her body that would assault my senses.

And when alone once, much later, with a girl behind the toilets, I was savagely hurled to the ground by a fire that rose from the base of my spine to explode for the first time in my loins, it was to Thembi I had run from the surprise and then cackling ridicule of the girl who was cause of it. Yet once at home, my pants congealed with my half-dried first issue and my eyes glistening with knowledge and fear, I had not known what to say to her and had turned instead to my brother who danced a dance around me in celebration of my adolescence.

As far as I knew, Thembi was never aware that my staring at her through the door as she washed became as much a part of my daily evening pattern as dinner, prayer and schoolwork around the kitchen table. My brother caught me once and threatened to tell, but soon forgot and was anyway always quick to fall asleep. In any case, Thembi had moved soon after into one of the outhouses and I was never again to have such unashamed access to the sight of her bold breasts or to the uncertain dark between her legs.

"Why are you laughing?" Thembi asked as we walked towards the gate at the end of the yard. Blushing, I replied, "I'm not laughing at anything. I'm just thinking back to you and Grandmother and Puso and me in this house before I left."

"There was nothing wrong in your leaving. Everybody leaves at some point," she replied, her eyes fixed firmly at the distant mountains. "I also went away and came back. You should have come back earlier, that's all. Anyway, never mind, we'll talk about it later."

She called out for her daughter who came skipping to the van and jumped in beside me.

Driving through the streets that led from our house to the main road to town, I looked at the houses which all used to be so perfectly familiar. Amongst them, the few of clearly recent construction stood proud in red brick or stone with well-trimmed gardens with flowers and vegetables and enclosures for the chickens and even sheds for the odd milk cow. However, most of the houses were ramshackle old structures held together by mud and wire, their roofs weighed down by rocks, scrap metal and old tyres against the strong winds that would come sweeping down from the mountains. I passed the house of a childhood friend and immediately spotted his lean and angular form amongst the men and women huddled under a tree in consumption of home-brewed beer. He raised a wasted hand in recognition but I looked away and hurried the van down the rutted road. How were we to connect the many years between us and the obviously different trajectories our lives had taken? I knew he would be offended at my inevitable disinclination to participate in the passing of the frothing jug of warm beer. I in turn would be embarrassed by his quickly gathered recollections of my departure for Europe, and the way he would inevitably, obsequiously address me "White Man" as a prelude to telling me about hard times and asking for money.

Like so many other towns in poor countries such as ours, the village clustered together to form our nation's capital is the outcome of colonial planning. Our former masters never imagined that the single thoroughfare named in usual fashion after a royal of the time might one day need to serve a far larger population of vehicles and people, or that state administration might require a smarter design and location of police stations, passport offices, departments of agriculture and such. Things did not improve much with independence and our town is now a place of half-completed infrastructure projects, their funds siphoned off by keen politicians, of congested and potholed streets ruled by uncouth taxis, of too many people in insufficient space and a few well-hidden quarters where our satisfied managers and their foreign advisors lived behind tall hedges and "Beware of the Dog" signs.

Along our capital's single central thoroughfare stand a garish mix of chain stores, cheap retail outlets, decrepit government buildings and aspirant business complexes. On the pavements, hawkers sit beneath smoke-billowing stalls and compete to sell dumplings, boiled corn, fruit and such, plastic and metal combs, nail clippers, small pots, paraffin stoves, all artfully displayed. At almost calculated distances between them, men shout their herbs and potions will cure all misfortune: bad luck in relationships, unemployment, poor success at exams, a weak penis.

At its southern end, the thoroughfare spills into what serves as a bus station and market. Large buses contest for space and custom, horns blaring the exultant music of homebound migrant workers, their destinations deep in the mountain interior of the country.

At the more civil middle of our capital's main road, Thandeka and I passed a hotel that used to be a favourite Friday and Saturday night haunt. My brother Puso, then at the beginning of virtuous employment, had spent many hours there and had always been good for a few rounds of beer for his younger brother. I would sit uncomfortably amongst his foreign friends and their local counterparts, their shirt collars sullied from the dust of the streets, their florid ties askew, as they would debate, with the free-at-last aggression of Friday night, the funding of the latest government project or the misdemeanours of some errant politician. Occasionally, emboldened by alcohol and to embarrass my brother whose voice was always too loud and sure, I would interject to sabotage their discourse. Later, humbled but still disgruntled, I would follow him and his friends to a party where no longer able or willing to understand their jokes or to dance, I would inevitably and to my brother's secret delight, collapse hopeless in some back room.

Opposite the hotel, I saw the run-down government complex where I had worked briefly as a trainee journalist. When three months into the job, a newly appointed minister had come to our offices to advise that those of us without party cards would be dismissed, I had been relieved that my scholarship had come through, and that I was to leave in a few months for Europe. In the event, those of my colleagues with keener survival instincts had applied for party membership, whilst the others who had not had paid the price.

My brother though employed elsewhere had also applied for a card and over the years had risen rapidly in the ranks of the parastatal where he worked, until just before his death, he had achieved the exalted position of Deputy Chief Executive. In fact the last communication I was to receive from him was to inform me of this, as well as of his separation a few months earlier from the woman I was on my way to meet.

At the northern perimeter of our capital city is the muddy river that is the border between us and the country neighbouring ours. It winds down many kilometres from the central highlands, where first a chain of white tributaries, it rushes down steep and narrow gorges, scouring its banks of what is left of the soil, until now the dirty colour of fresh mud, it calms down and passes our city as it heads off to the distant sea.

This river is not a great river. There are mightier rivers deep in the country that flush with the torrential rains of summer, carry away cattle, foolish men and even whole vehicles laden with provisions for delivery to far-flung settlements scattered about the highlands. But this river carries a particular meaning, standing as it does as the barrier to work and opportunity to the north and as the last obstacle to a place of refuge and a freedom of sorts to people escaping the predatory history of these parts.

I had crossed this river earlier today, tired, my eyes grainy and bloodshot, my clothes dishevelled after hours of rude travel, first in a train speeding under the ground, then by plane, and then finally by long-haul taxi, from cold, wet Europe to this disconsolate place in Africa.

My senses had been deeply offended by the shock of arriving at home. I was shocked first by the sky with its almost pointless enormity and the spiteful brilliance of the sun at its flaming centre. I knew that later, at night, the whistle of thousands of brilliant, brilliant stars, so close you could almost brush your ears about them would throw me about. I had then been affronted by the many, many people simply standing about, and awaiting the cross-border taxi to take me home, I had anticipated a riot, looting or some demonstration and held my bags firmer. But the real shock of so many people was in recognising them as if they were all relatives or friends, or people I had become acquainted to through the routine doings of daily living. I had stared at the men, their pants hung low in a manner of dress that had changed but could not hide a fundamental structure of bone and muscle and remembered how people here walk, how they hold their heads backwards and to the side and extend their arms as they bicker or stalk each other. I had stolen glances at the women too, and had been afraid of the suggestive challenge of direct eye contact and the rough jealousy of their men. The women too strutted about the bus stop, some unkempt, theirs a coarse and rudimentary provocation, whilst others were vain and tight, if cheaply put together for better opportunities than their sisters'. I looked at small children and wished them to throw themselves at me, to ask me for money or sweets as familiar children do, prefixing my name with Abuti, an appellation for the familiar or the respected, or simply for an older but not too old stranger. Here, in the teeming press and hustle of the station, I had known the power of origin, and knew immediately that I could never return to Europe. In all the people about me, I recognised myself as I had been, disrobed of the imprints and trappings of Europe and now reconnected to an inevitable and inescapable history, an undone and refuted future, but a future that nevertheless has to be cajoled for whatever hope it might offer. The bitterness of this continent is much too deep.

Not so many hours ago, a surly customs official had stamped my passport as I crossed this river to finally arrive at home. There were no dogs or large armoured personnel carriers at the border, and by the casual pose of the few policemen hanging about, I had known that the war was finally and truly over.

Thembi's daughter Thandeka remained silent throughout our journey except to reply in sullen monosyllables to my questions asking her to name or explain things to me as we drove. Passing the border, she pointed out the narrow dirt road that led to my brother's wife's house.

I immediately recognised Puso's children standing in the yard. I could see his shadow in the way their ears protruded, in their bulbous foreheads and the way they stood leaning slightly forward as if fighting a wind.

The boy of about five years turned away to retrieve the ball he had been batting against a wall. His sister, taller and lighter in complexion, her hair pulled together in two straw coloured puffs stood staring at me, her brow knotted at something half recognised. She called out, "Mummy. Thandeka is here with a visitor."

As their mother came out of the house, I could see why my brother had been attracted to her. Her inquisitive grey eyes, firmly settled above high cheekbones and a full, almost protruding brow and her small mouth turned up at the sides as if in a permanent smile, all framed by short blonde hair, must have had much to do with it.

"You must be the long-lost uncle. I am Miriam and this is Palesa and little Tsepo. Come children, say hullo to your uncle," she called as they gathered around her.

I shook her damp palm and ruffled the children's heads.

She turned to Thandeka, "We haven't seen you in a long time. Come inside all of you and make your Uncle and me a cold drink."

She herded me into the house and offered me a seat in a frail straw chair in the large room.

"What would you like? Tea, coffee, a cold drink?"

"Do you have a beer? I'm not used to this weather," I said by way of explanation.

"Of course. Let me get one for you."

The room was neatly put together. There were no children's toys strewn about as I imagined there would be. On the walls were hung various ochre and mud coloured prints and baskets and masks from all over Africa, testimony to her travels around the continent. Big-eared plants stood sentry around the wicker sofas and carved tables on which delicate stone and wood figurines were artfully arranged. On the imposing bookshelf against one wall were arrayed family pictures, books and a sleek black music system somewhat out of place in the earthiness of the room. I stood to examine the books, stealing a brief glimpse at the image of my brother at the paternal centre of a happy family picture on the shelf.

The bookshelf held many faded yellow books from the African Writer's Series, a variety of more modern novels from around the world, large paperbacks on unfashionable themes like race, class and socialism, and more current issues their titles loud with the key words of the current lexicon, postmodernism, globalisation, identity, gender and such.

These were not my brother's books. He had never had the patience, energy or inclination to exert himself in what he had always considered puerile attempts to fathom the unfathomable. For him, the world was an uncomplicated and simple place. It was devoid of the ambiguity and nuance implicit in too many considered takes on the condition of life. For him life was about attainable and clear success, to be planned, measured and duly purchased. Who you knew, what you knew, why you knew it, all in a very close and particular way and the manner in which you arrayed all of these extant variables was the key.

Why then he had chosen to marry and have children with this woman, I did not understand. On her part I suppose she must have been moved by my brother's happy optimism, and the way that for him, conclusions were easy if you asked the right questions and framed life around the unfaltering rhythms offered by a predictable sun, cool evenings, and the regular events that mark the passing of the years, the odd wedding, birth or funeral, promotion at work, the occasional excursion out of town and rarely even overseas.

Miriam entered the room, a gold beer and a mug of coffee balanced on a wooden tray.

"I read a lot, especially since I moved in here with the kids," she said in circuitous allusion to their separation. "Your brother's things are at his place. Have you been there yet?"

She carefully moved a stone statuette of a woman's figure huddled down in some agricultural activity on a side table to make room for the beer and her coffee.

"No, I haven't. Perhaps I'll go there later."

She shrugged her shoulders. We sat down and silently sucked at our drinks, the only sound the children talking quietly in some back room.

"When did you move here?" I asked, scanning her face.

I had expected to find at least latent signs of anguish inflicted by the passing of someone once if no longer dear. But not knowing her, I could not make out how recent the darkness beneath her eyes, inappropriate to what was otherwise an optimistic face. My brother had alluded to a spate of contained violence of the flung plate and slammed door type as her response to admitted and persistent sexual misdemeanour on his part. He had explained his taking a concubine in very simple terms; it was what, you know, men do in these parts, something inherent to our culture, not altogether a good thing, but something to be quietly tolerated because it did not have to break up families. It was something I would have found out, were I here, that was necessary to break the seamless passing of the years. He had touched on his wife's frequent travels and hinted that it had been a mistake on his part to take a foreigner, especially a white woman, as his wife.

My brother's letters had shocked me, briefly. Had we been together, his shoulders would have reared as he explained this to me, my dear, dear brother, cultural recidivist at mid-life. But I had then remembered again how practical he had always been and how for him what was appropriate was what worked for the particular ambition of that point in time. My brother had become a strange mix of a technocrat and a traditionalist just before he died, something not at all in contradiction I had mused. Indeed I had gone on to agree that the strange mix of the future and the past that my brother had become was inevitable in this place, on this continent at this time.

Europe from where I have recently returned remained a beacon. And yet Europe was unattainable, such that this place and its managers uncomfortable but committed in their white shirts and lurid ties, had no choice but to lean backwards to find explanation for a largesse promised but barely delivered. I rationalised my brother's eyes had looked ahead and had imagined a future that had pulled him, sufficient emotional accoutrements assembled, to marry a white woman. Later, the town and his view, dusty and congested from poor construction, his wife now less bright, her complexion turning to the ruddy and burnt red of the settler, my brother had cast his eyes backwards and had fallen on an amazing collage of myths to create a new picture for a way of living.

For this place, the past has not come to overtake the future. Rather, a new method has been worked into the practical equation, with a widely inclusive thing called culture and a reminiscent history now deposited and ensconced if a little uncomfortably on a future under construction. The future of this place is not Europe in a bright African print shirt. The future, like the print shirt, all bright and beautiful, and anyway probably made in China, hides more than it reveals and sneers at reality.

"We used to live in another place in Mountain View."

I briefly imagined a committee of the first inhabitants of this suburb gathered to name it and organise its administration and remembered also an exiled acquaintance who took photographs but never of landscapes once say, "I cannot enjoy mountains and landscapes if they do not belong to me."

"This place is all right for now, or at least until I decide what to do," she continued. Her eyes glazed over and she turned away to rub them with the back of her hand. I could see now that she was not unmoved by the recent course of events, and that what had come over almost as indifference was in fact the resolute containment of a great deal of pain.

She kept quiet for a while and then blurted, "It hasn't been more than six months that we have been here," as if to reveal everything and nothing.

"It's been a difficult time. I'm off work of course and I have been thinking of going back home. There's not much here for me anymore. If we do go, things will be difficult for the kids. They've only ever been back with me once and they were young then. They would probably miss their friends and all that, but they'd get used to things."

"It's not so bad," she concluded as if my face shouted a personal and general disillusionment with the place of her origins.

I didn't know what to answer. What could I say, stranger as I was to her and to her life with my brother and their kids? To have eagerly agreed would have been to mock at the choices she had made. It would have been to undo what must have been a cheerful stoicism in the face of the heat, occasional droughts, electricity blackouts, military coups and civil unruliness and all the other inevitable and daily affronts of her life here.

I could understand why leaving was a real option. I was here not only to bury my brother, but having failed miserably in Europe, I was here also to find a place of unconsciousness and invisibility. I could imagine that for her as for me, too much energy had been expended in explaining herself, in justifying difference, in hiding it. I remember how in Europe one night, in the loud company of a bunch of drunk and nostalgic exiles like myself, we had taken a night bus home, and gradually quietened as it dawned on us that it was the black boys amongst the group of youths who were loudest in mimicking us as monkeys.

Black boys and girls in Europe scramble about for ancestors, and there was a time when they took me for a messenger, a repository of the things they searched for, so that for a while I became a bright, original thing, genuine, from the source. My phone rang often and I was often asked the meaning of my name. But in the end I had to leave, my brother's funeral the final push, to escape from an image constructed for me, which however embellished, whether by anger, or nostalgia, or by an equally fanciful idea of the future, had little to do with the truth of my origins.

Similarly then, I could understand if Miriam left to return to the place of the Cassimir's – her maiden name, which bespoke a mixed ancestry my brother had never described to me. Beyond a vague holding out in the face of my brother gone, perhaps for Miriam too the idea and reality of this place no longer coincided. The light, the scratch of the dust, the gurgle of flowing water, the wind and its rumours, and most of all, death's disposition must for her be completely changed now.

My thoughts turned to Thembi on the other side of town and how she expected answers or at least a little sweeping away of the dust by my return. But I had no resources and had acquired little if any wisdom in exile to begin to change these lives. My brother's wife probably could not, but Thembi could see that I had returned home only because I had to. She could see that I had used my brother's death to disentangle myself from whatever it was that had kept me in Europe all these many years. In our brief moment together, Thembi understood why I was so afraid of the past and yet why I needed it so much. The past had shaped my, and all our individual and common, ambitions. And yet the past was a place we barely knew.

I took a large gulp from the beer perspiring in my hand. "Thembi asked me to tell you, you are expected at the old place for the wake tonight." I hurried the last of my beer to make a quick exit.

She turned away from me and I knew tears were welling in her eyes. As she stood to walk to the window, her shoulders jerking in tight spasms, the door to the room opened and a young woman entered. She stood as if to appraise me for a moment, briefly nodded and then rushed over to put her arms around Miriam.

She was not a large woman but Miriam seemed to fit into her arms as if into a blanket. They stood there shaking against the light of the window, the woman clicking her tongue to repair Miriam's broken breathing. She began to mouth words I couldn't make out as my brother's wife broke into a quiet, high-pitched wail that seemed to come from the deepest part of her. The woman began to sway her in a dance whose music was her own repeated "No, no, no" to the moan wrenching from Miriam's breast. I turned my head to the floor and studied the pattern of the carpet.

They stood swaying at the window for a while and then Miriam began to quiet and to disentangle herself from the woman's arms. She turned to look at me and for a moment we talked through our eyes. Behind their tears, I heard her eyes say, "See how much I have loved. See how much I pain." Mine replied, "I see your pain." She stumbled out of the room and the woman rushed after her.

The woman returned after a few minutes.

"I'm Ipuseng." She spoke in our language. "I'm a friend of Miriam's. I live next door." She threw herself into the seat opposite me. She took off her glasses and rubbed her face.

She was wearing a short denim skirt, a red faded t-shirt and cuffed, out-of-fashion shoes. Her knees stared at me like two black eyes. The irony of the meaning of her name, "rule yourselves", so similar to my brother's.

"I came to talk about the arrangements for tonight."

She interrupted me, "Miriam has had a lot of pain." She had her glasses on and glared at me as she spoke, as if in reproach.

"I understand."

We remained silent for a moment.

Miriam entered the room. Her face was scrubbed and slightly swollen. She walked over to the window.

"Shall I come and get you later or do you know where the house is?" I asked, standing to force us to finish so I could escape.

Miriam circled towards me, her arms wrapped around her bosom as if to hold herself against the turmoil inside her. Small beads of sweat on her brow glistened against the light of the sun through the window. She lifted a hand to wipe her eyes and then looked at me, her mouth pulled tightly down.

"Thembi didn't want to talk to me when I needed her to. I asked her to tell your brother to stop seeing that woman. But every time I went to your home she used to hide from me."

Her anger mounting she continued, "It was if she didn't want to see what he was doing to me, to us. Now she wants me to pretend to be his wife, as if nothing happened. I was alone before I was a widow. Tell her that."

She turned sharply to the window, holding herself once more. Her pain was almost palpable. I could feel it spread across the room towards me, as sultry as the breeze coming in through the open window. I could feel her anger and despair at a past rubbished and a future rendered hopeless by the scattering into a displacement of all the small things that had contrived to shape it. She moved away as Ipuseng tried to catch her again.

"I'll tell Thembi you'll come to the funeral tomorrow," I whispered to create a way for her and by way of the apology I would deliver on her behalf.

Miriam quickly nodded her back still to me and then rushed out to the kitchen. I heard her saying something in the back, and then re-enter the room with the children, confused expressions on their faces. She must have said harsh things to them. I searched for quick words of solace by way of farewell, but finding none extended my hand to Thandeka, and exited hurriedly into the blindness of the afternoon sun.

Two

THE EVENING BEFORE the one time Thembi left us those many years ago, my brother and I and a small crush of friends had been in the front of the house singing a song about bats to the flying rodents flitting about us. One boy, tall and moody and deeper into adolescence than the rest of us, was swinging a long wire in the air around him and had wagered he could bring one down.

Grandmother had stuck her head out of the window and shouted at us to stop. "Those bats will get in your hair," she warned. We ambled away from the front of the house to continue our little game. In the end, the boy failed to drop a bat and we gave up as Grandmother's voice had come cutting through the growing dusk to send me as usual on an errand to the shops. By the time I returned home, I had forgotten about the game with the bats.

Our evening rituals completed, I went to my room to change into pyjamas, small hand-me-downs inherited from my brother that squeezed me under the armpits and between my legs. I wore them more for form than anything else. Most nights, especially in summer, I would wake straitjacketed in them and hurl them angrily to the floor.

Lifting the pillow under which Grandmother put my nightclothes, I had been suddenly startled by a small dark thing hurtling into the air, clipping my ear as it flitted past me. I jumped onto the bed in reaction to memories of unknown things, mostly rats and such, but once a snake, that moved on the floor at night, my eyes rapidly searching the room for the intruder. I immediately saw it hurtling past me again, now clearly a flying thing and rushed shouting out of the room, slamming the door behind me.

Thembi and Grandmother had laughed at me and told me not to taunt bats again. They belonged to the devil they explained. That is why they only come out at night and so on, they continued. Bravado and adolescent cynicism notwithstanding, I asked Thembi to get it out of the room. Later that evening Thembi's tales had turned to the supernatural, and my brother and I had moved closer towards the light of the single paraffin lamp on the kitchen table, and away from the shadows where according to Thembi, tokolosies, hairy dwarfs with huge penises, hid.

I had stalked around Thembi as she went about packing her things for the trip home the following day.

"How long will you be gone?" I had asked, handing her a dress hung from a wire in the corner of the room.

"I don't know," she replied. "But I shouldn't be gone long."

"You still haven't told me why you are going," I remonstrated.

Thembi turned from the bag she was forcing shut, a small smile spread across her face. "My family needs me for a while," she answered. "My father is not well and I have to look after him. But don't worry," she continued cuffing me lightly against the ears, "before you know it I'll be here to harass you again. Anyway you won't miss me will you?"

"Of course I will," I blushed. I walked to the door leading into the still yard and hesitated for a moment before dashing out, shouting "tokolosies, tokolosies" into the dark.

The next day, my brother and I were busy weeding Grandmother's garden in the heat of early morning when a car with number plates from the country neighbouring ours and with two men inside drove down the road towards our house. In Thembi's lilting way of speaking our language they asked for Grandmother. I thought I recognised one of them from before.

I entered the house with them, but Grandmother, completely unlike herself, had shouted, "What do you want in here? Have you finished in the garden?"

She smiled apologetically at the two men, glared at Thembi standing sulking in the corner and ordered me to fetch a cloth from the garden to wipe the table. Angry with Grandmother and hoping to hurry back to catch the real explanation for Thembi's departure, I hurried to the bucket to fetch the cloth. As I lifted its lid a black thing again flitted towards me and away and this time, in the bright light of early morning, I saw it clearly as it darted about blindly before disappearing behind the house. It was a bat, and there was no cloth in the bucket.

I did not return to the house but instead sat under my tree in the corner of the garden, dazed still by the fright of the thing as it had flown out of the bucket, by Grandmother's and Thembi's twice repeated deceit and Thembi's impending departure with the strangers come to our house.

I ignored all Thembi's attempts to cheer me up as she walked to the car that was taking her away. One arm carrying a bag and the other extended towards me, she used my diminutive to call me to wish her goodbye. I stood up and made for and exited the gate, deaf to her and Grandmother's appeals for me to come back. Finally I turned but too late to see Thembi inside the car as it disappeared at the end of the road.

I spent the rest of day wandering about our township and stopped in for a while at Abuti Jefti's place. He told me to go away when a young woman arrived, and I had retreated to the river that runs along the bottom of our village. The sun set, I stole in hungry and tired, and ignoring Grandmother as she berated me for missing the evening prayer, I headed straight to bed where soon asleep, I was invaded by a strange, beautifully vivid dream.

The dream crept upon me quietly but quickly, such that I was all of a sudden conscious of standing at the edge of mountain above a deep valley with a glistening, snaking river at its bottom. The river gently gurgled its way across the length of the valley until in the far distance, it disappeared into the dark blue fog of mountains crouched against the horizon.

A hard, flat mud plane sat squat on the bank of the river on which I could see many small children running about, their blankets flailing behind them. I could hear their voices as they called to each other.

Above the plane on higher ground stood a huddled village of round huts and cattle kraals and a small trading store along the dirt road that passed through it and continued along the valley's edge. Women stood on trampled spaces in front of the huts, shouting occasionally to each other as they went about their chores between thick clouds of smoke billowing from wood briers. Others sang out their children's names who came running to them from the riverbank. Still others slid down the many paths that crept down the valley sides, heavy loads of firewood on their backs.

From the store, I could hear the sound of music from a shrill radio to which a small group of young men would occasionally break into dance, their sticks raised and their blankets dancing behind them.

Suddenly there was movement at the higher reaches of the valley. A small group of men on horseback appeared and began a slow downward descent to the village below. Other men also on horseback began to emerge on the paths cut into the mountains overlooking the valley. Rearing forward as their sure-footed mounts made their way down the paths, the men were resplendent in lavishly coloured blankets of mustard yellow, bright blue and deep red, and conical straw or old felt hats garnished with feathers or countless small dull coins and medallions.

The children cavorting on the plane along the riverbank noticed them and stopped playing to point excitedly at the different groups of horsemen making their way down the mountains. Their mothers, their attention also caught, straightened up and hands held against their mouths began to ululate, jig and sing praise songs at their resplendent husbands and sons descending the mountains. At the trading store, the men previously entranced by beer and the harmonies of the radio also saw the men and began to dance in file towards the flat plane below the village.

Gradually the hundred men on horseback began to arrive at the river's edge. Cautioning excited dogs with their switches, they dismounted and tethered their horses against trees and stones at the edges of the plane. With large gestures they slung their blankets around their mares, slapped each other's backs, turned briefly to smile at their women folk and reached down to ruffle the children dancing between their legs.

Finally composed, sweat glistening on their muscled arms despite a sun now low on the horizon and the chill of the wind that sweeps down the mountains from the east, they approached a particularly large hut standing alone at one edge of the plane. In front of it was a massive cylindrical object of grey stone as large as the hut. Around it were tied ropes whose ends lay on the ground some distance away.

From where I stood in the dream, my senses as sharp as I have ever remembered, I could see rats and other small animals bolt from between the tufts of grass and weeds growing from under the stone cylinder. It had obviously not been moved in a long time.

With some confusion and much shouting and hearty jostling, the men arrayed themselves in lines along the three or four ropes tied to the cylinder and lying on the ground. They lifted the ropes and twisted them around their arms for better grip. They then started moving and leaning backwards and tautening the ropes to pull them. Once they appeared ready, a stout man who had all the time stood aside from them began to shout a call. He repeated it until it found a rhythm, to which the rest of the men soon joined in response. The woman too joined the single man so that the song was soon a shrill, rising call, followed by an affirming, confident response.

All along the valley's sides everything seemed to have come to a standstill except the shiver of bushes against the growing wind. The only movement I could make out at the bottom of the valley was the slow billow of the fires around the huts in the village, the flickering tails of the cattle as they bent to the straw in their troughs and the shimmering waters of the river. A few goats paced about restlessly at the periphery of the plane, whilst the dogs tripped excitedly between the legs of the women and children.

Abruptly, the stout man stopped singing and began to shout

against the now established rhythm, his arms waving wildly above his bald head. The men slowly stopped singing and looking at each other in puzzlement, began to loosen themselves from the ropes.

I could see the stout man remonstrate and shout at them and then use his no mean size to bodily shift a few men from one line to another. Around them, the women and children had fallen silent and still, except to hold each other against the gathering cold and to whisper into each other's ears.

The stout man, by all appearances satisfied by the way the men were now arranged, extended his chest and raising his head to the sky, started the refrain again. The men flexed their arms, dug their feet into the earth, and leaning back away from the stone, began to pull on the ropes. The stout man screamed again and slowly the chorus began to swell again as the women, disentangled from each other, began to wail and clap the call, to which the men responded in deep, resonant voices.

Almost imperceptibly the tempo of the song picked up. I saw a dog take fright and bolt towards the perimeter of the plane, its ears swept back. Others followed, scattering bleating goats as they ran.

My eyes returned to the image of a hundred men pulling at a large rusted stone in the middle of a darkening valley. I heard the chant quicken, the women's ululation rise, and saw the massive stone slowly tremble in the ground. The leader groaned a loud noise, lifted his legs and started a low twisted dance in time to the singing. A horrible sound surged from the men and then suddenly, I saw the cylinder tremble and then turn, hesitantly at first and then with growing momentum on an invisible axis, but without moving forward in space. The men began to lift their heads at their success and turned to look at their womenfolk and children, their faces beaming in the last rays of the setting sun.

As they continued to pull against the ropes, I began to notice a change in what was left of the light. The sun, its remaining half peering over the shoulders of distant mountains, began to grow until it was quickly whole, the dull egg-yolk yellow of its last moments brightening as, slowly but perceptibly, it began a contrary assent across the sky.

On the valley floor I could see some men stand away from the ropes and shielding their eyes with their hands, stare into the backward rising sun. They stopped singing, as did the women, who began to ululate and shrill and dance with their children around the stone. A few men remained at the ropes to maintain the stone's momentum. An excited boy bounded between the men and attempted to reach for a rope but was cuffed about the ears by an elder and retreated hurriedly between the men, who were now prancing and laughing around each other.

The sun continued its backward, contrary ascent across the sky, faster and faster, the shadows shortening until they were gathered closely under whatever they stood. At a sign from the stout man, who was laughing with a woman who had rushed to bring him water, the few remaining around the stone reigned it in, whistling as if to their horses, until it came gradually to a dead stop.

Arm-in-arm and slapping each other's backs the men began to make for their horses, the women and children tumbling and dancing about them. Slinging their brightly coloured blankets around their shoulders they mounted their horses and still waving at the women and children, quickly regrouped and began to move away from the valley bottom. In no time they were well up the paths that led out of the valley, until soon, I saw the last of them, his bright-red blanket shouting in the brightness of the sun, disappear over the cusp of the mountains on the other side of the valley.

As I awoke from the dream I was conscious my mouth was stretched in a small smile. I had never before dreamt a dream as vivid as this one. It was if I had been in that valley or that I had been one of the children running around excitedly at the miracle of the sun turned back, the day restarted.

For a while I had been afraid to open my eyes. I was afraid the dark of the room would erase the intense colours and sounds of the dream. I rushed through the dream again in my head – the long valley, the village at its bottom, the winding river, the men as they rode down the mountains and pulled ropes tied around a large rock, the women and children running about, and the sun, its yellow brightening as it moved backwards across the sky.

At school later that day, it had been more difficult than usual to concentrate and, unable to answer a string of questions on a subject in which I was usually adequate, the teacher had banished me to labour in the school garden. But I did not mind, as I was able to build a rhythm between lifting and sinking the pick into the moist soil to savour the dream.

I wondered why I had had it and puzzled over what it meant. Thembi's departure must have had something to do with it I reasoned, even though from the little she had told us about her home, I knew she had not gone to a place where villages sat beside rivers, or people used horses for transport. Thembi had gone to a place of many cars on big streets and thousands of people living in densely packed rows of identical houses.

I tried to think whether I knew such a village, but thinking about the few times I had been to the mountains, either on school trips or occasionally with Grandmother to visit her brother – a priest at a rural mission – I could not remember ever having seen it before.

I had finally decided that the main thing had been the sun and how the men had pulled it from its dim departure to a warmer inclination at mid-morning. But did this mean then, that, as in the dream, things could be started again? If so, what was it that was to be restarted? Who would be the men to turn and the women and children to applaud my grey sun machine? And why did things have to be restarted? Apart from Thembi's departure, the only thing I wanted to undo was the fact that my brother and I had never known our parents. However, never having known them, I wanted them only in order to be like other children who would come to school with stories of what their fathers or mothers had done and would do for them, because in every other way, Grandmother and Thembi were enough.

I never talked about the dream to anybody. The only person I could ever have told it to was Thembi and she had gone away. Grandmother would have referred me to the Bible, and my brother would not have had the time to hear it. Only Thembi could have found and explained its meaning.

In time it faded as all dreams do. But occasionally alone under my tree at the corner of the garden, our village quiet and deserted before the traffic of people returning from work, I would think of it. The valley in the dream became a secret place I would run to, away from the pointlessness of school, from my brother's arrogance, Grandmother's growing senility, and the dull ache of Thembi's long absence.

Thembi's occasional letters to us had brightened my monthly trips to the store that served as our post office. I would immediately recognise her handwriting and in my excitement would almost stop searching the old shoebox for other letters. The first time one arrived I was tempted to go to that place where I had read the stolen letter to Adelina, sure that its contents were addressed only to me. But instead I had rushed home to Grandmother, who, her eyes failing, asked me to read it to her.

Thembi's letters always started by saying that her family was well and that she missed us. They would ask after us and close by asking Grandmother to kiss us for her. She must have forgotten Grandmother was finding it increasingly difficult to read.

It was with a bit of a shock, then, that I discovered the real reason for Thembi's departure from us. In her third or fourth letter she announced she was finally leaving for the school of tradition in the rural areas and that, although she did not want to, she was glad that all the waiting was over.

As I read that part of the missive, Grandmother sat up in her bed and demanded I stop and give her the letter. "I will read it myself," she harrumphed. "Do you think I am blind?"

"What is it Grandmother?" I asked, fully aware that

Thembi's description of a circumcision school had upset her. I wanted to make as if this thing she described was nothing new or shocking to me, though inwardly, I was thoroughly shocked that Thembi could have agreed to such a thing.

"Get out, hear," Grandmother ordered. "These things are not for children."

Grandmother had not wanted to tell us the real reason why Thembi had left and was angry now that I knew it. She was proud and protective of our upright Christian upbringing, of her husband who had been a lay preacher and all that stood for. I imagined she did not want us to think of Thembi as part of what she considered that "heathen, backward" world that existed everywhere around us. Grandmother maintained that despite the common enough practice of traditional rituals in our neighbourhood, she would only allow us, my brother and I to participate over her dead body. She always become agitated at any discussion of such things, and threw me out of the house when I once came home with a strip of goat fleece tied around my wrist – for protection, I had explained.

After that letter, Grandmother never asked me to read for her again, but would chase me out instead, as if I had been rude or disobedient. She called us in after I had delivered the next letter and told us that Thembi was on her way back and that Thembi had talked about some of the troubles we were increasingly aware of in the country neighbouring ours. Thembi had not been personally affected she said, but it was a good thing, nevertheless, that she was coming back.

I waited impatiently for Thembi's return and on returning from school, rushed into the kitchen always in anticipation that she would be there, as she always had been, making a meal or washing dishes at the kitchen table, or the back of the house, drawing water from the tap.

And soon enough she was. Dawdling up the walkway from our gate I saw her standing in the door of one of the outbuildings. She had her one hand on her hip and the other against her face as if balancing herself to get a measure of this place once again.

Grandmother had finally asked the lady with too many visitors to leave, saying she was keeping the room for Thembi. The last straw had come when we were awoken one night by loud noises in the yard. On Grandmother's instruction shouted from her room, my brother had peered through the window and then carefully opened the door leading out of our room to see what was going on. I followed slowly behind and saw two women, one of them our tenant, wrestling on the ground in front of the row of outbuildings. Other tenants were peering through their windows or standing about enjoying the spectacle of the fight. On seeing my brother and I, the old man who always came to prayers drunk rushed to the women and proceeded to separate them. Finally standing, their breasts heaving through torn clothes, lips swollen and bloody, the women continued to shout at each other. I saw a clearly very drunk Abuti Jefti of the letters from Helvetica come out of our tenant's room. He smiled sheepishly at my brother and I and, ignoring the women, staggered towards his house. The fight had ended soon afterwards and once quiet had been restored we returned to bed.

Now, seeing Thembi, I think I was stopped in my tracks for an instance, then becoming aware, continued as normal, so that she wouldn't see. I didn't know whether to rush to her and throw my arms around her, or to calmly approach and greet her formally, as I would a tenant in one of the rooms. Smiling despite myself, I walked towards her, briefly held the hand she offered and ducked my head as she reached for it.

That evening she recounted what had happened in her township, her voice dancing in the strong accent of people from the country neighbouring ours. She had changed in the time she had been away. She was taller and her legs and shoulders had grown stronger underneath the African print dress she wore. Her hair now hung behind her in a simple plait, and framed her dark face with her perfect white teeth shining between thickened lips.

Grandmother, tired and frightened by Thembi's stories of tear gas and shooting and police vehicles rushing about, had retired earlier than usual. Reaching for the bowl under the table to wash the dishes as if nothing had happened, Thembi had turned to me smiling and asked, "So, how have things been with you?"

My brother had rushed in all bluster. He boasted, how he had made a little money at 'Me Thuso's shop, filling in on weekends for the old man who had fallen ill. At some point Grandmother had shouted from the other room for us to go to bed, and as we rose to go Thembi had whispered there would be time for us to talk the next day.

Thembi and I never did get the chance to talk, or rather, I always found something to rush to do in the house or in the yard when we found ourselves alone for a few moments. I avoided Thembi because I knew her eyes and the way she would talk to me would touch that part of me for which I had built a silence. She had caught me once under the tree I liked to sit under in the quiet of the late afternoon before our township woke to people returning from work, and rolled a rock to sit on beside me.

"This is a nice place to sit," she started. I nodded and turned the piece of wood I was carving in my hand.

"What are you making?" she had continued.

"Oh. It's nothing. I'm just waiting for a friend to come." I looked at her through the corner of my eye. Her strong legs were spread out in front of her and for a moment I caught the white of her underwear. She must have noticed because she adjusted her skirt.

"It's so nice to be here," she repeated. "Where I'm from, there are very few places you can sit quietly alone."

I didn't answer.

"Sometimes I miss home, though. It's not so much my family, although of course I miss them. Its much more that things happen there, there is so much to do."

"Like what?" I asked staring at the piece of wood in my hand.

"Oh. I don't know. There are just so many more people to see, places to go and things to do. I sometimes go to town with my mother on Saturday mornings. That can be fun, looking at all the shops and the people in their fancy clothes."

She noticed I wasn't impressed.

"And then sometimes in the evenings I sneak out to parties and things." She continued, "Even here, the good thing about not living in the main house is that I can sneak out sometimes. My friends come and collect me. You haven't heard me leave or come in have you?"

"Ah, there's my friend," I said, indicating a boy walking down our street. I jumped up and apologised before skipping away to meet him. He wasn't a friend, just another boy from the neighbourhood, but he would serve as sufficient excuse for me to get away.

The only thing that consoled me about the way Thembi and I now were was that I thought she recognised and acknowledged things between us that were not for sharing with my brother or Grandmother. I used to eavesdrop every time she would be alone for a moment with my brother and was secretly happy that all they ever talked about were quite ordinary things.

Sometimes I would think to concede and imagine how I might approach her. Grandmother had become too old and spent too much time locked away in her room to provide any comfort. I would sulk at the way, her eyes failing, she would call me to read the Bible or a letter to her, or when she insisted I lead our extended household in evening prayer. She would cluck at my protests and tease that I now thought I was too old to be her favourite. She would remind me that I was named after her husband, a great man, a schoolteacher, and that I would one day be like him. Such things only made me angrier.

My brother was no friend either. He was hardly ever at home what with new friends, physical after-school activities to which he had taken with a passion, and other things we never discussed, but which always kept him busy.

Many children came in and out of our yard all the time, to visit Puso mainly, though amongst them were some whom I could call friends. At school, I had few friends. I had tried many times to hang about after classes were out but had always found the inevitable discussions of cars, sports and girls a little repetitious. There were limits, after all, to how many times we could retell our limited sexual encounters, and since in our family we did not have and were not likely to get a car in the foreseeable future, I did not see the point in discussing the merits of one model over another. The future in which such things might accrue was too distant and uncertain.

Books were useful and I spent many hours locked away in my room, or hidden from Grandmother behind the outbuildings, devouring them. Apart from the few I would borrow from the very limited school library, I would steal some of the many on an old, rickety shelf in Grandmother's room. They belonged to her late husband, who had amassed a fair collection. Covered in dust and rat droppings, the black and burgundy books exuded a musty smell and many would not open to my fingers. The books were of a wide range of subjects from animal husbandry to religion and there were even a few novels amongst them.

Often I would sneak to Abuti Jefti's house to browse through his torn collection, barely upright between bricks collected from the yard. Abuti Jefti would send me to fetch a few beers for him, then dropping a record onto his old turntable, he would choose a book for me and sit me down on his small stoep to discuss it. He would inevitably veer away from the subject of the book at hand and instead sing along to a hoarse bluesman wailing the blues or a saxophonist tripping all over his instrument.

Abuti Jefti had come here from Europe with many books. There were many by African writers and these I fell to, finding them easier to understand than the numerous others in his scattered collection. At school, I would sneak into the staff room to locate the countries from which their authors came. I would gaze longingly at the few photos of modern Africa in our shared textbooks on geography and history and try to imagine what those places were really like and whether I might ever see them.

The more beer he ingested, the more difficult the books Abuti Jefti would recommend to me. He would suggest books on the history and politics of distant places, warning me not to show them to anybody. As much as I enjoyed history at school and try as I did, I couldn't understand these books. They were too full of long words whose meanings I did not know. I would flip through them in an attempt to find passages or sections that made sense but invariably failed.

And when I returned them, Abuti Jefti would ask me what they were about, to which I would stand in the dust in the front of his house, one leg drawing in the sand, unable to answer. He would shout how clear and straightforward they were and how the young people of today had become so stupid. He would then ask me if I had ever heard of so-and-so and so-and-so, great writers I suspected, and then shout the names of faraway places like Ghana and India and China and the momentous things that had happened there. He would rave on that the problem with this country he had come to for refuge was precisely that it did not have wise men and women, at which point he would again intone the names of obscure heroes and epic places as if to prove his point.

Thembi had tried to use the books to start us talking again. She would ask me to tell her what the book I was reading was about. I would mumble that I was tired and move away, pretending I had something urgent to do for Grandmother.

I don't know at what point Thembi decided to give up on me. It might have had something to do with the growing influx into our town of people her age, some of whom she knew, from the country neighbouring ours. They would visit her occasionally in groups of two or threes. She would sneak into the house to fetch bread, biscuits, juice concentrate and such and serve them. I would kneel below the window of her room and listen to their strange language, making out a few words here and there, but unable to follow the gist of what they would talk about. Sometimes Thembi would sneak one or two of them to sleep with her, almost always girls, although one day she did bring a boy, whom I heard slinking away to the bark of the dogs as the first rays of the morning sun peered over the mountains.

One evening around the kitchen table, I hinted at the strange people who came to our house at night. Thembi stood frozen for a moment then glared at me and turned, her feet scuffling angrily on the floor, to busy herself with pouring tea. My brother had raised his eyes from his schoolbooks and looked at me disapprovingly. Increasingly unaware of the goings on in our compound, Grandmother thought I was referring to our tenants, and threatened that she would evict them just as she had the woman with too many visitors.

At any rate, all our lives were changed in many small ways by the arrival of these young people from the country neighbouring ours. Whatever special consideration I arrogantly believed Thembi might have had for me simply dissipated in the face of their arrival.

My brother found a new girlfriend amongst them at school and every night begged Thembi to teach him terms of endearment in her language as well as other words he would giggle to her, at which she would click her tongue and scold him.

I too was intrigued by the new students. Some of them scared me in the way they carried folded knives in their back pockets and were so quick to turn to violence. Others were impressive in their knowledge of all manner of worldly things. They would go on about how they were on first-name terms with the gangsters, soccer players and musicians who appeared in the monthly magazines which we would share among us, and we had little choice but to believe them. The girls were particularly impressed and for a while running battles broke out between the new students and small groups of aggrieved locals.

I was impressed most of all by the knowledge of a slightly older boy who I quickly took to. He was tall and light skinned, with badly set teeth that forced his mouth open in a permanent grimace. The titters of the class would quiet to his amazing knowledge of places and things. He had a stutter and would often repeat words for which he was soon given the nickname "Twice".

Twice was one of the less self-conscious of the new students. He would never volunteer to say anything in class, clearly on account of his stutter, though it soon became evident that there wasn't much he did not know. Neither did he participate with the other new students when sparked by an incident in their country relayed through the press or via an invisible information trail that led from there to here, they would gather to discuss its ramifications and then to sing and dance in celebration or defiance of it. Nor did Twice come to our house amongst the small groups that would visit Thembi until one day I pressed him to, among other reasons because I secretly wanted to impress her with my new friend.

On the long walk home from school, Twice had not said very much, except to ask me about my parents whom I had never known, about Grandmother and about Thembi who I had used as bait to get him to come. I had told him that like him, Thembi was from the country neighbouring ours and had hinted at promises of opportunity in the attractive and understanding half-sister that she was.

Our township was usually a quiet and still place towards the end of the afternoon. A few bouts of real and feigned sickness had offered me the opportunity to listen to the passing of working days. In the mornings, after the hurried departure of working people and school children to town, routine domestic activity was about all that ever happened. The women would shout greetings to each other across falling-down fences, recount dreams and visitations, or boast about the rare amorous feats of their husband against a backdrop of dirty water being spilt or the swish of straw brooms as they meticulously swept the dusty yards around their homes. By midday, in summer, apart from the screams of some infant with colic cloistered away in a back room, or the emissions of a radio around which out of work men gathered to pass the time, the ring of the sun was the loudest thing as it blistered its way across the sky. In winter, the wind whispered cold threats or rustled countless discarded bits of dirty plastic hanging against fences or blew to dance the trees.

At the end of the afternoon, our township would gradually awake to the noise of children returning from school and the increasingly voluble excesses of the out-of-work patrons of scattered shebeens. From the priest's home a few houses away, a bell – the rim of a tyre hit with a metal rod – would ring out to call the faithful to four o'clock prayers. At the peal of that bell, Grandmother, then less infirm and more participatory in her devotion, would raise herself from the large armchair daily settled on the stoep, rush into the house to fetch her bible and book of hymns, and make her way to the house, where squeezed amongst others in a dark and slightly fetid front room, she would listen to the Word. The priest's alleged involvement in a scandal one day put a sudden end to that daily pilgrimage.

When Twice and I arrived at our house, the streets were still empty of the frenzied rush of those returning from work. We found Grandmother ensconced in her armchair, vessels of peeled potatoes and carrots at her feet. She squinted her eyes, grey with cataracts, against the sun and stared quietly at Twice as I introduced him. It was not often I brought home someone unfamiliar.

Twice haltingly answered her questions about where he was from and thanked her for the prayers she promised to pray for him, so that he could return home, she explained. Grandmother then sent me for her bag in which she rummaged until she found a tightly bound handkerchief, which she then slowly untied. My friend and I stood patiently as she chose a mix of copper and silver coins, which she then gave to me, whispering to me not to tell my brother. The fruits of being her favourite sometimes ripened at the sweetest of times.

As Twice and I walked to the row of low, dilapidated shops on the main road, the working day had clearly ended. Numerous tilted buses and barely held-together taxis ran up and down the road, disgorging passengers in swirling clouds of dust. The sides of the road were congested with poorer workers, men mainly, in faded blue and red overalls and hard hats, walking briskly home after a day of labour in firms and on construction sites in town.

On the narrow side-streets off the main road, children scampered about at play, their songs and chants cutting through the growing dark, whilst their older brothers and sisters held hands and whispered arrangements for secret assignations deep in the night. At the shops were scattered groups of youth, some simply hanging about for the chance of a cadged cigarette, or for a few cents for half a loaf of bread and a small plastic bag of milk. Others, sullen in unemployment and the effects of glue or marijuana awaited a more brazen advantage. Friday nights were their best days, when after a week of few spoils, they would like silent and patient predators pounce on the pay-day reckless.

I knew the boys well. I knew who was alleged to have killed, who to have waylaid and forced himself upon a young girl one dark night, who was alleged to have served time, for as young as they were, survival was a desperate thing for which they and sometimes the innocent had to pay the price. I knew too what was their due by way of a certain obsequiousness, a tail-between-my-legs, an eye-to-the-ground stooping on my part. I knew too that I occasionally had to offer a street tax of sorts, to buy free passage around the township. When I refused, the almost daily trek to the shops became something I came to dread, for however long I attempted to put off Grandmother's errands, I eventually had to go. And they were inevitably there, rude in hand-me-down clothes that had not seen water in a long time, their muddy eyes quick to every movement, their hands rough and familiar. I sometimes mobilised a friend or two to accompany me, but that never helped because they would weed me out nevertheless, grab me by my shirttails, search me for the coins Grandmother would have given me and hurl me humiliated to the ground.

So I paid, in Grandmother's change and some of the coins she would give me by way of small bribes for doing her bidding. Then they would leave me alone for a while and turn their attention to some other hapless boy sent to buy candles or paraffin or a tin of fish for the evening meal.

Walking out of the shop, our arms laden with booty of chicken feet and fat cakes just out of the oil, I saw Abuti Jefti, his arms heavy with bottles of beer. He had just come out of a doorway that opened into a room where men and a few rowdy women sat to drink white man's beer.

I could see from the way Abuti Jefti put his legs down in front of himself as he walked that he had sat for a while in the room. Abuti Jefti was also mumbling and singing to himself, a sure sign that he had indulged in immodest quantities of beer. I thought to ignore him, but then thought to let Twice meet him. They were both, after all, from the country neighbouring ours, and Twice would probably think more of me for knowing Abuti Jefti, or so I reasoned.

I called out to Abuti Jefti and reached for two of the large bottles he was carrying to help him.

"Today I'll let you carry them, my boy," he laughed. "In a few years you'll be like those boys over there," he continued, pointing with his thumb over his shoulder, "and then I wouldn't trust you to carry anything for me," he laughed.

He turned to Twice. "Where does this one come from? I don't know this one."

I tried to introduce Twice, but a bus thundered past in a cloud of dust and exhaust fumes, almost running over us.

Abuti Jefti, shouted an expletive and staggered in the road. "It's safer to stay at home, my boys. I'd rather stay at home. There's something about the brains of bus drivers, taxi drivers, not so?"

We arrived at Abuti Jefti's house that stood huddled against trees in the dark. He pushed the front door open, entered and rummaged about for a match and then lit a candle on a brick propping up a dishevelled row of books.

He proceeded to an equally dishevelled pile of records beside the bookshelf, chose one and placed it on the battery-powered turntable, also on the floor.

Still bent above the turntable he shouted, "Don't just stand there, get some glasses."

The gramophone scratched for a while then blared a music becoming familiar with every visit to Abuti Jefti's. I could make out saxophones and other blown instruments, drums, and thin clusters of notes from a piano. I was no longer that ignorant. Abuti Jefti often tried to explain to me the music he listened to during my occasional visits. He would laugh that, ignorant native that I was, the best thing would be to start with the drums. He would snap his fingers, get up and tap his feet at a dance whose reason eluded me, which was made no clearer by the strangled grunts that would come from his gaping mouth.

"Get it. Get it," he would shout, his arms held out one above the other, his fingers flexing at an imitation of someone playing the saxophone. Or he would extend his hands and play the piano.

Sometimes I think I understood what he was going on about, and when he would go out to piss against the hedge in front of the house or to fetch another beer immersed in a large bucket of water at the side of the house, I too would extend my arms to play the saxophone, drum or some other instrument. The main thing was, I could sometimes get the simple yet impossible logic of the beat of the music, and for a while I would smile at the understanding.

I blurted out the name of musician I had heard Abuti Jefti often call.

He choked on the beer Twice had just given him. "Bloody fool. Can't get anything right."

I turned away, embarrassed at getting it wrong. From the corner of my down-turned eye I saw a small rat at the end of the bookshelf.

"Maybe this fellow knows who it is," Abuti Jefti said turning to Twice.

Twice mumbled a name I could not make out and I was secretly shocked and delighted as Abuti Jefti shouted, "That's right, that's right," and stood up to look more carefully at

Twice who like me had turned his eyes to the floor. Maybe he also saw the rat behind the bookshelf.

"Now who is this chap you are with?" he said, head tilted, eyebrows raised, an arm extended to point at Twice.

I tried to repeat the introduction attempted on the road when the bus almost ran us over, but Abuti Jefti his arm now on Twice's shoulder was shouting something at my friend. He pulled Twice down to sit next to him on the thing that passed for a sofa, and reached for a dusty glass on the floor into which he blew. The dust from the glass shot into his eyes and for a moment he was blind and spitting, his hand wiping at his face. He thrust the glass at me and ordered me to rinse it out with water from the tap outside.

By the time I returned to the room Abuti Jefti and Twice were talking in the language of people from the country neighbouring ours, the formality of introductions clearly over. Twice looked at me as Abuti Jefti handed him the beer-filled glass. He pursed his lips around his protruding teeth and took a noisy sip. When Twice passed his glass to me Abuti Jefti clapped his hand and shouted I had not been to the mountains and was not to get any.

They ignored me when I remonstrated that Grandmother was probably wondering where we were. Outside I could hear the last of the buses making their way up the main road, the occasional bark of a dog, and in the distance, the dull repetitive thud of a drum of one of the many evangelical churches in our township at prayer. Between the eager clamour of the music from the turntable on the floor, I could make out the high-pitched squeaks of bats lodged somewhere in the ceiling of the house.

As Twice finished his beer I stood as if to announce our departure. "Abuti Jefti. Twice and I have to go. I'm sure Grandmother is angry, where she is." I looked at Twice, my eyes imploring that we really had to leave.

In the end I ran home alone, leaving Twice behind, to talk, "...and to finish the beer," Abuti Jefti added, refilling their glasses. I would lie to Grandmother that Twice and Abuti Jefti were related, even though I knew she did not approve of Abuti Jefti. He was a drunk and completely the wrong person to be teaching children she would remonstrate. But there was nothing to do. I could not begrudge them their newfound friendship, or whatever it was that kept them, especially Abuti Jefti, talking with so much heat. Neither could I force Twice to come home with me. He would probably have refused anyway, and I would have been upset that he chose this falling-apart house with no food, cockroaches swarming around the dirty dishes in a pan on the table, and the smell of cigarettes and beer for comfort, over our house with Thembi, Grandmother and my brother.

The next day I helped Twice carry his few belongings from the hostels where he lived with others from the country neighbouring ours to Abuti Jefti's. From then on, I was an almost daily visitor except when Twice would come to our house, for comforts unavailable at Abuti Jefti's and, I suspected, to see Thembi.

Three

I HAD FORGOTTEN how it rains here. In Europe, rain seeps out of a low, parochial sky. Nothing is defined or mitigated by it, and sometimes all it seems to do is to extend the flat grey sky down to the level of the streets, so that you wouldn't even know it was raining.

Here, the rain is an enraged, indiscreet thing that comes down in a violence that defies the sun and scatters all living things to run for the nearest available shelter. And it can catch you by surprise if you happen to be overly taken up with whatever you are doing. You may miss the thick white clouds as they begin to boil and mass like a horde for an assault. You may, your head turned down at some activity for commerce and success, miss the first rumblings of thunder at the corners of the sky. But, sooner or later, you will raise your head and, seeing people scurrying from the spit of the sky, you will rush to close a window, or to bring in the washing or a child.

Midway along the thoroughfare that services our town, the sun disappeared behind a cloud and it started to rain. Thandeka rolled up her window and I threw out my cigarette and turned on the wipers. On the streets, the people spilt out of the government offices and shops that line the thoroughfare and began to run for shelter, some with their bags or bits of plastic on their heads for protection. Hawkers battled to cover their makeshift stands with black tarpaulins and plastic sheets. The sky crackled and lit up, and an instant later crashed to a clap of thunder. Someone screamed in the street and I saw a man and a woman seeking shelter on opposite sides of the street collide in front of our car. The woman banged her arm against the hood of the car and went down. The man stopped for a moment, then turned and rushed off. From my side window I saw a red shoe bobble down a river of water, its gold buckle glistening at another explosion of lightening and disappear down a drain. The woman appeared in front of us, her hair pasted against her face and her heavy breasts visible through her blouse that clung to her body. She limped off to the side of the road, lifting her red-shod foot high out of the water. She paused at the side of the road and turned back to look for her other shoe, but quickly resigned herself and began to walk up the street, her shoulders pulled down by the weight of her clothes and parcels, heavy with water. The man she had bumped into was nowhere to be seen.

Some distance in front of us and vaguely visible through the steamed-up windows of the car, I saw a man struggling to push his van off the road. He was not making much progress and no one amongst the many sheltered under the corrugated-iron overhang of a shop selling coffins, the words "Six Feet at Last" vaguely visible against it, ran out to help.

We remained stuck in the traffic and deluge for what must have been half an hour. I sat in the car with Thandeka, my eyes wide to the violence of the rain and lightning, my tiredness all forgotten. At each explosion of thunder, I would flinch and involuntarily duck my head, and Thandeka would steal a secret smile at her uncle afraid of the elements. I saw a small flock of pigeons with no formation hurry across the sky, their wings flapping urgently. I looked at the water charging along the sides of the road, and the things it swept along – bright soft-drink cans, muddy bits of plastic and newspaper, twigs, the leaves of somebody's cabbage for dinner. A little ahead of us, an old woman was sitting on the pavement in the rain, her arms raised above her and her face turned up at the pouring sky. People were laughing and calling for her to get up and out of the rain.

I remembered then that there are many mad people here. Too much hunger and the anger of an overbearing sun, and winters so cold people sometimes die in them, has much to do with it. They survive in clothes hardened and blackened by years on the streets, and subsist on the occasional organised charity of foreigners and middle-class women or more mundane daily refuse-bin acquisitions. I looked at the woman, her black cloak heavy and clinging to her and remembered her, a former nun, made mad by her expulsion from her order for giving birth to a child. She had kept her habit and her wooden cross and walked about the streets selling little yellow jerseys she knitted. Sometimes she would walk about with a man who carried a burden of two large flat stone tablets on his back who went by the name of Moses. I remembered how, sitting at some bar overlooking the thoroughfare, we would joke about them and wonder who amongst the citizenry of this town would be next to join this religious order of the streets. For a day or two, a former, quite senior government official, scandalously and suddenly gone mad, almost did. But he was quickly rushed off to our only sanatorium for the insane.

A young couple broke out from under the shelter of a shop and ran arm in arm into the rain, which had started to abate. They stopped by the old woman and tried to help her up, but she shouted something at them and they left her alone and continued on their way. Ahead of us, two men peeled out from under a shop front and put their shoulders to the van stuck in the road. The immobile traffic began to move. Arches of water sprayed from their wheels as they cut through the deep puddles of water. I opened the window and started our car and heard the rushing water swirling and gurgling under us. The sun peeped out from behind a cloud and shot rays of light through the now lightly spitting rain. By the time we approached the junction that leads to our village on the shoulder of the town, with the exception of a few huge clouds hung high against the far horizon, the sky was clear and the sun was out once again. But as we moved up the road that leads to our house, I noticed it didn't seem to be so wet there. It had rained, but not with the intensity of the deluge we had met at the centre of town.

I remembered then that the rain often discriminates here, that it is said to choose gardens. I chuckled to myself at the thought of the partiality of the elements here. Households would flourish because the scourges of nature would pass them by, only to come in various unrelenting forms to undo the opportunity of a neighbouring home. In some households, the women were fecund and bore children who lived, grew up and moved away, to return from time to time for the occasional family ritual. The man of the house did not run away to set up house with some young girl, and the mother of the children did not suddenly and inexplicably succumb to some unknown ailment.

In other households, locusts would descend on the fields and destroy the crops, the fruit trees would fail to blossom, and the horse would be found keeled over dead in the morning. The father of the house would be useless in alcoholism and the daughters would be the first amongst the girls of the village to fall pregnant, or to move to the district town, where they would spend their time in the commerce of selling laughs and brief moments of happiness to truck drivers, government officials out on field work and other itinerants.

There are no patent reasons why some families flourish whilst others flounder. Maybe that's why there are such strong beliefs here in the power of the supernatural in shaping destinies. A perusal of a family genealogy might unearth where a particular act, a birth, a death or a deception on the part of an important elder might have dislodged the trajectory of lives connected by blood and marriage. Gathered at some recreational affair, men and women and even children will often, with an appropriate click of the tongue and a weary shaking of the head, attribute blame for the particular misfortunes of a household to the marriage of uncle so-and-so to that woman from across the valley, the failure of a son to go to the mountains for initiation, or the fact that a household did not unveil the tombstone of an important progenitor. But even when the bitterness of all this falling apart becomes too much to bear and due solicitations are made to the deceased, apparently wrathful at being forgotten, things are not always repaired. Or where they are repaired, a permanent veneration is required of the life patterns of every day; the rising and setting of the sun, the taking of food, that somnolent time after the evening meal when the candles and fires have been put out but which is not a time that is asleep at all. And what of the bloody demands of a birth or a death to make it propitious beyond itself? Life is blood. But what is the meaning of its spilling beyond a young girl's first blood, the blood of her first invention of life, the blood that anoints a birth, or the blood that dries and clots in the collapsed veins of a cadaver? And if this is not blood enough for those who are to be placated, then how demanding they are. Death is a very near thing.

I wondered which type was our family. Our parents had not featured, and perhaps that was the first manifestation of a trajectory derailed. But Grandmother had held us in her clutch and my brother and I had grown and lived and moved on, though Puso was dead now. And Thembi had come into our lives and added to them in so many ways. Yet here I was, driving up a rutted road to a yard where my brother's corpse lay in a box, a carcass was hung and dripped blood in a back room, and various barely familiar relatives and neighbours busied themselves in preparing for his interment. And here I was returned from a little frightened woman, the design of her and her children's lives broken by the simple reality of her husband's death. And what of me, my eyes red and sore from too many harsh events in too short a period, my body dumb and aching, my hands shaking slightly from insufficient sleep and the shock of my transplant from that place to this? I needed to sleep a little. I rubbed the mud off my shoes on the old coal sack that serves as a doormat as I entered the house.

I was woken from a short and listless sleep by singing in the yard. It took me a moment to remember where I was, but the sliver of light through the door that led to the kitchen shocked me to the present. Under the curtain drawn against the window and unchanged all these years, were my bags. Next to them stood the sideboard, and on it the straw basket in which Thembi used to keep her vanities. In it were a few toiletries – Thembi's daughter's, I supposed. Above me I could make out my old bunk-bed with its grid of wire and springs holding up the mattress and familiar pink and yellow sheets and blankets.

The song in the yard outside was an old church hymn, translated from English into the vernacular but almost unrecognisable in the singers' way of playing with its melody.

In the kitchen were three women whom I barely recognised. They drew back a little and greeted me softly as if afraid of me. One of them, Grandmother's cousin or something who used to visit from time to time, remarked she had heard I had returned and that my brother's death was such a sad thing, he was so young, and his poor wife and children. I asked where Thembi was and they directed me to the back of the house.

She was amongst a group of women around a row of tables set up in the backyard. Preparations for the day to follow were clearly well advanced. One or two of the women were shuffling about the fires, stirring the large steaming pots on glowing coals, occasionally adding this or the other condiment or licking at the wooden spoons for taste. The others simply sat around, their arms heavy on the tables or in their corpulent laps. I heard Thembi, her back to me, shout at them that several bags of vegetables and some meat seemed to have gone missing and that this was not the sort of thing she expected at a funeral. She turned, saw me and came towards me, wringing her hands and shaking her head at the apparent theft.

"There's somebody who's been taking food here. Two bags of cabbages have disappeared," she said, her brows knotted in a frown. "You can't trust people these days," she continued turning to glare at the women at the tables.

She sighed, "Anyway, we'll see. Come let's go inside and get you some food. I hope you are rested." She took me by the hand and led me round the house to the front where a large tent stood, lit up by a naked globe on an extension lead from the house. Inside, the men and women huddled in blankets on rented plastic chairs were singing another hymn. A group of young people, the print of their t-shirts extolling a commitment to shrift, service and God, sat to one side and swayed and clapped as they sang. At the table in front of them, a balding old man, his arms clasped and rested on a pompous belly, stood swaying gently to the hymn. He unclasped them as the hymn began to fade and lifting them skywards shouted, "Let us pray." The people in the tent bent their heads as he began.

Thembi and I passed on into the house. The front room was much the same as when I was last in it. My brother's coffin remained firmly closed where it had been. I thought I could make out the faintly medicinal odour of whatever it is they use to keep dead bodies from rotting too quickly. Thembi told me to sit down and went out to the kitchen to prepare a meal for me. I heard her say something disapproving to the women still busy in the kitchen. She was clearly tired. But there was still a lot before us before the business of my brother's funeral was finally done.

I went out on the stoep that had been Grandmother's favourite spot and lit a cigarette. From the tent I could hear the old man's voice rising in entreaty to God and the flock murmuring after him. Beyond the tent I could make out the many yellow lights of neighbouring and more distant houses, a sure sign of progress since my departure. Ours was not Dark City any longer. Above the tent the sky was clear and lit up by a thousand whistling stars. It was a long time since I had seen so many vividly clear stars.

I flicked my cigarette at a scruffy dog scavenging for scraps at the edge of the light from the stoep. It bolted into the dark and yelped as a figure approached, arm raised as if to hit it. A young man took off his cap as he came into the light and greeted me cautiously.

"I don't think you remember me. I am Teboho. My grandfather and your grandmother were cousins." Links travel far here, I remembered.

He said, "I just thought I'd pass round before I go off to the graves. I thought you might want to come, see how they're doing." I remembered him, a relative who used to visit from time to time. He was younger than I was and I had never paid him much attention.

I called him inside and we sat down across the room from each other, silent after a stilted exchange about my trip, how his family was, what he was doing with himself, and the tragedy of my brother's death.

Thembi entered the room, greeted him and handed me a plate of food on a colourful tin tray. She returned to the kitchen and came out with another tray of food, which she handed to him.

"Miriam will not be coming tonight," I started.

Thembi did not say anything.

I shovelled food into my mouth. I didn't feel I could explain. The boy sitting with us averted his head to the silence of the room and dug his spoon into the plate on the tray balanced on his knees.

Thembi wrung her hands and sighed. "These are painful things. A person is supposed to be buried from the place that was his last home. But we couldn't go to the place he was living before he died. We couldn't go to her place either. It isn't his home."

She stared at me. I turned to my food and chased a congealed piece of meat around my plate. It fell off the plate on to the tray. I slid the tray onto the table beside me. I couldn't eat.

Thembi continued, "I know they were not living together. But to us, they were still man and wife. And they have two children together. What if I was not here or if you hadn't come back? Who would have buried your brother?" Thembi rose and reached for my tray. "She should have come," she said, rushing out of the room.

The boy and I sat in the room silent save for the hum of singing from the tent outside and from Thembi's words, hanging in the air like the smell of something dead. There was a knock at the door and a small group of men in long coats and blankets shuffled in. They held their hats in their hands. I recognised some of them. One of them announced they were here to take my brother's corpse to the tent outside. He stared at his scuffed boots for a moment and then shuffled towards the coffin. The other men squeezed in behind him.

I got up and looked to the boy, who was also standing. We

exited into the heavy night air. We made for the gate, past the hanging tent, my eyes blind and unseeing in the heavy dark, my feet searching their memories for the places to step. I stumbled and the boy reached over to save me from falling. His voice came cutting through the dark. "It's not far where we're going."

We passed the shops where I used to go on Grandmother's errands. They stood closed and morose and a little rundown in the glare of the light against them. An old watchman hunched over a brazier watched as we walked past, and murmured a greeting.

From the last of the shops, whose door was slightly ajar, I made out the sound of drums on a radio, signature to the news about to be read. I remembered how, when I brought Twice to our township for the first time, we had met Abuti Jefti here, his arms laden with beer, his walk that of a man already drunk.

I reached into my pocket for money, handed it to the boy beside me and asked him to buy us a whisky or brandy to see us through the digging at the grave. He knocked at the door and entered the yellow light of the shop. I heard a snippet of the news, about a massacre somewhere on the continent.

Apart from the wailing refrain of the hymn drifting through the dark from our house, the whine of a labouring truck in the distance and the bark of a dog even further away, our township was asleep. Sounds carry easily here, especially at night. They seem to come like isolated rays of light, so that it is possible to hear at which house a dog is barking, at which an ongoing argument is started once again. By now, they must have carried the coffin to the tent.

Even in the dark I could see that our township had changed much in the years I had been away. I could see how the rain and the thunder of the wheels of trucks and buses had eaten into the dusty road, which was now cut deeper in the ground. I could see that the trees dancing in a sudden wind reached taller into the sky. The house that had stood opposite the shops was no more. In its place was a shed of corrugated iron, the words "A1 Shoe Repairs" painted above its door. I could make out the brighter lights of the more developed part of the town, broken by a large structure that was the stadium, built during my absence to host Independence Day celebrations, colourful political rallies, and soccer matches on Saturday afternoons.

The shop door opened and my young relative walked out. I heard the newsreader intone, "...the service will commence at eight o'clock..." and knew it was my brother's funeral he was announcing.

The boy handed me the bottle. I opened it and lifted it to my mouth. I choked on the burning of the alcohol and spilt a few drops against my shirt and to the ground. "A libation," I chuckled, offering the boy the bottle. He smiled, took a quick gulp and returned it. We continued up the road.

We were guided to where they were digging my brother's grave by the glow of a fire and the deep thud of picks digging into the ground. The graveyard was not fenced off or marked by any sign that I could make out. We were just suddenly amongst mounds of earth randomly crouching in the ground and the occasional gravestone standing upright like a sentry in the night. The first graves were low, squat things, overgrown with weeds and grass. Deeper into the burial ground the graves were taller, the round stones heaped on them less burnished in the dim light, their occasional wreaths less battered by the elements. These were the fresher graves of people not so long in the ground.

· At the edge of this row of graves was where they were digging my brother's grave. About ten young men took turns with picks and shovels at a growing hole in the ground. A man in the hole jumped out, handed his pick to another and came over to me. I recognised him as a friend of my brother who had lived a few houses from ours. They used to sell fish they caught in the little dam at the bottom of our township.

We exchanged greetings and he mumbled something about the tragedy of my brother's passing. He called out to the men that I was Puso's brother. I could feel their eyes as they peered at me, and for a moment we all stood perfectly silent there in the dark, the only sound the fingers of the grass scratching against the tombstones. I offered the man out of the hole the bottle, to take their eyes off me, to break the stillness. He took it and the men waist-deep in the hole resumed their digging.

"This graveyard is getting full. It's rocky here and getting more and more difficult to dig. It's a good thing it rained earlier." My brother's friend put the bottle to his mouth.

"Soon they'll have to find another place," he continued, handing it back to me.

The boy who was my relative sighed. "We've buried a lot of people this past while. This Kgodumodumo will finish us all."

I remembered the story of Kgodumodumo. We all grew up hearing it. A story about a huge and hairy beast that devours all the inhabitants of a village, save a young, pregnant woman, whose son grows to manhood in minutes to confront the beast, cut open its belly and release everyone. He becomes chief, is gifted many cattle and takes as his bride the girl with the dimples in her cheeks.

I could not claim ignorance at the general ravaging of this place. My brother's occasional letters, and Thembi's too, spoke always of someone who had passed away. Their letters, as letters are to someone far and long gone away, were held breaths, still points of silence, pauses against motion and movement. And like all still points, their meanings were quickly shelved like useful but barely used implements to mend houses, in places reserved for their storage, so that I had now to open doors, put a light to the darkness and rummage about to find meaning, or if not meaning, then at least a way to connect.

This was a still place I had come to. It was a place pursed in holding in air: a place going faint and hallucinating slightly in the sun or against the slice of the moon; a place paused against movement, so that there was a modesty to the violence of the digging in the hole, so that the men around it, blind already with alcohol, laughed when one of them slipped and fell into the grave, but indecisively, humbly, their fear visible in their wide shining eyes. This was a place stilled by much dying and the dying still to come, and I, accustomed to the stalwart forward movement of a foolish displaced optimism, was thrown about by it.

"Who has died?" I asked.

My brother's friend took off his cap and scratched his head. "Last week we buried Cheevas. And three weeks ago it was Limpho. Remember her? The fat girl of the shop. They moved away."

I remembered Limpho, her father's favourite amongst the large family that owned the shops we had passed on our way here. I caught her and my brother behind the shop one day, his hand groping between her shining thighs, her elbows in front of her to push him away. She would sometimes give him steaming fat cakes or a handful of stolen sweets.

A man opposite us with a deep voice called out some names and they came bouncing to me across the hole in the ground like so many thrown-away things.

The names he called were familiar, everyday names. I could not attach faces to his morbid roll-call, but every name shocked me to associations dimmed by too many years away from here. Every name assaulted me with an image, a girl balanced by two buckets of milk in her hands, the setting sun a halo above her head; a boy shooting his knife into the soil under the shade of the back of a house; a fat woman fighting her way off the bus from town; the boy with sores on his head, who was always snivelling and who we always chased away.

I remembered Nthabiseng, the girl who used to tuck her skirts into her panties and jump about a tennis ball on the stoep of her home. Or was she the girl who years later used to chase me around the sweaty floor of the place we used to go to for beer and the chance to hustle a lucky stolen fuck on Friday nights? Was the Lucky he called the Lucky who went to jail for stealing a car, when everybody knew he hadn't been there when it was taken? And who was Simphiwe? His was not a name from these parts. He must have come from the country neighbouring ours.

Another familiar man digging in the grave stopped to catch his breath and called a name and reminded me that I knew its owner. "Remember the day we tried to hit bats out of the sky? In front of your house? Remember that tall boy with the wire?"

I remembered, and remembered the bat I found under my pillow that night. Thembi had left us the following day.

I asked when the bat catcher had died and someone replied he had passed a few months ago.

They resumed the digging, working a good rhythm, one of them at one end of the hole digging with a pick, another at the other end shouldering the moist soil out with a shovel. After a few minutes they would break and jump out, and another two would take their place, so that progress was quite quick.

Their work would be done when the tallest amongst us would measure himself, six feet or thereabouts, against the depth of the hole. I thought back to the shop Thandeka and I had passed in town in the rain, the words "Six Feet at Last" immodestly painted on its front.

The proprietor wrings his hands, bends his head and frowns, suitably dejected, appropriately humbled. But life must carry on, he consoles, the business of living must and will continue and, at least for this dearly departed soul for whom arrangements are now being made, it is six happy feet at last. He holds his hands behind his back and ushers the two or three come for business about his shop, explaining that it is only proper that the deceased be interred in coffins appropriate to their standing. He hands out catalogues embossed in gold and stands beside those come to do business to explain the various payment options, cash discounts included. He reaches to his breast pocket, takes out an expensive black pen, removes its cap and holds it out with two hands like an offering. Papers duly signed, he springs on gleaming black shoes, skips across to a well-thumbed ledger and promises the coffin will be delivered to the mortuary at such and such a time and that the hearse will arrive as agreed. He shuffles the relatives of the deceased out of the shop, rues that, sadly, death is for us all, but that six feet is a place of rest at last. He waits until they are no longer visible among the people streaming along the pavement, then turns into the shop and shouts instructions to the man in a dust coat at the back, reminding him not to forget to collect the children from school.

Six feet at last, the last men in the grave throw out their picks and shovels and are helped out by the others. An empty bottle rolls into the hole and one of the men jumps back in to retrieve it. In silence, we make our way back to the road in a single file that snakes between the mounds of earth in the ground. Once at the road we pause and shuffle about, the men expectant that I might offer them a drink in return for their labour. We head for the rooms at the shops where, on my way to the graves, the radio had spoken of my brother's funeral.

After the darkness of the streets, the room was bright with the light of a long neon tube hung from the ceiling. Thick cigarette smoke floated in the air, blurring the forms of the men assembled inside. At one end of the room was a wooden counter that served as a bar, behind which stood the owner and a small woman who I assumed to be his wife. On the shelves behind them stood a radio and a line of empty beer bottles and small nips of gin and brandy. They looked at us as we entered and responded heartily to our greetings, though they stared at me for a moment, until, satisfied I was with the familiar men come into the shop, they briefly nodded.

The room was full of men seated on low plastic crates and broken chairs at the edges of the room. They all wore hats on their heads, hard hats and balaclavas and some amongst them, formal hats they once must have been proud of, but which were now misshapen from too many years of use. They wore overalls and dustcoats, though the dejected postures and more randomly assorted garments of a few others spoke of their probable unemployment. Three men sitting slightly aside from the rest were in grey suits, white shirts and ties, and I guessed they were junior civil servants or clerks from shops or the post office in town. I zipped up my coat, a casual black anorak, to hide the formality of my shirt and consciously trawled one shoe across the face of the other, to be as dusty as the others.

We found a space for ourselves and borrowed stools. I offered cigarettes and then money for one amongst us to fetch beer from the counter and we tilted our plastic tumblers to receive it. The beer was cold and sweet with a hint of yeast. I picked a bottle from between my feet and studied it, its long, dark elegance and its bright labels, which, I noticed, offered no warnings for health but only displayed volume and alcohol content. Beer was food, not fashion; effect, not process, though for these men and countless others, meaning was in escaping from their houses, shouting and receiving communal greetings on entering drinking houses such as this, the first draught quaffed, hitching onto the extant banter, and then, hours later, money gone, an earlier optimism dissipated, stumbling out into the darkness, to their hopefully stilled homes.

We talked and laughed and joked into the night. I explained many things and was interrupted often by men come to introduce themselves, some of whom I vaguely remembered, others whom I understood to be more recent arrivals to this place. The men in the suits and ties were disappointed that, though I tried, I could not remember them. They called for a glass for me, explaining that beer did not taste as sweet in plastic tumblers. They soon turned away to resume their discussion of the attributes of some young women, as men with time and opportunity are prone to do.

I was most often interrupted by the more randomly attired men, itinerants who walked the land, I guessed, whose tumblers were empty when they would come to me. Some of them understood how to buy my face so that they could return, half an hour or so later and, telling me a sad or naughty story, would pause mid-sentence to reach for the bottle in between my legs. Others had less guile and were rebuked by my companions to leave me, to leave us, alone. One man amongst these itinerants stood out. He wore his clothes tight, as if to hide a disfigurement. He had the bulging eyes of one afflicted by some mental illness. Around his neck on a dirty rope hung a portable radio, against which was tied, on the same rope, a disfigured child's doll with one leg and one arm and two blue eyes that moved with his every moment. He would occasionally hold the contraption to his ears and turn it on. The men would shout at him to turn it off. I offered him a bottle at which he turned and pressed himself against the wall, lifted the radio-doll thing to his head and pointed at me, his eyes seeming to bulge even further out of their sockets. He mumbled something until one of our group took the bottle and poured him some beer. He drunk lustily but would lift the radio doll thing to his head and point at me every time our eyes met.

Another gaunt, polio-disfigured man danced and stuck out the corners of his amazingly flexible limbs and bent his frame for our amusement. He stole beer, which the men tolerated because he only ever took off the last of a bottle and because when he seemed especially inspired, he would dance like a devil full of angles to the music from the radio. He would sometimes even stand briefly on his hands and threaten to kick the men with his legs.

At first, none of the few women in the room would approach me. Two of them were young, wearing brightly coloured trousers, equally bright if mismatching tops and scuffed, dusty shoes. Their faces were almost turquoise with make up. The older women were more modestly dressed in matronly clothes and headscarves, but were nevertheless undone by the scars on their faces that did not look accidental and their muddied, darting eyes.

I thought at first the women did not come to cadge a drink because they were the partners of the men whose lively company they kept. But I soon noticed how they moved around the men, teasing and mocking them to ingratiate themselves, or how they sometimes even sat on their thighs, as if by way of down-payment for a suck at a bottle. After a while, one of them, who was clearly drunk, came up to us and without introducing herself, held up an empty, brightly labelled bottle – a cider or some blend of fruit and alcohol – and demanded I get her a fresh one. Men drink beer here, though occasionally flush with good fortune, they would buy and sip a small bottle of brandy or cane spirit and get rowdy and aggressive. The women also drank beer, though I remembered how they were also the easy victims of the marketing strategies of our single state-subsidised manufacturer of alcohol and importer, from the country neighbouring ours, of exotically branded and brightly coloured drinks. I reached past the men and offered her money. She stumbled off to the counter, returned and sat close to me and responded randomly to whatever was the subject amongst us, so that we would not chase her away.

I suppose I got quite drunk. I was tired and vulnerable and easily intoxicated by all the new things around me, the odour of the men and their unwashed clothes, the smell of spilt beer, the clinging sex-infused odour of the woman sitting beside me, who had left the room with a man, to urinate I had assumed, but had returned after longer than it would take to lift her skirt and bend and piss behind the shop. My jaws were numb from smiling too often, as people do to ingratiate themselves amongst unfamiliar others. I could feel the vein on my forehead that throbbed when I was tired or stressed. My eyes were scratchy from the dust of digging at the grave and the smoke of the room. But I was nevertheless exhilarated. This was a safe place to which I knew I could always come. Here the talk was not too bitter, though I knew I was still to relearn the real meaning behind the words the men spoke. I was still to know these men and understand the significance of their laughter, because laughter is often a veil. I was still to understand how it was their inevitable stick-raised anger could be so quickly settled; why they were so caringly possessive yet almost abusive of the shouting women amongst them; what was the scorecard against which beers continued to be offered to a currently insolvant one of them. This could be the place I could scurry to, to get away from our house. The men and coal stove and the smoke would warm me against the bitter winters of this place and in summer, it would be cool I knew and the beers cold and wet.

We stumble into the night. I and the boy who was a relative broke away from the rest of our group and made our way down the road that passes the shops, our feet crunching a tattoo on the gravel. I can make out the faint drone of people singing in the tent in the yard outside our house and, further away, a sangoma's drum beating like a heart.

The wind rustled the trees beside the road as if wise to where we'd come from, to what it was we were going to. The cry of a child squeezed out of a small house of mud and stone squatting under tall reeds swaying in the wind. The man of the house swore. A woman, the child's mother, answered back, her voice cheap and defeated, and a faint yellow light came on in the window of their single-room house.

Further down the road at the intersection that leads to our house, I make out the barely visible figure of a man standing against a pole holding up a fence. A second figure brushed through the dark and joined him and for a moment they came together before separating and walking in a direction away from us. I made out a young woman's voice and knew they were lovers.

He must have blown her a secret whistle or thrown pebbles on the corrugated-iron roof of her home to call her outside. She must have slipped on a jersey and soft shoes, peered about to make sure the others were asleep, squeezed quickly through the door, crouched down to quieten the dog and then skipped out to the road, her heart pumping, her blood coursing, to meet her lover.

These are the usual sounds of the night in this place. The air is dense at this time. It sits like a blanket over the village. Things pass through it. Animate things like bats and night birds, and when the wind is very strong, dust and debris and bits of paper and leaves. And things also that we do not have names for. Things that occasionally insinuate themselves through the walls of our houses, into our dreams, so that we are convulsed awake to horrific memories of bloody-eyed things with rotten breaths that licked our faces with rough, lascivious tongues and sat on our chests until we choked.

Sometimes it is we who pass through the air to places inhabited by strange beings. Translucent young girls, each with a single, blinking eye, dancing in a circle; horses without hind legs but standing perfectly in a rain of blood; a dwarf with no arms who giggles and runs away; an infant suckling on its own fecund and distended breast.

And the dead. Talking to us from a firmer place, though their message is never clear. Someone thrice shouting your name in the middle of your slumber, but there is no one in the next room or in the yard outside. A pungent odour of sweat and old urine following you around the house. A sliver of light or a shadow that bolts across the corner of your vision. Private ghosts, whatever their umbrage, whatever their discontent.

But in this and countless other places like it, how does a plurality of the dead talk to a plurality of the living? How do those not yet consumed by the Kgodumodumo account? What is the rhythm of a generalised mourning, or are songs for the dead scattered by being too often sung? Is bereavement a jealous thing? My loss is greater than your loss, we speak with our eyes, because my loss is the more recent, because it was of a child or a truly, truly dearly beloved, or of someone fallen in battle. Your bereavement was inevitable, our eyes scold, and anyway what did you expect the way you lived your lives?

Who, whose life is otherwise on a generally forward-looking if precarious trajectory, is not sometimes pained by a sore at the centre of their heart and is not compelled therefore to try and dull it? And what of those who, unsettled by a foresight of things to come, burst screaming into the world, or arrive with memories from the womb of a tumbling and a falling about hard objects? That first pain is no insurance if "nobody knows the trouble I've seen", nobody sees the trouble I've known, at the tent, outside our house, they wail. The man at the table in front of them wipes the sweat off his brow and implores the lord not to judge this our son, too harshly, even if for now, we should not address ourselves to this man in a box, at least not publicly. To call the dead is to recognise, is to make recompense to the living, and our recompense is not yet due.

To call the dead is to call the sun.

And the sun is a powerful thing. It cures and regenerates. It is a balm, a tonic, a first rate detergent. It demystifies hypochondria and is antagonist to all affliction. It is an antibiotic, an antidepressant, an antihistamine, an aunt who descends on a fractured home, cleans up the living spaces, kindly rebukes the father, consoles the mother, puts the kettle on for tea and buys the children sweets, so that everything and everyone can be remade. The sun wipes away most anything.

I am drunk and stagger past the tent to the house. It is very late. I see the first intimation of light against the mountains on the horizon. Tomorrow's sun frightens me.

Four

OUR LIVES CONTINUED pretty much as usual with Grandmother, Thembi, my brother, Twice and the ever-changing tenants in the outhouses at the back of the yard. Thembi, Puso and I were emboldened by Grandmother's increasing infirmity. We constructed a secret pact for the running of the household. Most things were allowed, as long as they were kept out of Grandmother's view and did not upset her, our tenants, the neighbours or this or the other relative to descend on us occasionally to see that everything was in order. My brother and I generally deferred to Thembi, who established the boundaries of the permissible. Not that there was much we did, really, although my brother's tended to be a sometimes elastic understanding of our new arrangement, as when he brought home the girl from the shops and locked her in our room, in the middle of the afternoon, as if there was absolutely nothing wrong in that.

Over the years Thembi had transformed her room in the outhouses into a warm and lively alternative to the main house. She had acquired a fair-sized bed, a plastic-topped table with four chairs, a radio, a sideboard and a cupboard for her clothes, a smelly paraffin heater to put the room to sleep, and a few other things besides. She would dust the surfaces and sweep the room diligently every morning, and at night would hurry to it from the main house at the first onset of dark to draw the curtains and light the lamp. Later, the evening meal consumed and the dishes and Grandmother cleaned and packed away for the night, she would hurry back to it, to begin her other life.

Twice became as much a part of Thembi's separate life centred on her room as he was, at least initially, part of the life at the main house. When he and Thembi first met they had circled and sniffed at each other like animals. Eventually, names, places of origin and histories established, they had sat at the kitchen table across from each other and talked haltingly in that dancing language of the country neighbouring ours. Twice had been particularly reticent and I had not known if that was his nature with girls, or if it was because of Thembi, her broad walk, her dark smiling face and the way she tilted her head to the side when she concentrated to listen.

At first, Twice would come to visit with perfect timing, just before the evening meal was served. He would scratch his head in a greeting at Grandmother, loudly mention some subject to do with books and then suggest that he and I go outside for a moment where he would quickly engage me in some story of an occurrence of the day or an obscure idea he had just thought of. My interest aroused, he would point out that the food was probably served and that we should go back inside, promising that we would talk of the subject later or the next day.

I knew he told me these little secret stories to secure his presence amongst us around the dinner table. He needed me to call him to sit down, to pass him a slice of steaming bread, to offer him more of the little that might have remained or to break the silences that exposed and rebuked his presence and the reasons for it amongst us.

My brother did not take well to Twice. They were about the same age and height, but I noticed that in my brother's company, Twice would lower his head, assume a shuffle to his walk and move quickly out of the way whenever my brother would move about. Once, during a silent moment, when the news on the radio had been about the abuse of a local girl by a young man from the country neighbouring ours, my brother had blurted out they were all troublemakers and should all be sent back. On another occasion my brother had insisted on a discussion about Abuti Jefti's drinking and how he lived his life to implicate Twice, who lived with him. Twice hardly said a thing that night and left as soon as the meal was done.

After a while he stopped coming to the main house, but would pass directly to Thembi's room, where he would throw himself onto her bed and read a book or lie with his hands under his head listening to the radio until she came. At first Thembi would keep a plate for him and take it with her when she left for the night, but she stopped when my brother commented loudly we couldn't go on feeding the whole neighbourhood.

I deeply resented my brother for driving Twice out of the house. My brother had come to understand the allure and magic of power and in expelling Twice, he had exercised it perfectly over me. He had always bullied me about a bit, but I accepted that as normal. He was never ever cruel about it except occasionally, amongst friends, for demonstration purposes really. Soon after Thembi came to live with us, he tried to dominate her, but she brushed him off and he was chagrined by the fact that then, her age endowed her with more authority than his maleness gave him. But now a second bull threatening the kraal, and the fleece on his chin suggesting manhood and the possibilities of a new order, he was emboldened to take us all on. I suppose Thembi understood these things if only instinctively. Perhaps she calculated that authority forgone in the main house was sufficiently compensated for by the freedom to live a second life, as she wanted, in her room in the backyard.

My brother brushed past the insolent silences and monosyllabic responses I adopted as revenge. And neither was Thembi much impressed. She treated me as always. As for Grandmother, her life was dark and dim and she could sense little of the new tenor of the household. I remained in a brooding, self-conscious funk, thick and festering like a mound of cow dung in the garden. I needed to invent a reprisal that would dilute his arrogance and castrate the bellow in him.

Soon after my brother had barred Twice from the house, Grandmother sent me one day to restock her pills and medicines from the government dispensary in town. Now that she was no longer able to make the trip, a young doctor, like all doctors educated abroad, would come to our house at the end of the month for her check ups. That was not the normal thing, but he explained that Grandmother's husband had been his teacher and that he felt obliged to help in some way. Like Grandmother, he would call me after my grandfather as he handed me his heavy doctor's bag to carry into the house. I would lead the way, shooing the dogs and explaining, the irony not lost to me, how Grandmother had been since his last visit.

Whatever the diagnosis, the young doctor always made out the same prescription. His visit over, he would stress to me the importance of Grandmother taking her medication as indicated. I would then hurry to put on clothes reserved for excursions into town, for visitors, weddings and other occasions such as those. I would jump into his smart car and wave at the neighbourhood children at the sides of our township streets, to be sure they saw me as we rushed into town. Once at the hospital, just off the main thoroughfare of our little town, I would follow in the wake of the doctor's dancing white coat, through the crowds of mothers and children come to be weighed and inoculated and through the emergency ward where men with broken and bleeding limbs sat about awaiting the nurse with the imperious bosom to call them in for attention.

The doctor would push me through the throng of people crowded against the window where medicines were dispensed. He would flirt with the nurses, undaunted by the hapless victims holding vials of urine or faeces, like reprimands. He would sometimes stop by some old lady to enquire about the state of her arthritis or high blood-pressure, and cluck a soft admonition at her for not taking her medication as instructed.

Once in the dispensary, I would squeeze myself against a tall metal shelf with vats of colourful syrups and buckets and plastic bags with pills and steel myself against the glares of the throng jammed against the service window. The chief dispensing officer, a grey man in a grey suit and meticulously polished black brogues would enquire about Grandmother as he put together her medicines. He would write the instructions for their ingestion in precise handwriting and insist that I read them back to him.

"Two pills, three times a day, after meals." He would squeeze his eyes behind his glasses and nod his head, "Good. Good."

"One pill, once a day, just before sleeping," I would read from the second packet. The chief dispensing officer would pat me on the back.

From the first bottle containing a dark, sticky syrup I would read, "One tablespoon, three times a day, after meals", and from the second, "As required, but not more than two times a day with meals".

I knew these instructions well. Going to the hospital had become as much a ritual as going to the store that served as our post office. Grandmother's current doctor and whichever doctor she used to see when she still had the wherewithal to undertake the trek to the hospital, always prescribed the same medicines, such that they seemed to work not so much to make her better, but to maintain her in a stable if slowly deteriorating state of health. The young doctor, fresh from training overseas and keen to establish himself as a more learned healer when he first started seeing Grandmother, did briefly prescribe something different, a pale yellow potion to be taken once a day only. But Grandmother had complained of headaches and pains in her joints and he was obliged to concede the efficacy of her established remedies.

From the hospital I would walk along the thoroughfare that is the spine of our town and make for our township, Grandmother's medicines in a plastic bag firmly clutched in my hand. I would make a quick detour to one of the many cafés at the bus stop where I would count the coins Grandmother would have thrust at me and purchase steaming fat cakes, or chips soaked in vinegar and garnished with too much salt. I would wait until I was at the hillock at the outskirts of town, looking across the valley to our township, before I would settle myself on an appropriately elevated rock to consume my fare. My repast done, my greasy hands wiped carefully against a tuft of grass or a discarded bit of paper, I would continue on my way.

The plan came to me as I made my way up the path that leads to the main road at the centre of our township. I stopped suddenly as its possibilities became apparent, ignoring the greetings of the children toiling in the vegetable garden at the back of their home. The risks were high, the dangers real, but if it worked, it would exact a perfect revenge on my brother. No one would ever discover what I had done and my brother would have to live with the very dire consequences of an act that would reflect a negligence unbecoming of someone claiming authority on account of pale wisps of hair on his chin and a breaking voice. He would be undone and would not know why or how, though I would leave a whisper behind the curtains, a smudge against the table or a faint trail of drops on the floor to hint at my hand at the act.

I arrived home to Grandmother on the stoep in front of the house on a low armchair with an animal's claws for legs. I showed her the medicines clutched in my hand and hurried to put them in her room. Thembi was preparing our midday meal and I knew she would be too preoccupied to notice that I would remain in Grandmother's room for longer than necessary to simply place the medicines on her table. I entered the room, dark and cool with its curtains drawn against the heat and sat on Grandmother's imposing bed. I took the pills out of the plastic bag and spilled the contents of the first sachet on the bed on the one side of me and the second on the other side. I then quickly scooped the first spill of pills and poured them into the sachet and repeated the action in reverse for the second batch. I replaced the two sachets in the plastic bag, which I then placed on the bedside table.

The job was done. The plan was in place. There was only one thing left to do and that I would do later in the evening when it was time for Grandmother to take her pills. Until then, I would remain about the house and act the filial grandson. I would offer her cool water from the tap and perfectly sweetened, perfectly whitened tea. I would listen to her complaints about one or the other of our tenants. I would bound into the house to fetch whatever she needed – her bible, the radio so that she could listen to the drama about the wicked man who was deceiving his family; the red and white can of vaseline to cream her hands and face; her shawl to comfort her against the chill of the late afternoon. Thembi saw this and teased I was overly enamoured of Grandmother's breasts.

As was his wont, my brother would not appear until the shadows were long. But I knew he would be back in time for my plan to work. Sitting beside Grandmother on the stoep, I saw him come skipping down the road that leads to our house, his frame barely visible against the fiery glare of the setting sun. He bounded across Grandmother's garden, ignoring her shouts that he should use the driveway and skidded to a dusty stop in front of us, wide-eyed and boisterous with a story about a fight at the café up the road.

It had not been a normal Saturday afternoon. On a normal Saturday, chores done, I too would normally sneak away from the house. I would go to Twice or, if he was irritated, to another friend or to one of my favourite places – behind the outhouses where the earth was cool and slightly damp under the shade of thick pine trees and where the sounds of a radio from one of the rooms would sing me reason and displacement at one and the same time. Or to that place at the bottom of our township where I had read the letter to Adelina. Or to town where I would stare at the wares in the shops or follow white children about and mimic they way they talked, until a watchman with a stick would chase me away.

But I had remained at home and made myself available to Grandmother, though I sometimes did not hear what she said, or sometimes forgot what she had sent me into the house to fetch. I dug a hole with a stick in the ground against the stoep. Grandmother had noticed and asked me what was bothering me. I ran inside to refill her jug of water.

"Grandmother," I started, making use of goodwill purchased, "Twice wants a book of mine" – something to do with school would do. "I will be back just now," to be available again as I had been and as I would always be, because of, despite of today.

"Go 'Lefe, but do not delay."

I dashed into the house to fetch the book and made for the streets, my heart beating, my limbs weak and shaking, my head heavy and dull with a foreboding of what was to follow. I stopped at the gate and made to rush back to undo the plan, but saw my brother dancing with the dogs and remembering his arrogance, resolved to carry it through and bounded into the growing dark.

In common with many elderly women in these parts, Grandmother suffered from high blood-pressure and a weak heart. The condition was so common I always assumed there was something of a fashion about it. To the accompaniment of breaths sucked through teeth and knotted hands patted gently against breasts, old women, gathered outside a church or at a wedding or funeral or at a monthly savings association meeting, would complain about the ailment, the dizziness that comes with it, the threat of strokes that would claim them all one by one, and console each other in the knowledge that it was a shared, inevitable affliction.

It was a condition Grandmother put to good use. Shaman as all old people are, she would conjure up its effects whenever she needed to remind us that she, and not Thembi or my brother, was the centre of the household. She would call to us in a faint voice like a kitten stuck behind a cupboard every time the sounds coming to her from the kitchen suggested an ardour that defined her out of the life of the household. We would at first ignore her, aware that all she sought was a little attention and to have us bustle about her to retrieve the blankets wilfully pushed onto the floor, or to offer her a jug of water which she would accept and then reject for tea, and then reject for soup.

Her estate re-established, her room straightened and settled at last, Grandmother would inevitably ask my brother and Thembi to leave the room. She would ask me to sit at the edge of her bed, clasp her hands that resembled stranded bullfrogs around mine and eyes uncommonly still, would rue the genealogy of our lives. She would peel away at the years and talk of being brought many years ago from the country neighbouring ours to this place to be married, her late husband's rectitude, our parents' fate, stories all that I had heard many times before, but which I would obediently listen to at each retelling. She would lift her heavy hands from mine and raise them to my head as if to anoint me the final repository of the bones and blood that had named this family.

"You 'Lefe must hold this family together," she would whisper as if telling me a great secret that my brother and Thembi in the room next door were not to hear. She would pull me closer with suddenly strong arms and go on, "It is good Thembi is here. She has been a great help to me. I don't know what I would have done with you and your brother if she were not. When I am gone," she would sigh, loosing me and tapping at her breast, "she will be here for you."

Thembi's voice would come bursting through from the room next door as she shouted at one of the tenants in the back yard, forgetful of the solemnity and quiet demanded of grandmother's recent indisposition. Grandmother would click her teeth and shake her head. "But she is still a young one and she came here with things from the country neighbouring ours," she would sigh regretfully.

She would remember my oblique association with that place and warn, "Watch out for that friend of yours. He is a good one, but many things follow him from the country neighbouring ours and may come to do you harm."

"And your brother. He is like your father. He wants things quickly. He already wants to rush away from here and leave us all behind," at which almost by illustration I would hear the front door open and my brother bound away across the stoep, slide across the narrow lawn skirted by flowers at the front of the house and make for the gate, the dogs panting and yelping behind him.

"You 'Lefe must never leave this place."

I would turn my head to the floor, away from the glare of her grey cataracts that made her eyes like white people's eyes, my bent and mute disposition a tacit acquiescence to her demands. Finally done, Grandmother would lean back into her bed, whisper a faint prayer for our absolution and hurry me out of the room to fetch water for her medicines.

Grandmother's taking of her medicines was something akin to a ritual. It was even more structured after one of her fainting spells. Even though there wasn't a clock in her room, she would call for me at exactly the same time in the evening. If for some reason I was not available, she would ask my brother to make the preparations, something he would try to fob off onto Thembi.

For water, Grandmother would only use an old dented metal jug with imperial measurements on one side and a handle on the other. Once, when it was misplaced, she almost screamed the house down. She also insisted on water from the tap outside and would not drink water collected each morning by Thembi and stored in a bucket under the kitchen table for drinking, cooking and other light household use. It was not cool enough or fresh she would complain. Grandmother would also demand a thick slice of bread and butter, because "You shouldn't take pills on an empty stomach." These were all to be carried to her on a metal tray with a cloth and her favourite old silver spoon with the British royal coat of arms at its end.

The tray was to be placed on the bedside table, after which whoever was administering the pills would then retrieve the medicines from a shelf under it and place them on the tray. That done, Grandmother would mumble her approval as first two pills were taken from the one sachet and then a single pill from the second and also placed on the tray. She would then lift the pills from the tray, a slow task given her thick arthritic fingers and the size of the pills, and scramble them into her mouth. She would extend her hand for the jug and, eyes closed lift it and slowly drink, her throat squirming and gulping like a bound animal. Her eyes still closed, she would then extend the jug to be taken by whoever was ministering to her. For a moment she would remain still as if to guide the pills and water to her stomach by an act of concentration.

Abruptly, she would open her mouth to reveal toothless gums because she always removed her false teeth for the occasion. Her breath, a heady distillation of sticky saliva, old tea and pills despite the water recently swirling in her mouth would rise like an aura around her. Whoever was tending to her should by now have poured green syrup from the first bottle into her favourite spoon. Slurped off the spoon, she would open her mouth once again for the second syrup. Finally done, she would cough once or twice, pat her chest, open her eyes and look about as if seeing the world for the first time and then settle back amongst her pillows to suck and masticate at the slice of bread.

I was late in coming home that night and arrived to a quiet and put together house. Grandmother had retired to bed and my brother and Thembi were huddled around the kitchen table playing a quiet game of cards to the backdrop of the radio and the hiss of pots of water simmering on the coal stove. I explained I had been at Twice's, which was true and enquired about Grandmother. They ignored me and continued their game. I shuffled about the room for a bit and then feigned drowsiness and announced I was retiring. Thembi pointed with her chin at a plate covered with another on the stove and asked if I had eaten. I answered I had and stretching a yawn, I slunk off to the room I shared with Puso.

A settled house as ours has habitual patterns of sound and movement to announce it awake: the crow of the cock; a rush of water from the tap outside as someone collects water for washing; scratching and scraping as the stove is emptied of ash; the radio blaring promises for the day just begun; the rumble of the first bus in the distance as it takes the faithful to work or to early morning prayer.

But I awoke to scuttling feet and much coming and going in the adjoining rooms. For a moment I lay confused in bed, my eyes sticky from a restless, dreamless sleep. I knew something was amiss and remembered suddenly what I had done.

I did not walk directly into the kitchen. Instead, I put my eyes to the crack in the door through which I had spied

Thembi when she first came to live with us. Standing by the kitchen table was one of our tenants, an elderly woman who worked as a maid for white people in town. It was Sunday, her day off. The woman was ringing a cloth into a vessel of steaming water on the table. Thembi burst into the room, a towel and a bucket of water in her hands. She put them onto the table and snatched at the cloth from the vessel, wincing as she burnt herself. She glared at me as I entered the room.

"'Lefe, Grandmother is not well. Put on some clothes and go and phone the doctor."

"What has happened to her?" I asked, my heart drumming, my thoughts turning to the possibility of Grandmother being dead.

"I don't know," Thembi replied, rushing into Grandmother's room.

I had to go into the room. I had to see for myself what Grandmother looked like. I had to see the effects of my act of revenge. But most of all I had to see to be sure that she was not beyond repair, that she would recover from what I had convinced myself, was not such a drastic measure. I rushed into the room after Thembi.

Grandmother was lying back against her big pillows in her bed. Her eyes were tightly shut and from her gaping mouth, a string of saliva hung and stretched to her breast. Her breathing was irregular and her hand resting on the bed beside her twitched like a dying thing.

Thembi wiped Grandmother's brow with a cloth. "Grandmother. Grandmother. What is the matter?" she said, the tone of her voice rising in worry.

"'Lefe, run and phone the doctor and tell him to come. Grandmother is not well."

I stood fixed to the floor, my eyes wide as I stared at someone I imagined dying.

The cloth in Thembi's hand splashed a trail of water against my face as she bolted from the room. She shouted for my brother still asleep in our room, her voice angry and in a panic.

His name shocked me to my plan, and I remembered what still remained to be done. I stole a quick look at Grandmother who remained supine in her bed and rushed to her bedside table. I had to switch the pills back. In the next room, the door leading to our room opened and I heard feet scuffle into it and knew that I had this chance only.

I bent and reached behind the curtain on the table and took out the sachets. I spilled the pills into two small piles on the table and stuffed the first small pile into its rightful envelope. Beside me, Grandmother suddenly convulsed and groaned. Her eyes were open and were fixed at me.

"Who is that? Is it you 'Lefe?"

I stood frozen beside her, the second scoop of pills in one hand. "She can see me," I thought. "She sees what I am doing. She sees it is I that has done this to her."

I forgot myself and called to her, but her head swivelled away towards the wall and I did not know if it was because she saw what I had done. I funnelled the pills into the sachet, dropping one as I did so and pushed the two envelopes under the bedside table. Thembi entered the room as I straightened up.

"What are you doing 'Lefe?" she asked in a pinched voice.

My voice caught in my throat and I didn't say anything.

Thembi thrust coins and a slip of paper with a number on it into my hand and shouted at me to run to the store that served as our post office to call the doctor to come. I bolted out of the room and almost knocked down my brother standing vacant and bewildered in the kitchen. Well down the road that leads to the store, I paused and looked between blinding tears at sweating coins and the slip of paper yellowed by the pills I had just held in my hand. I would call the doctor and everything would be all right.

Grandmother spent two days in hospital, "For observation," the doctor said, when he returned to explain to us how she was. He had asked whether Grandmother had taken her pills as usual and why it was one had been spilled onto the floor. My slightly irate brother explained that yes he did give Grandmother her medication as indicated and that, no he did not know how the pill had fallen out of its little envelope.

When they brought her home the doctor explained that either she had not taken her pills or she had taken them in the wrong combination. He turned to my brother and tapping him lightly on the back, urged him to be more careful the next time, adding that medicines were not things to be carelessly played with. My brother shrugged the doctor's hand off and replied sulkily that he had done as indicated on the packages. I offered the suggestion that, in future, only Thembi and I should dispense Grandmother's pills. The implications of this statement were clear and my brother bolted out of the room, ignoring the doctor calling after him.

Grandmother repaired soon enough and was quickly her usual cantankerous self. I had the sense however that she called for me more often than before, and that there was a change in her tone when she talked to my brother. For a while he was not himself and it was quieter than usual around the kitchen table in the evenings, after we had prayed and eaten and Thembi had cleared away the dishes. I cajoled Twice into coming to eat with us again, lying that Grandmother had said it was all right and for a while he did. But the spaces between my brother and Twice remained thick with tension and a nervous call and response of movement. The one would be unsettled by the dropping of a spoon by the other. The one would stop his scraping at his bowl at the sneeze of the other. Twice would squeeze himself unnaturally against the table to allow my brother to pass behind him, or would shut up to my brother's every interjection and not continue afterwards even when I pressed him to do so. My brother would eat in a hurry and rush out to the room we shared, and only reappear once Twice had left for the night.

Puso deferred to me, at least for a while, so that it was I who would interrupt his languid telling of an occurrence at school or on the streets of our township and in so doing define it irrelevant, insignificant, of poor comparison to other fables of truer resonance for this household. His pain at his emasculation before us was visible. He became a gentler, more patient, slightly defeated creature, like a bird at the point of realising the futility of flying into glass. He became a hesitant whisper of his old self around the house. He spent more and more time out on the streets and would return bitten, scratched, soiled, his life out there still rude and brittle. But his entry into this yard or this house would force on him a taciturnity and self-consciousness so that his stories from the streets were less ribald in their manufacture, less profusely adorned, less contemptuous of his own or some other hapless soul's defeat. He learnt to listen to the noise of my silences and for the first time, I felt that when the time came, when he and I would be without Grandmother, and Thembi, that we would survive, not in a simple practical way, but in a more profound way, that we would sing meaning to each other and connection and fortitude for our lives to come.

My guilt at the act of revenge was like a swamp. Sometimes I felt I could clutch at its reeds and pull myself above it and walk to its other side. At other times it was muddy and fetid, so that sitting in the sun, or in the shade behind the outbuildings where the radio and the talk from behind a drawn window would conflate me, I would be drowned by it. I would remember the thread of saliva hanging from Grandmother's mouth and the way she had stared at me as I switched her pills and remember that I had been prepared to risk her illness to undo an inevitable and finally trivial affront. I dug holes in the ground like a small burrowing animal and pissed in them and looked for patterns in the froth of my urine. I stamped my foot behind a stranded toad and laughed as our dogs barked and sniffed at it. I stared at classmates seated in front of me at school and divined their fortunes by the shapes of their heads. I yearned to squeeze the boils and pimples on Thembi's face as if to excise poisons in her. I listened to Abuti Jefti's records and unravelled the mathematics of their rhythms, the sorcery of their melodies. I opened Thembi's drawers and looked at her underwear. I shuffled behind my brother and wished he was what he had been before I had undone him. I looked at Grandmother and wondered who she was, what she was beyond a failing matriarch ensconced with pillows and blankets on a propped up bed funky with the smell of her effluence. I wondered at her and our histories and where they would carry us. And always, the sun continued to shrill. The moon scratched at the darkness. The stars danced like an initiation of pubescent girls in mockery of me.

Five

IN TIME, THE act to half kill Grandmother became like even the most vivid memories. It receded and dimmed and became as a place of reluctant personal pilgrimage. It became a place to wash away guilt, a place for the occasional haphazard return, a milestone to measure the years, to mark the passing of my early years.

My brother's beard grew to beyond a whisper. He came to construct a Saturday morning ritual to shave it. A bucket with steaming water placed carefully on chair in the back yard, a jagged hand-held mirror for the memory, a towel to wipe at the suds of soap on his face, a large black comb for the hair on his head, his shirt off for acclaim and the radio and our ageing, frailer, still yelping dogs to bless the proceedings.

I would skulk about to learn his ritual and steal away to study my face, and wonder when it might sprout as his had.

Thembi danced about and talked and laughed in the language of the country neighbouring ours. She came to smell of soap, cheap perfumes, and other cloying, sweet odours. She cavorted about and was strong in the leg. She balanced jugs of milk to take to a neighbour's sick child, clutched coins and scraps of money, salt, evidence, advice for a household about to be evicted. She sculpted her hair, sometimes with poor success. She asked for funds additional to her weekly stipend for activities whose purpose we could not guess.

Sometimes her face would cloud up and she would sulk off to sit alone in her room. She would let me in and tell me stories about her mother, her tall brothers, her father, her yearning to go back to her home in the country neighbouring ours.

She would ignore my ineffectual attempts to dilute her pain. I would mutter recollections of her charms, her successes, the way she had constructed a world with herself at its firm centre, like the sun. The way her room was like a queen's castle, a hidden place of camouflage, bubbling water, soft music and not so bitter memories.

I would make a connection of Twice and suggest his uneasy and fought-for existence amongst us as contrition on our part. I hugged him into the house and offered him scarce available things, when my brother was not about or was too occupied by an event out on the streets to care. I was tempted to tell her I had switched Grandmother's pills the time she almost died.

I learnt a little of her language and humoured her by speaking it. I brought her little found gifts. Bright or dull things – a perfectly freckled stone; the tail of a slaughtered goat; magazines full of colour stolen from a café in town; a tin drinking vessel discarded by the white people in town, empty but worthy by reason of its previous ownership. I enjoyed the songs she liked that would blare on the radio and copied the way she danced so that I would tell her whole life by the lay and intent of my step. And she knew it, so that sometimes she was languid and blissful, and sometimes angry and shattered and shout me out of her room.

Thembi's room become a second place of refuge for those come over the river from the country neighbouring ours. Almost daily, sullen groups of two or three young men or women would pass the main house and disappear into her room in the backyard.

I got to know a few of them, her regular, tighter friends. There was Ace, a football player apparently, though you wouldn't say so what with his buttocks that jived and twisted behind him. Ace always came with Thami, a quiet, shy boy who never said anything, and sometimes with a fellow with a bad odour they called Skunk. They would sit on her bed and on her few chairs and smoke cigarettes. Occasionally Thembi would send me to fetch cool beers from the room adjoining the shops up the road. They would turn the dial on the radio and listen to distant music from the country neighbouring ours. They would sing along, each claiming a separate harmony for identity and to augment the whole. Occasionally their arguments would erupt into brief spurts of violence and a knife would emerge to cut harsh, spat words. If Twice where there he would intervene, his proprietorial instincts aroused. He would come between the warring boys, shout them down and eject them from the room and the yard.

The girls were more familiar. They would call to tease me and speak to me in our language and laugh when they got it wrong. They were all about Thembi's age, ripe girls with breasts and thighs that would shiver when they moved about. Sometimes, on weekends, they would sit outside in the sun and take turns to scratch and pull and tie each other's hair. Occasionally they would come with a squawking chicken, potatoes, bright-red tomatoes, a cabbage or two and Thembi would hurry into the main house to fix a succulent, yellow meal, full of pepper and hot to the taste, which they would consume in a hurried silence.

Once in a while, most often at night, I would catch the sounds of deep, deep wailing coming from Thembi's room and would know that one of them had lost someone dearly beloved – a parent, a brother or sister or lover – and would be chagrined by the fact that they could not return home to bury them. I would make out Thembi's lowered, patient voice between the bitter choking and understand that our house and her room in it had become, for them, a home of sorts. I would hurry to the main house and steal juice concentrate, scones if there were any about, anything that might soothe their pain.

Twice would also seem to hear the crying and appear suddenly. He had cut a path along the hedge that separated the outbuilding from the neighbouring yard so that he did not have to use the gate at the bottom of the yard. He would just suddenly be there, quiet as always, like a soft breeze or a scent. His was to stand and shuffle about, his hands in his pockets, his lips chewing against his jutting teeth, his head rocking rhythmically as if to conjure himself or the anguish away from this place.

When not at school, Twice was most often at the house he had come to share with Abuti Jefti. He didn't venture much into the dusty streets of our location. Nor did he ever really go to town, except to sell to white children the little wire cars and toys he made. I would come across him sitting on a bench under a tree at the corner of Abuti Jefti's small, contained yard. He would raise his eyes quickly to acknowledge me and turn his attention back to his hands, efficient, callused things, quick to bend wire or to lift a tool from the sand below him, or to swat at a fly.

Our conversations were almost always hesitant and stilted and sometimes I wondered what it was that brought me to him. I would talk about simple things, about occurrences around the township heard from my brother, embellished for better effect; about a new girl that had come to Thembi's room, at which he would stop for a moment and smile; about Abuti Jefti's most recent scandalous performance under the influence of alcohol at which we would laugh and feel connected.

Sometimes, on particularly somnolent afternoons, when everything was battered and stilled by the fierceness of the sun, he would, like Thembi, talk of his home. And, as when a girl would break down and wail in Thembi's room, I would be saddened once again, because as a backdrop to the softly buzzing tenor of his fond recollections, his anecdotes, his sudden mimicry of a friend's walk, was a canvas of a brutality and hunger greater than I had ever known.

"And where is he now?" I would ask him of a friend perfectly described.

"Oh, he died," he would answer, his voice coming to a simple full stop. I would know by the silence or the way he reached for his tools that his friend had been undone by some pointless act of violence.

He offered to show me a picture of his mother once and had ambled deliberately into the house to fetch it. He wouldn't give it to me but had held it carefully in his two hands as if afraid for it. The woman in the picture was a thin, awkward woman. She wore a long, shapeless dress that hung to her ankles. A small wooden cross was pinned to her depleted breasts, and on her head was tightly bound white scarf. She was staring defiantly out of the picture, but her half-raised arms and feet placed one slightly in front of the other suggested flight.

"And your father?" I asked.

"We didn't have a father," he answered, and I hummed beside him to remind him that neither did we, Puso and I, have a father, or a mother.

He pointed at the picture. "She's standing in front of our house."

It was a small house of brick.

"We had to move out when she died. We went to live with relatives."

I knew they had moved not to a better, warmer place, but that they had been scattered to live with poorer aunts or with an uncle's discarded wife or with friends of the family, connected by place of origin or a significant, remembered act of kindness.

Twice never received a letter or a message carried by someone come over from the country neighbouring ours. He never explained whether this was because his brothers and sisters were illiterate or because they did not know where he was or because they did not care.

Abuti Jefti was almost always about, though he tended to stay indoors with his records and books, and his condition, invariable somewhere between a surly hangover and the induction of the next one. His lover sometimes visited, a fussy woman with carefully made up hair, glistening glasses and reproach in her voice. She would bundle him out of the house, search about for cleaning things and proceed to dust, scrub and generally put the place in order. She would appear every now and then to draw water from the tap, take out dusty beer bottles or to hang a washed shirt on the line.

"Bloody woman," he grumbled. "Can't keep her hands off anything. Thinks she's my mother."

Abuti Jefti would send Twice into the house for more beer. Settled, he would enter into one of his monologues on the state of the continent.

"Mengistu is on the offensive. Apparently got new guns from the Soviets. Hopes to contain the Horn. Can't read history that fellow."

He sipped from his glass.

"One emperor for another. The Ogaden won't buckle. There are not many things you can teach people who live on camels, especially foreign things. And they'll fight you all the way. For all that desert with nothing in it. Doesn't matter that they are supposed to be your subjects or that your money works where they live, if they use it at all. They'll use anybody's money that works."

He lit another cigarette. "They've got it all wrong. Nkrumah was the man. We should have listened to Nkrumah. Met him many years ago."

"Oh. Did you? What was he like?" Twice asked.

"Do you know who Nkrumah is?" he pointed accusingly at me.

I had heard the name but remained dumb.

"Typical. But you know who Cecil John Rhodes is, right?" Another sip from his beer.

"I met them all. Nkrumah, Nyerere, Senghor. In London. Paris." He was silent for a while, the glass of beer held against his lips, his eyes focused on distant places in his memory, when he was with Nkrumah in London and was handsome and excited for the future.

He called out other names.

"And all we have now are the Mengistus of this world. Men hungry for power who murder this continent. Armed with foreign ideas and paid in foreign money. And they're not much better here," he continued staring at me again.

"You see, you can use any pretext to justify things. Twice comes here running away from the country neighbouring ours and so our dear leader here is absolved. But trucks come at night and take people away, and nobody says anything, because our leaders have their excuses, their justification. And those who are taken away? What did they do? Except to suggest a different way?"

It makes a vague sense to me. The war. No, not war. More a relatively bloodless state of unease with a barely visible trickle of victims. People like Twice and the boys and girls who come to Thembi's room. Fathers from our township are dismissed from their jobs or are briefly taken away for questioning by men in trucks that rumble through the night.

"My friends joined rag-tag armies and disappeared into places I have never heard of. Or became governments, or run large companies making beer or mining tin. You'd be surprised at the people I know," he laughed.

"Nkrumah talked about borders. He was one of the first. And they got rid of him for doing so. And now everybody is happy to keep them, or to extend them because you can't be a president without a border."

Twice sometimes participated.

"I agree. But what do you put in their place? To what do we go back once we have removed these borders? To the village, the chief?"

Abuti Jefti was dismissive. They had debated many times before. "You and your socialism. Think the ideas of an old German Jew will save us. We can't go backwards, but we can't look for salvation in ideas that come from Europe. We are what we are because they are what they are."

I could make no sense of it and was happy to go into the house to fetch Abuti Jefti a bottle. The woman followed me out and shouted across the yard, "Isn't it a little early for so much beer?"

Abuti Jefti looked at her silently and turned back to Twice to advance a point.

"We have men and women we should have listened to. Not the false prophets who come here with good things to dish out in exchange for our lives, our souls."

The beer was taking effect.

"You young people, you burn Credo Mutwa our noblest seer, our greatest healer. Say he is in the way of change. Just watch. Modjadji will stop making rain, because we forget who she is. We don't read Odinga's books, or hear what Aime

Cesaire says, son of a slave, speaking to us from across the ocean. Or Fanon who died before he turned forty, but explained how you can use blood to clean everything."

Twice's tools lay untouched on the ground below him. The woman was done with cleaning the house and pulled up a bench to sit with us.

"And I teach at a mission school and simply stay here." He stared about the yard.

"I drink my beer, listen to my records, talk to you boys. It's not much of a life, but better than most. I haven't been home to the country neighbouring ours for many years but I know what's going on. I look at young people like Twice rushing here and will tell you their history. One day they'll be bitter like me. Or they'll forget. The clever ones will forget and accept whatever works. Because our lives are short and when a little opportunity offers itself, why not, why not jump and take it?"

The woman sitting with us interjected: "But Jefti it's your fault that you are bitter. There are so many things you could have done, could still do."

She was afraid to look at him in the face but continued. "You did not have to come back. Or you could have done more. Put away the drinking and that music you listen to. Gone with all those people you like to tell us about and done something. Instead of sulking in this place."

Abuti Jefti got up from his perch and made to urinate against the wall of the house.

"That's why I love you so much," he laughed back at the woman. "You're the only one to put me in my place."

"Why don't you use the toilet like everyone else?" she responded, as if to illustrate his point.

A moment later he shuffled back to where we were seated, drops of urine freckling the leg of his trousers.

"I was there," he carried on, reaching for the bottle and squatting down. "I was also huddled down in those cold, wet places amongst people who claimed to be with us, but who would always run to more comfortable places when things got tough. I got tired of too much good advice, too many people somehow with the credentials to tell us what to do and how to do it, what to be, what to fight for. I got angry at the way there was nothing they did not know. They way they could tell me more about myself than I could. The way they knew more about us than we did. So that when I would suggest a course, a position, it was ridiculed. Not because there was anything wrong with it, but because it wasn't their invention, their suggestion. It wasn't put in their language."

He was roused.

"You should have seen us. We had money, their money generously parted with." He laughed. "We were all over the place, meeting and talking, and drinking a lot. But that was all right. We were young and were taking over the world. Everything was bright. Anything was possible. We learnt how to milk them for money, and their women for sympathy." He laughed again.

"We danced a lot, in between a lot of talk about the future. Rumba and all sorts of music from all over the place. Black music. Jazz. We were special, you must remember. The first to go over there in big numbers. We were doing anthropology. Studying them in their environment. We made our own space, had our own places to meet, determined who was allowed in and who was not. And if a new fellow arrived, ugly and badly dressed and black from too much sun," his teeth flashed as he laughed, "we would welcome him, show him the ropes, where the best drinking spots were. We would take him to the market when he felt homesick and show him where to buy fufu, cassava, plantain, whatever."

He stopped and rearranged himself on the stool.

"I remember I had a collection of records, by Franco, the chap from Congo. Franco had a song for each African head of state. So when a fellow from say Ghana came in, we would dance to Kwame Nkrumah ah yeh. Didn't know what to do with the thing when they couped him."

He pointed at the house. "I still have some of them somewhere in there. I'll could play them sometime, but they wouldn't make sense to you."

I imagined dozens of dusty records in torn sleeves, pictures of black men in long robes on their fronts.

"But then it all went wrong. Nkrumah was ousted and the whole continent went astray. I stayed on and watched them leaving. Left girlfriends and good times behind. Some wrote for a while, but soon stopped. Too busy making money or running governments. I'd hear about some of them on the radio. Big bunch of crooks they all became. Some died."

He stopped. Sweat glistened on his forehead. He looked exhausted. He stood up and stretched to retrieve the bottle and glass spilled around his feet.

"I tell this boy not to do as we did. But he doesn't say anything. He doesn't know anything. I've told him everything and don't know if he hears me. It's not my time anymore."

He looked down at us, his face a dirty plaster of pain. He turned to the woman. "Come let's go inside. I need to lie down." She got up and followed him into the house.

Twice and I remained outside. We sat staring at the ground, still and battered by a lesson of history.

"Come let's go look for wire," he said, gathering his tools and wire and carrying them to where he kept them in a wooden crate at the side of the house.

We walked into a low, staring sun.

Everything was elucidated by the memory of Abuti Jefti's story. Eddies of dust grabbed at our feet as we walked the streets. Dry, flapping things hung like bats on the fences that separated yards. The voices of children playing about came to us like loyal, unforgiving ghosts. They echoed and shrilled and cut through the growing dim of late afternoon, but remained without meaning. The buses rumbling up the main road were choked and apologetic, like bearers of bad news.

Twice and I were huddled against the bustle and walked as if we were two untouched, untouchable apparitions. As if we were discarded, unwanted things. Like blood.

We didn't find any wire.

We found my brother instead. Lounging and laughing against the wall of the shops. Hidden between the flapping coats of the boys who made a poor living there.

"Let's ignore him," I said, conscious of the stillness his reason would burst, but aware that he had seen us.

We walked past the shops, our heads bent in greeting to the boys and my brother amongst them, fidgeting at the side of the shop. We continued silently up the road, the growing darkness obscuring our original purpose. We might trip over wire. But that was highly unlikely. We could peel wire off fences, but that was dishonest and would bring us ill-will. So we just walked, the shuffle of our feet a fanfare to our purposelessness.

"She, she's right," Twice blurted out, and for a moment I did not know whom he was talking about.

"Abuti, Abuti Jefti should not have come here. Look how he's rotting away."

I thought back to Abuti Jefti and his house in the small square yard and the bent trees, hanging protectively over it.

"Abuti Jefti's the devil. He, he makes me angry. That music of his and all his talk, talking when he's drunk. And the number of times I have to carry him to his bed when he's had too much. Like, like, like the time we carried him from the shops."

I chuckled at the memory.

We had come across him, soiled and damaged on the ground outside the shops. A crowd was gathered around him, swearing and baying at him. His pants were dark with urine and blood, which we discovered much later. We had saved him from a beating and carried him between us to his house. It was only when we lit the lamp that we discovered he had been stabbed. The wound, low under his armpit had stopped bleeding and was clotted. We had washed him and changed his clothes and put him to bed, not too worried that he might bleed again during the night. And all the time he had kept up a mumbled stream of invective against his fellow drinkers in the pub and the whole world as he slowly began to fade.

He woke up scratchy and irascible. Twice and I spent much of the day consoling him by many small acts of appeasement that healed and taunted him in equal measure. He had finally forced himself off the cushions and pillows we had laid out for him in the front room and chased us out.

"And when that woman's there. At, at night. They, they kick me out of the house. You can hear everything. But they don't, don't do much. The bed squeaks for a while then he fall, falls asleep and snores."

He sucked a laugh between his teeth.

"But he's alright otherwise. He gives me money sometimes. Beer, beer. Cigarettes."

We continued walking.

"I don't know why he took me in, but it's much better than the hostel where the others live," Twice continued.

The others, young people from the country neighbouring ours, shared rooms in dormitories behind dilapidated schools around our town, or in draughty pre-fabricated buildings hastily erected by a government ministry with funding from overseas. For a while, some even lived in tents. Others had, like Twice, found better accommodation in single rooms scattered around the townships.

"I, I don't know what will happen to me. But I know I won't end up like him. I won't, won't stay here forever, though I don't know where I'll go. But when I return, even if it's back here, I promise I won't be like, like, like Abuti Jefti." His steps were heavy in the dust of the street.

"Leaving home was only a first step. I, I have to turn my running away into something. Because without doing anything, things at home will simply remain the same. And here too."

He was silent for a moment.

"You think because people can do pretty much as they like here, this is how things are supposed to be." He swung his arm as if to illustrate his point.

"You, you forget how many people leave this place to go over there. They come back with things for you at Christmas and you think it's worth it. You forget what they leave behind, why they have to leave in the first place."

I was upset. I didn't know what I had said or done for him to accuse me.

"Twice, I haven't been over there. I know only what you tell me and Thembi, and sometimes the others in her room. But I do know that it's wrong. Even this place. Do you think we simply live here without seeing things?"

"But, but, but what do you do about it? Since I have been here, I have not seen anybody do anything about it."

I did not know what to say. There was nothing I could say.

"I will do something about it. I won't be like Abuti Jefti. There have been too many Abuti Jeftis. Drunk and broken and useless. Memories are fine, but we have to go beyond them."

I tried to look into the future to imagine him, older, better held together, better defined than he was now.

He started to gently hum. His song carried to me on the back of a rising, ruffling breeze. He hummed a song I might have heard, in Thembi's room, or at school when battered or resolved by the news of some incident, the young people from the country neighbouring ours would gather to sing themselves a comfort. His song held and firmed as a sentinel in the gathering dark. It called me in as friend, and my voice, an illiterate, poorly tutored fellow traveller, conscious of general origin, aware of general purpose, but ignorant of finer meaning, was joined with his.

Dogs did not bark at us. The shapes that became men as they approached did not hesitate as men do when they come across each other in the dark. The houses seemed bent into the ground like humble things. Chorus, said the wind and brushed us about the ears. A small crawling thing darted past and scratched at the grass at the edge of the road.

We sung a song that marched to our beating, yearning hearts, that washed surfaces, that burrowed beyond the outer flesh, the protective epidermis, beyond the lacunae of our histories. It roused old forgotten spirits. It joined those yet to be born with those dead and born again and still stumbling about behind the sun. It sounded the shape of the light that will light the future. It laid bare the history of the future. It guided us, so without knowing how, we were suddenly upon the part in the hedge that was the entrance to Abuti Jefti's yard. The song ended like a sleep and we stood sweating and shining and embarrassed, but returned from the centre of the world and elevated by the fact of it.

That was one of the last times I saw Twice. Not long afterwards, flying things and men came from the country neighbouring ours and poured fire into the night. Against Thembi's injunctions and Grandmother's bedridden cries, Puso and I climbed onto the roof of our house and watched as balls of fire and smoke rumbled and roiled across the horizon.

The next day, we participated in the public survey of the damage and offered our accounts of the events of the night before. In Thembi's room, there was much whispered and hurried shuffling about. Twice was not at Abuti Jefti's who shouted at me to go away and slammed the door in my face. In the evening, Twice rapped quickly on the kitchen door and entered the house. He remained standing as he told us he was going away. Thembi turned her back and spilt water on the dishes. My brother chewed a pencil and swung his legs under the table. I walked Twice outside. We stood silent for a moment. He suddenly hit me on the shoulder and without a word bounded off the stoep into the night. I stood there for a long time, his fading fleeing feet the only sound and movement of the night.

Six

WHEN THE BREEZE rises, the ears of the tent flap and for a moment the hanging odour of soap-chased sweat is dissipated. It is early and not yet very hot, but already I can feel the tent begin to sulk. It is quiet inside the tent, except for the odd whispered exchange, or child's outburst, or apologetic cough.

I am seated at the front of one of the two columns of chairs in the tent, with Miriam and her children on one side and Thembi and her daughter on the other. Next to Miriam and her daughter are her few foreign friends, yellow and uncomfortably conspicuous. Beside me are old men, elders holding their hats in their hands like begging bowls.

At the front of the tent is a table with a starched tablecloth. On it is a chalice, a bowl containing the bread and a flask of wine for the communion and two candles flickering against the faint breeze. Beside it, my brother's coffin stands closed and faintly humming. The priests from the wake the night before are wearing faded grey suits and navy blue waistcoats, clutching bibles, and gently sway behind the coffin like sentinels. The tent is nearly full, but people still arrive and bend their heads and quickly scurry to the back.

I am aware of massaging a protruding vein on my forehead. My mouth is dry and I can taste the obstinate reminders of last night's drinking at the shebeen. I search through the corners of my eyes for familiar faces. The huge, unblinking eyes of an old man staring at me from behind bottle lenses for spectacles jolt my heart. I catch the eyes of a woman and neither of us knows if in lieu of some other, more obvious act of acknowledgement, we should perhaps simply smile. Her eyes lash me as she turns away.

An adult's face in grief is a slack, dumb, hanging muscle. Or it is grimacing and grinding at the teeth as if against a cold buffeting wind or against a light that shouts and bounces off the surface of things. A child's face on the other hand, does not know the shape of grief. There, amongst the mourning, a young boy will know by a quick slap on his well-greased thighs to hold himself in. He will look around and catch another child's eye and they may fashion a game. Or he will swing his legs beneath his chair to a private song, which, if he could ever keep, would redeem him. Or forgetting himself for a moment once again, he will turn in his seat and make faces at the people behind him, until his mother sticks her sharp elbow into his ribs.

A child does not understand the shape of grief. A child's world is undiscovered. It is too much at the point of commencement; too full of possibilities, too unbounded to make sense of the irrevocable. A child does not have the language or a sufficient history of emotion to make sense of beginnings and endings.

A child will appear to grieve, but it will only be in recoil to the tears and wailing around him, in shock at the quake of something previously firm and steadfast, or simply because the normal everyday patterns are disrupted by the comings and goings of so many strangers.

For a young child's elder siblings, for his parents, his relatives, senses can be rendered singular. They can even be made antagonists. A bright light deafens the ears. An old scar on a lover's body at first has no taste. Noise, if there is enough of it, can wipe away the smell of the dead. Slightly older children will wisely use a surfeit of energy to hide away current truths.

But for this particular permutation of siblings, friends, neighbours, older children, senses are compounded. An old man next to Thembi scratches at a wart and sighs because of it. Another man excavates his decaying teeth with his fingers and holds what he finds to his nose for the smell. A matron fans her face with her hand, but her eyes glisten nevertheless with a currency of tears. A young man with a large shining forehead brushes at a fly and frowns in annoyance at its persistence.

In this tent, senses are not separate. The light diffused through the yellow rubber of the tent canopies too many odours of too many people in a space cloyed with a broken, over-expectant silence, an over-impatient shuffling about. In this tent, for this permutation of siblings, friends, neighbours, young and older children, senses are rendered intimate relatives that contour the inner and outer boundaries of grief.

The priest who is to conduct the service enters the tent. His eyes are bloodshot from the wake the night before, but his otherwise dour face is broken by a tight, enlightened smile. For a moment, he gazes at the people gathered in the tent then turns and whispers to the two men beside him, now steadfast and earnest for the serious business about to begin. One of them raises his hands, bangs his bible against his hymn book and starts the verse of a well-known hymn. The people in the tent scramble to their feet and join him at the second line of the verse. The women's voices are high pitched and lead. The men respond in deep, sonorous voices.

Thembi does not stand and neither does Miriam, though her boy gets up briefly, stares about and then embarrassed, sits down, aware that all of us at the front of the tent have remained seated. I look across at Thembi and then at Miriam and we share a quick, guilty moment of recognition at whom we are.

Miriam is dressed in black. Her knees are pressed together and her dusty black shoes are crossed beneath her. In her lap is a small, shining and obviously seldom used black bag. She reaches into it for a tissue, which she trawls across her face. She puts a hand out to hold her daughter sitting beside her. The girl squeezes her hand out of her mother's and stares at the ground. I look to where she stares and make out scuffled, hesitant shoeprints of women and children's shoeprints between the heavier indentations made by the men when they entered the tent. The girl's brother cocks his jaw and holds his head up. He stares back unblinking at my attempt at a smile.

The hymn comes to an end and the gathered sit down. In the rows directly behind us are my brother's friends and some of the men from the digging at the graveyard and the private wake we held in the run-down drinking rooms at the shops.

My brother's colleagues wear striped grey suits that are almost a uniform and some of them wear bulbous, dark glasses on their faces so that they appear as giant insects come to sniff at something rotting. Abuti Jefti is amongst them. He has not changed much since I last saw him, when I took the chance to run away from this place. Except for his hair, which is grey and receding and his alcohol glazed eyes that never settle to be seen. Behind them is the less well-decorated assemblage of ordinary men of the village. Some wear faded overalls, or second- hand, white-man-died jackets over previously bright jerseys. Others are barefoot and carry children in their arms.

In the opposite column are the women, my brother's friends' wives, all put together in hats and costumes and clutched bags and polished shoes. Behind them is a bright group of elderly women in the black skirts and stockings, red blouses with large white lapels and white hats. They are members of Grandmother's burial society, still faithful these many years later. At the back are arrayed the youths, with their white t-shirts extolling a commitment to shrift, good service and God, and the old women of the village.

The priest begins the sermon. He slowly lifts his arms as if in invitation to the congregation to enter his world. He shouts, "Molimo!" and for a moment we are all shaken.

He continues, "Molimo who is almighty, who sees all things, who is everlasting, be here with us today as we deliver this your son unto you."

A good service is like a journey. The priest is its guide, its shepherd. A good service starts with a hymn that calls the assembled to order. It uses rhythm to find the lay of emotions and to haul and distil them to a central place. It is patriarchal and assigns difference to men and women, but promises a common, greater purpose. Its stalwart rhythm shames the cynical who are forced to look about themselves and finding no comfort, sway in remembrance of its meaning. It is affirms the converted who scramble to it as if to a last place of sanctuary.

The first prayer is outward and backward looking. It marks the journey's furthest boundaries of origin. It is a whispering, plaintive, guilty invocation. It summons current memories and unfolds dark recesses of human baseness. It shadows the lightness of being and points to contrition as the place of beginning. Then gradually, softly, gently, it turns away from a backward purview, raises a finger and points to a place of renascent intent, to absolution at journey's end. The believers open their eyes in wonder. The dissenters wring their hands and look at each other over their shoulders, through the corners of their eyes.

A bold "Amen" resounds in the tent.

The priest smiles his satisfaction. He pauses, hangs his finger in the air for a moment and plunges into the sermon, the common enough parable of a father's absolution for his long-lost son. He stands above us at the front of the tent, close enough so that his swinging robes ruffle the air around us. He splays his finger about like a sword and rubs his other hand across his stomach when he stops to collect himself.

When he speaks as the father of the son who is lost, or sometimes as God himself, vengeful and unfaltering, his voice booms and brilliant drops of spit shoot out of his mouth. Appropriately advised, probably by Thembi, he speaks in a hesitant but liturgical English, interspersed, when he is impassioned, with words from our language. He pauses at the parable's end and raises his head to the roof of the tent as if to find judgement encrypted there.

He approaches my brother's coffin and looks inside.

"Every son has a father and every father has a father. Time immemorial."

He holds his hands to his chest. "To this our dearly departed son, we are father."

He extends his arms to encompass the gathered.

"To this our dearly departed son, we are father. We are father because the Father is all of us." His eyes light up.

"When we pray, we call upon the Lord as if he is not amongst us. We pray to him as if there is a place he goes to that is not here. But he is here, always, even when we forget him in the mad rush of our daily lives. The Lord is the blood that courses through all of us. He is every muscle we lift. He is all our tears. He is even that child who knows nothing except the comfort of his mother's breast. And in that child's grandmother who can barely see but who sees the most."

A woman from the burial society stands up and begins the refrain of a hymn but is waved down by the two men beside the priest.

The priest smiles at her.

"It is our mothers who know this as an everlasting truth. They know because they have reared us, they have extended their breasts to nourish us, and because even in the most difficult times, they have never failed us."

The women from the burial society wipe their eyes and nod their heads in agreement.

"This our son returns to the Father. He will squeeze himself amongst those gone before us and find his rightful place beside the Father. The Father will look him in the eye and know him. He will lift His arms and wrap them around him."

The priest rubs his stomach.

"Let us not forget. We are never alone because the father is always with us. He is in every one of our dreams. And even in our nightmares, when we might consider Him absent. He is the sculptor of every injury that befalls us, every insult, every rude undoing."

"Sometimes we forget our good fortune, our success at work or in love or in simply living lives that are not fraught with too much misfortune. The father is also there then and for this too we must be grateful."

"But most of us live hard lives. We live in a world in which evil finds its way easily amongst and between men. We live in a world in which we too often succumb to the effects of ignorance. Too many of us go hungry too often. Many of us do not have safe, warm places to rest our tired

118

bodies at the end of each toiling day. Many of us are bitter at the poor chances offered us. But sadly, this is not always evident to us all."

A woman in the corner of my vision takes off her hat to fan herself. It is a large, bright-green hat with a red band. It pulls her hair as she takes it off so that two greying strands stand like horns above her head. She pats at them with little success. The matrons from Grandmother's burial society turn as one and glare at her.

The priest puts his hand in front of his mouth and coughs, and then pats his stomach.

"And all of us, irrespective of our station in life, have lost or will lose a loved one. The reaper does not discriminate and will steal like a thief into all our homes and take the most loved, the most generous, the kindest of us away, when we least expect it. And we will be shattered by his coming."

"And so what of us whose turn has not yet come? What of those of us left behind?"

He shuffles in the earth and approaches the front row of chairs in the tent. He passes his gaze over us, over Miriam who lowers her head, over Thembi, over the children.

"We are none of us so selfless that our thoughts are only for the departed. We sit here after all in deep pain because of our loss, our bereavement. And we have to live on, to continue, to daily reckon with the new emptiness in our lives."

"And for all of us, that loss comes with many things. A father is not just a loved one. He is also the keeper of his family. He fights off the wild beasts that take siege of our homes. He hunts for us and feeds us. He teaches us much about the world. He scolds us and plays with us. He shows us that we are to follow him, as he followed his father and as we in turn will be followed by those to come after us."

He points at Miriam's son. "This boy, this son may not fully understand now. But he will grow and will ask why his father was not there to lead him, to guide him, to help him make sense of all the mysteries of the world. What will we answer him? What will we tell this boy or this girl or this woman?"

The priest is standing above Miriam and her children. They are taut and unmoving, their faces glistening in the growing heat. A trail of perspiration slides off Miriam's face. Her daughter stares at the ground. The boy frowns at the priest who turns and shuffles to the table.

For a moment, a hung silence pervades the tent. Outside, it is also quiet except for the distant struggle of a truck making its way up the road that leads through the township and a woman's voice as she shouts to someone to fetch water.

Suddenly, one of the men at the front of the tent bangs his bibles and starts a hymn. The gathered rush out of their seats to join him, their voices scattered and disjointed. The second man shakes his head angrily. He also collides his bibles and begins to stamp his feet into the ground. The singing is unsure, hesitant, as if few know the hymn. Then, a voice at the back of the tent takes the lead and cuts through the discordant singing. It is a treble, bitter voice, of a woman whose husband might be cuckold. It imposes pitch, commands tempo, and exhorts the congregation to fuller voice. The frail, arthritic, phlegm-clogged women from Grandmother's burial society scrape their voices and join in. From the back of the tent, the voices of the young people in their red t-shirts find themselves and begin to swell. Soon, the singing is joined. The priest too begins to lift his feet. His robe is flicked up by his rising knees and falls down in a twisted, devilish dance.

At the front of the tent, Thembi and Miriam and their children and I sit huddled against the barrage of the hymn. I remember it – an obscure, sometime favourite of Grandmother that we used to sing with little success with the tenants from the outbuildings. Twice had also known it, though he had known it in the language from the country neighbouring ours. When he was amongst us, he would hum its melody and Grandmother would reward him with a smile afterwards, for the effort.

I raise my head to look at Miriam to see what the priest's questions, the swell of the singing, the shiver of her husband's coffin might have done to her. She has her arms wrapped around her bosom and is leaning forward in her chair. Her hair hangs down the side of her head like a curtain so I cannot see her face. A wisp dances across her nose and she raises her hand to brush it away. I see her face then. A trapped, pulled-in, frightened face, unable to escape from itself as faces do when they lie; an interrogated, translucent face whose bitten mouth and shining, scattered eyes seem finally ready to scream its truth.

The hymn ends like a strong breeze will, if you are listening to it.

The priest sways against its memory. He lifts his hands and slowly lowers them to his sides as he starts to speak, as if to lower us gently from the place we have just been.

I look across at Thembi. She is leaning back in her chair. Her eyes are shut but shiver slightly beneath their thin lids. Her one hand is clamped firmly against her mouth as if to hold in a terrible secret. Her other is pressed against her stomach as if to cause the stillbirth of something inside her.

The priest enjoins the believers to the front to receive communion. The men beside him are pouring the wine into a chalice and signalling the congregation to come to the front. Someone starts a hymn that serves to hearten them to rise and move to the front of the tent. The women from Grandmother's burial society are first on their feet and shuffle past us to the table at the front and then men and the youth with the righteous t-shirts. Thembi also stands and beckons her child to join her in the queue. Miriam and her children and her foreign friends remain seated. They look at me as if to seek some comfort, some solidarity in the fact that I too have remained rooted on my chair. The men and women cross themselves, bow to the priest's "the body and blood of Christ", open their mouths to receive the wine and bread and then bend and hurry to the back.

My brother's broken, blood-stilled body.

Wine as blood, bread as body. Drunk blood, though I do not know, would be thick and glutinous. I would retch I think, or be warmed by its magic, if I could feel it course down my throat, into my stomach, through my whole body to magically dissolve a hardness. Bread would stick to my palate and I would afterwards pick at with my fingers, or feel it as a weight in my stomach, so that I would be weighed down and indolent. But these men and women trip away. They swagger. Their eyes are alight. They are sanctified, blessed, reinvigorated and louder in humming the hymn, as cannibals would loudly bay at the dazed tribe across the valley from where they stole their victim.

They're all finally seated and the priest starts another prayer. But I do not hear as he closes the prayer. Instead, I am conscious of the gentle swirl of blades of grass against a wind stolen into the tent. The walls of the tent collapse inwards, then balloon out, then collapse in again, like a breathing lung, and I am squeezed and released. I am slapped by a child's single, horrified cry. The light darkens. A cloud must be passing.

Spirits begin to gather and murmur. At the roof of the tent. At its corners. Beneath the lined up chairs. Nameless absconded, intimated spirits. Dancing, impatient, beckoning spirits. Spirits that call my name. Spirits that know me and have no fear of me. That rub their moist flesh against me and spit at my face. That knead and sniff at my groin. That begin to pull me, at first gently, then eagerly, chanting and making quick teams to take me away.

They pull me to a trampled path along an undulating, moon-drenched landscape with large boulders strewn about it. They push me along the path and slowly, one by one, though I am not aware of them as individual identities, they disappear and I am alone.

The path dips and rises and shines across the landscape, then disappears into the armpit of a jagged mountain on the far horizon. Apart from scattered, stunted, leafless shrubs shivered by a whistling wind, there is no life, no movement on the plain. No animal darts amongst the rocks. No night bird breaks the brilliant shine of the moon, or hangs for a moment on a shrub, or calls for a mate.

I turn to look behind me, but the path disappears into a perfect, unfathomable darkness so that I know I cannot turn back. In front of me it stands like an invitation, an inevitable choice.

I begin to walk along the path, stumbling at first despite the glare of the moon. I slip and slide in its moist earth and the round stones strewn along it roll my feet so that I am unsettled and think to turn back. But I soon learn its treacheries. I learn to read the depth of the shadows along it. I learn to ride the pebbles, to slide across its softer surfaces.

I am drawn along the path by a force I do not recognise, a force that is one part fear, densified by a darkness that remakes itself as I move forward, one part an eagerness to walk where I have never walked before. I walk a great distance, that in the absence of other motion, in the absence of other fonts of measurement, I can only assess by the weariness of my limbs.

Occasionally, I stop and look up to scan the vast terra around me. Sometimes the land appears to slope down into the distance, so that the path seems to lie at the top of a ridge. The wind does not pick up as it would on a ridge, but I imagine it does. At other times, I am at the bottom of a gentle valley, at a place where the waters would be sieved from the ground and the grass would be thick and sweet and perfect for cows in fattening for a dowry.

My feet are worn and bleeding and I stop to rest, but am drawn by an irresistible force and resume my walking. A heavy load like a sickness grows on my back, but it is not there when I turn to reach for it. It adjusts itself across my back as I walk, leaning forward into my neck when I descend a slope, rearing back as I walk up an incline. My joints swell and a shivering fever rises in my body.

I do not know how much time passes but I know that I walk for a considerable time. Minutes chase minutes, chase endless hours, days even. And all the time, the moon remains motionless in the sky. It hangs like a lamp to light my way. The wind, too, keeps up its steady, endless whistling. The stars are bitter at the dark edges of the sky.

Suddenly, out of nowhere, I hear my name shouted. Startled, I stop and look about me. I search the shadows behind the rocks, the dip of the path in front of me, the jagged branches of a solitary tree along a slight rise in the plain, but apart from the stirring of the leaves, there is no movement.

My heart beats in a panic and I look for a place to hide. I scurry off the path and jump into a shadow behind a rock, but the shadow is narrow and my edges are mocked by the light of the moon. I dart behind another rock but the light is even stronger there. It remembers me. My trembling bloodied limbs. My cloying, telling sweat. My eyes for ghosts.

I rush back on to the path and continue walking, my head raised, and my eyes wide in search of whatever it was that called my name. In my rush I slip and slide about the path and forget the pain that stabs at my feet. I hear a voice again, and a moment later another, then another, quiet murmuring voices that do not shout like the first voice. The voices do not listen to each other. They talk together, past each other, as many disparate, gathered voices might do, in preamble to a debate that will be chaired, gathered, organised.

The landscape is unchanged, though for a fleeting moment I think I see something dart behind a rock.

Other voices join the babble. They speak in a language I have never heard before. Sometimes they speak as if from behind me and I turn towards the source of the chattering. At other times, the voices are ahead of me and draw me as if to confirm my bearing. Sometimes they are rude and violent in the bitter language of revenge. At other times they are like the soft singing of women bathing at a stream or collecting wood. Occasionally, from the midst of the hubbub, I make out my name being called. "'Lefe. 'Lefe. 'Lefe", softly, plaintively. At other times, it is spat out and I am frightened and hold my arms about my head, as if to ward off a blow.

The voices harass and comfort my journey. They push me forward and I feel my walking as a gentle falling, a perpetual, unguided forward movement. Or they bully me along the path and I trip and stumble about it and feel tears splashing across my face. I walk for many hours, the wind, the silver light of the moon, the endless chatter of the voices, my faithful, solitary companions on this bleak landscape. I grow weary, but when I stop to rest, the voices darken and encircle me and swirl about me like a storm, so I am quickly on my bloodied feet again.

Gradually, an immeasurable time later, I become aware that the path is now always rising and that I am approaching the mountains. I continue on my way, my muscles balking at the endless raising of one foot after the other. I clasp my hands to my back to ease the pain. My breath is a short sucking at dry air.

I stop to rest for a moment. The voices are angered and clamour around me but I ignore them. Ahead of me the mountain looms like an impossible obstacle and I am angry that I am still at its foot.

Then, suddenly, in the depth of its darkness, I think I see a movement, a light. I stare into the gloom, but there is nothing there. I proceed unsteadily, my watch lifted from the path so that I might discover if there is anything there in the darkness. The stars hang thrown and frozen above the mountain and glisten in my eyes as if to mock me. But then I see a light again, a yellow light, like the light of a fire. I stare and stumble towards it, tripping against small rocks and edges in the path.

The light wavers. For a moment it disappears and I rush forward, knowing that it is my only salvation in this bleak place. It reappears and my heart jolts. I stop again to be sure the light is really there, to be sure it is not a trick of the moonlight, or a play of the light of the stars. It is there, yellow and upright and rising and warm, though it warms only my desperate yearning for an end to this journey.

The voices shout and sing my name and other words I do not understand and I am thrown to the ground. They circle around me in a chorus, in a dance, but there is no form to their raving. A babble of devils and beautiful, unimaginable creatures. The voices brush my hair and slap my face and pull at my arms and legs. They pit insults against praise. They bury me into the ground and suck me as if to hurl me to the sky. They flush me with a stinking liquid and singe the hair on my arms. I scramble to my feet and run, towards the light. The voices chase after me, giggling and laughing. A solitary voice ahead of me screams an ambush and I am hurled to the ground. I scramble up again and rush on, towards the light, brighter now, a deep yellow with red-flamed heart. The voices lisp and stutter and fall away as I run.

I approach the light. I begin to hear a steadier, different sound than the sound of the previous voices. It seems to come from the centre of the light. Voices again, but not the warring voices that accompanied me across the plain. These voices wait for each other and pitch in call and response, as in conversation or singing.

It is singing. The voices are singing. They are singing a song I know but cannot trace. It is a patient, lilting song that never resolves but is always released to continue as if it has never been sung before, as if it has always been sung, as if it will always be sung.

I hurry towards the sound in the light, towards the light that is a fire.

I stop.

Behind the fire is a man or a being that passes for a man. The man is tall and thin and is wearing a blanket. He holds a stick that is taller than he is. He is completely still. He has a delicate face and a brushed beard yellowed by the light of the fire. His eyes are perfectly oval and have a lazy blink as if at a lame time of day. His eyes are soft as if unassaulted by too much seeing, or as if, having seen everything, they are no longer afraid.

Slowly, the man moves towards me. He moves easily, as if his feet do not touch the ground. He appears to have no weight. He plants the stick into the ground at his side as he walks. His hand is knotted around the stick.

He stops a short distance away from me. I can smell the heat of him under his blanket.

He does not say anything. Instead he raises his stick and

motions with it in the direction of the light, then turns and throws his blanket around his shoulders and begins to walk towards the light.

I hesitate, then follow, slowly, at a distance, but close enough so that his blanketed back remains visible.

His stride is long and he moves with an easy gait up the slope of the mountain.

The path is easy now. The voices are gone and do not follow behind me or lead me forward in entourage any more. The only sounds now are the scuffle of my feet as I hurry after the man ahead of me and the dry whistle of the wind.

The man reaches the top of the mountain and stops for a moment. He looks over to what would be its other side, then turns towards me. He smiles a faint, unconvincing smile that is lightness at the centre of his bearded face. He turns away and disappears between jagged stones at the top of the mountain.

I follow. There is nothing else to do.

I come between rocks standing like sentries at the top of the pass and stop to look beyond them. On the far horizon, jagged mountain peaks point to abjure the sky. Strips of clouds like scars hang above them. The land falls from the mountains into a deep, quietly murmuring valley, with crevices and faults and shivering leaves against its fertile sides, and a frightened plain where the river must be.

I know this valley. This is the valley of the dream I had the time Thembi left. This is the valley of the men and their horses and their bright, shouldered blankets, who descended out of its growing shadows; of the women with loads of wood or water on their heads; of children playing along the river; of the rock in the ground that returned the sun.

The man is descending the valley. He is a scatting figure that appears and reappears between rocks, bushes, between the rising and falling of the breeze that rises up from the valley's floor; a breeze thick with the scent of burning bushes.

I rush after him on heavy feet. My arms cut through the air. My eyes are widened to gather the changing contours of the darkness; ears open to my crashing bounding; blood coursing for a torn soul. My arrogant sphincter holds.

I follow him to the edge of the plain at the centre of the valley. It is dark, but from the red light of fires in front of them, I can make out the same throw of huts as in that dream. Behind them I can hear the soft sounds gathered animals make at night. A dog comes to the edge of the light of a fire and barks at me. A voice calls to it and it creeps back into the darkness. Another says something. A female voice, that would normally be weary and low, to put things to sleep. Here it is awake and not yet ready to hide.

I walk towards the hut. Against the light of the fire, I see the man who brought me here standing behind it, his staff in his hand. There are people around the fire. Numerous dark shapes huddled in a close circle around it.

I am drawn towards them. They are all turned and silently staring at me. Huddled in blankets that hang from their shoulders to the ground. Thin, tall people, with shaven heads, round foreheads and thin ears pulled down by large circular rings.

Their eyes are like the tall man's, shining and smiling when they blink and modest, so that they look often to the ground.

The tall man murmurs something I do not understand and walks around the seated people towards me. He points me to a rock and motions for me to sit on it. He sits down beside me and turns back to look at the people gathered around the fire.

A figure, a woman, gets up from the group and disappears into the mouth of a hut. She comes out holding a bowl in her hands and comes to where I am seated with the man. She bends onto her knees and offers it to the man. All the time her face is averted to one side. She hurries back to the hut and returns with another bowl, which she offers me.

The woman has no hair on her almost perfectly round head. She has the large earrings that they all wear and bracelets on her thin dark wrists. A smell of sweat and the acrid fat of an animal, of a goat perhaps, rises from the ochre blanket draped across her shoulders.

I take the proffered bowl and she rushes back to the group around the fire.

I look at the man seated beside me. He twists his mouth into a smile and bends his head to drink from the bowl in his hands.

I lift my bowl to my lips. Cool, bitter sour milk, with a perfect consistency. I finish the milk at a go and wipe my mouth with hands. I can feel its weight in my stomach.

The man has also finished his milk. He puts his bowl on the ground between his feet and I do the same. The girl fetches the bowls and carries them back to the hut, then hurries to rejoin the group as if afraid to miss something about to happen.

The man stands up and makes toward the group, motioning for me to follow. The group shuffles about on their low perches to make space for us. I lower myself to the ground between the man and one of the group, who remains staring at the fire. I am assailed by an old smell of burning wood and unwashed blankets and curdled milk and blood; a smell hanging about the gathered like protection or the beginnings of a rumour.

The group gathered about the fire consists of men, women, and children also, though there is an evenness to their features that makes it difficult to distinguish them. They all wear the same ochre-coloured blankets. I cannot see what they wear underneath, but from beneath their blankets, each one holds a little wooden stick, forked at the end and pointed at the ground.

Then suddenly, rudely, the man who brought me to this place points at the group. "These are people you know." His voice is soft and clear.

I am shocked and stare about the group as if by doing so they might become recognisable. I do not know them.

He continues. "These people, you know by blood."

"That one there tripped you the time you fell." He uses his hand that is not holding the stick to point at one of the people assembled around the fire.

"Remember?"

I do not remember when I fell, nor that round smiling face, smiling gently beyond itself.

"That time you forgot to listen to yourself, that one over there shouted at you. Remember?" I remember a scurrying voice in my sleep, "'Lefe. 'Lefe".

A man, who in another place would have a grey beard and a belly and would own a shop or buses, nods his head.

"Shouted at you and you were not asleep, though you tried to be."

I look at him to make sense of what he was saying. He does not turn to me but continues.

"That one," I look to where he was pointing, "yes that one," a tall thin man like himself, "that one walked with you. That one stepped before you stepped. As if you could ever know where you were going."

A figure gets up from the gathering and makes for the hut.

"And that one saved you."

The figure turns towards us. It is a woman.

"When you almost finally fell. Finally, for the last time. She would not have your falling."

I notice my heart is thundering in my breast. My forehead is coated with sweat though the night is cool. I am frightened. When I almost finally fell?

When did I almost fall? That one time? No. Many times. I have fallen many times.

I have lain many times shaking in my bed or on the floor of some room in whatever mix of mortar and brick then stood for my house, shaking and frightened for my life. I have stood in the dust of places without restitution, in a dust that insinuates itself into your nostrils, your ears, bloodies your eyes, scrapes at your ankles like some small suppliant, domesticated, uncared for animal. I have scuttled along wet, densely peopled, rain-slicked streets in cold, wind-blustered places and been rebuked many times by the lashing eyes of hurrying strangers hurtling past me. I have been rebuked, too, by being left behind by acquaintances, friends, lovers, who moved on and in doing so belittled the brief, hectic connections we made. I have rushed about to make everything a blur, to dull the glare of the light, to motivate stillness to movement, to make moments into lines. I have been battered and dissected and tortured by my own stumped, stooping, bent-down ignorance.

Falling down could be a song children would sing. Children say things so simply. Falling down could be the scuffle of a return from a vindictive passion, or a coward's discovery amidst ribald talk of brave deeds and a noble selflessness. Or the simple wasting away of someone once considered the most beautiful in the land, but now less firmly held together, less sprightly, now overtaken by other, fresher creations.

In the real world, nations fall down, tripped by their own ambition. A once-proud, tree-lined avenue is now the domain of sedentary vagrants, migrants from places with unpronounceable names, which we used to claim as our places of origin, then. Vagrants so long there now, they rise from their perch in perfect timing to the turn of the traffic lights, if they are working, to raise broken limbs and lacerated faces for a few coins, hungry sir, no mother, no father, hungry sir. "Thirty seven people were killed and scores of others injured at yesterday's Independence Day celebrations when a stand at the stadium collapsed. The Minister of Housing and Construction has played down calls for his resignation and has said a commission of enquiry will be set up to investigate why the stand collapsed. Sources blame the foreign company responsible for its upgrading last year." Men gather daily for work, at what was once the periphery of the town but is now its angry centre, and disappointed, hang about and bicker and fight but nevertheless survive somehow.

"Finally, finally fell down." The man rubs his shoulders against me and I am brought to the present, to this place at the other side of a mountain, now a certain reality.

"You are too knowing for yourself. You know falling, so you rubbish this wind that carries my voice to you, this place where we sit, these people who you do not know but who you know more intimately than you would remember."

I am perplexed and frightened. What is this finally falling down?

As if he reads my mind, the man responds. "Finally, finally falling down?" His voice is bitter as he laughs, a shock after the comfort of the milk and the fire and the beings gathered around it, at the end of an endless walk across a place I have never been.

"For everything there is always more. More, in any way you would express it. In years, or light or thunder. In distance. Further from this place where you are but should not be. In blood. More blood than would fill a river."

"In everything there is less. Less than what you are. Less than what you can see. Closer than you can be to yourself. Less than we are, though it would take me to tell you that."

He pauses and looks at the gathering around the fire. "You have never looked at the sun. If you had you would be blind. And you are not blind. Men are not blind. They see the sun through us, just as we see the sun through other mists. A mountain is tall because it stands above a flat expanse of land. A spring that gurgles down a mountain where you would bend and drink is only a spring because you bend and drink."

"For you," his voice accuses me, "falling is falling because everything falls around you. It is all the time falling around you. It is falling because a mountain is tall because it sits on top of a plain, a spring is bounteous because you have arrived at it and its coolness slakes your thirst. And that final falling, which you would do everything to keep at bay. As if there could ever be a final falling."

He pauses for a moment. He looks about him like a priest would at the mid-point of a sermon. His voice is low and melancholy as if at the kernel of a lesson.

"We are all merely intermediaries. You, you know this place as it is now. You do not know its real winds, its real sun when it is quietly enraged and ravages us. How else can I draw the boundaries of our being except to talk of them as things you would know? This place, this time amongst us will not, can not remain with you."

The man looks at me, his eyes now soft and smiling.

He continues, "You cannot remain here unless you choose to do so. Even though you did not choose to come here. And even if you do choose to remain, you will not be here in body, you will not know this place by seeing, or hearing or feeling, but in another way."

"To remain here you must unlearn everything that you know and begin to learn a new language, which is not the language that we now speak. You must begin to learn its essence, which is not the force of the wind I tell you about or the fall of the path that brought you here from the mountain, or the taste of the milk in your mouth. You are not blind. Yet you must see this place with the eyes of a blind man. Dream the dreams of a blind man."

He points at the gathered. "The language is not even in those seated over there. They are merely intermediaries, much as you are, though you would not know it. Intermediaries to pass things along, as men would pass things across a river. Held above their heads to avoid the raging of the current. But sometimes, often, also deep within the current's powerful, surging waters, and straining against its force that would sweep everything away, steeped in a conviction of the purpose of the passing of things from one side to the other."

I tried to imagine what things are passed across a river.

"Fragile, nebulous, changing things, without firm centres or outer contours or trajectories in time or movement or shape or colour; things with endless, disputed, uncommon meanings; random, strewn-about things; sacred things that might be hidden in the depths of a forest or under the earth; most favourite things, available only to be polished or for the purchase of select emotion; poems, stories, fables, histories, because there are no names for these things that are passed along. And because the act of passing is as much about origin as destination, about movement as arrival, about histories as portents. Hardy things also. Like blood."

The man is quiet for a moment. He twists his long stick into the ground between his feet, then turns to me once more.

"Men fail. Men are weak. Distracted, they drop things into the raging waters. They lose the line and fight to hold it. Some break to retrieve a thing dropped and carried away and are themselves carried away."

The man stops and lifts his head to peer at the sky. It is as before, bright and perfectly still and empty of movement. The valley, too, is immobile except for the shiver of trees against its side. My eyes are teased by the play of dark shadows that are even darker in the distance.

I expect him to say more, to come to a point where I can understand what he is saying. He does not continue. He stands up instead and directs me to follow him. "Come," he says, "there is something you must see."

We walk briskly around the fire and through the humble odour of the group gathered around it. They all briefly raise their eyes towards me. As we pass them, I hear them rise and follow us. They begin to talk, quietly but in a tone of excitement rare to this place.

The man makes towards the flat in the valley of the dream where the rock had stood that turned the sun. As we walk, I make out a darkness separate to the darkness of the other shadows in the near distances of the valley. I know then that this darkness is the shadow of the rock that returned the sun and am confirmed that this is the place that I came to in the dream of the time with Thembi and Twice and Grandmother and my brother Puso.

The man stops to one side of the rock. Behind us, the group also stops. For a moment they continue to talk in excited but muted voice, as if in attendance at a rare but solemn occasion. The man stands still and frowns at them, and the group quickly scrapes and coughs itself to quiet.

I look at the rock, firm and heavy in the earth and immovable except by the exertion of great force. It appears as if surrounded by a faint halo of light. A barely audible sound begins to come from it. It is the sound of singing. A low diffused singing, without a clear point of origin, like a dull untouchable pain. A plaintive singing of repeated words in an unbroken, returning harmony that is slow at its edges and more eager at its centre, like a turning wheel.

A force compels me past the man, towards the stone, towards the ropes still hanging from it, which the men had pulled to return the sun.

I walk around the rock to the other side. Two bent figures – a man and a woman – sit in its shadow. They resemble the others that had sat around the fire, with blankets and the same perfectly circular earrings. They are the source of the singing.

The man has followed me and now raises his hand and points to the couple still softly singing.

I hardly hear him as he says, "These are the people you know. These are the people who have been waiting for you."

They rise from the ground and raise their hands to hold the ropes that pulled, had returned the sun.

Singing again. A hymn. The gathered are on their feet. The priest and his two accomplices are swinging beside my brother's coffin.

Seven

HOW DOES A LIFE reveal itself to itself? At what point does a life pause to listen to itself, to take stock of itself, to measure the deceit of past and present failure, the limits of present and future opportunity? What are the objects or single occurrences of that accounting, of the encounters that tell a life?

Old people, who have learnt the settled and recurrent if sometimes broken nature of time's passing will use an unremitting drought or a month of tornadoes those many years ago as a milestone to mark the onset of a heart condition, or the point at which things ceased to be as they always were.

For those with a more forward-looking purview, the thrill of a first journey beyond the limits of a narrow, known horizon may be the mark against which everything is measured. And against these canvases, a suitably ritualised birth or marriage or death will occur to pattern everything.

For us, then, at the peri-urban edges of the burgeoning political and administrative centre where we lived, the seasonal imperatives of agriculture still figured, though in the wider scope of things, seasons finally, simply only tumbled into each other.

Our lives were not the same after Twice left us. For a few weeks, embellished narratives of the raid did the rounds and we looked about us to see what changes it had wrought, beyond the destruction of houses and the deaths of furtive people whose names we did not know. The radio was shrill in condemnation of it, to the point where even weather reports assumed overtly political overtones. An advancing cold front was somehow the fault of the country neighbouring ours and our vulnerability is all the more revealed.

A dusk-to-dawn curfew was imposed which we at the periphery of the town at first did not take seriously. However, a few days into the curfew, soldiers in a white Land Rover roared through our township and shot their guns into the air. Everyone panicked and the roads were soon deserted. The next day, we heard that one of the boys who frequented the shops along the road, his instincts dulled by too much sucking at his plastic of glue, had been shot in the ear.

Grandmother was frightened by the raid and its aftermath and would call us in as soon as the four o'clock bell pealed at the house where she used to go for prayer sessions. Earlier, my brother and I returned from school, she would insist that we remain in the yard. She would recount stories of the times, both here and in the country neighbouring ours, when younger and then still part of the real world, she had been caught up in various eruptions of public violence. She would clench her fist and hold her forearm out and shout "Qwa! qwa!" – the sound the guns had made. She even lifted her dress once to show us a scar on her white mottled thigh where a wire had torn her as she had run from the guns.

Old people, like all people, are either generally quickly frightened by things or bold and reckless with their chances. Grandmother, cloistered now for many years in and about our house, without the counsel and shelter of her wise husband who was a teacher, was afraid of the world. Her view of it was now almost totally shaped by our lives and the lives of the tenants in our yard. Thembi, my brother and I, and Twice before he left were finding our way out there on the streets. She was quietly envious of how quickly we were learning the world, how available it was to us. On any occasion that we would attempt to explain the logic of a progression of linked occurrences or how a thing worked, she would sniffle about her bosom in a show of disinterest.

For her, our tenants made up that other, greater, peopled part of the world. But they were of its more obviously fallen parts. They fought and came home drunk and failed to pay the rent, despite their upright occupations as teachers and nurses and newly inducted junior civil servants.

Even the organised church was damned. She had stopped

going to the house down the main road of our township where the bell pealed at four o'clock to call the locals to worship, because she believed the truth of the rumours about its priest. She would rather, she explained somewhat imperiously, worship her God alone with us and our tenants, sinners though they might be, in the kitchen of her house, than amongst a community of hypocrites.

For the first few nights of the curfew we sat caged and irritated around the table in the kitchen. Grandmother would call us often, partly to ensure we had not gone outside and partly in simple enjoyment of her increased access to us.

However, we soon learnt that the curfew really only applied in town and in the more communal spaces of our township. It was not safe to venture along main roads. Men, inevitably drunk, were picked up there often and taken away to dark places where they were terribly beaten, or so the rumours went. It was safe however, to skip along paths between the houses, taking care to keep low. I burst into Abuti Jefti's house one evening, who was at first displeased, then promptly sent me out for beer.

Stuck in the kitchen from the moment the sun went down, we would spend much of the time adding to the growing legend of the raid and its aftermath; stories about new abductions or about the few individuals who fought back – whom my brother invariably claimed he knew; stories about our own impotent soldiers, who were, it was said, warned by the invaders not to respond, and duly remained in their barracks.

My brother boasted about how he would have acted had he been a soldier or one of those under attack. He would describe the capacities of different guns and explain how had he been there and in possession of a particularly murderous piece of hardware, he would have taken them on and come out alive, his enemies scattered on the ground around him.

I was not convinced by his sudden knowledge of weaponry and military strategy. I wished Twice were here to temper his bravado. To explain, on the stoep at the front of the house, what was really going on out there and then to follow me into the house for one of Thembi's steaming soups.

I missed him. I missed the way he repeated words; the way he knew most things and would let me into his knowledge without revealing everything; the way he would sometimes dismiss me with his anger at my protected existence, my lack of experience of a larger, truer world out there, my lack of faith. I even missed the way how at those times, I would make to a quiet place in our township, like the place where I read the letter to Adelina and sift the crumbs of my deficient knowledge of the world.

Twice was gone, as were many of our schoolmates from the country neighbouring ours. A number had remained, but we never dared to ask what distinguished them from the others. There were intimations of political differences and that those who remained had not come amongst us to escape the predatory politics of these parts, but rather for the better opportunities for schooling and such to be had in this our nominally protected, independent state. They huddled amongst themselves and adopted a new privacy or learnt to speak our language to camouflage their foreignness. They lost their erstwhile brashness. They learnt to walk more softly on the earth, to hug its corners, to find shadows even in the glare of the midday sun.

Meanwhile, as in households in our township, other children ran in and out of the yard and sometimes even into the kitchen, if a pot happened to be boiling on the stove. Barring one or two of her favorites, Grandmother would chase them all out.

My favourite interlopers were two little girls, toddlers who could barely walk, but were wiser than their years, who would shout to me from the end of the yard. I would walk them to the house, each clasping my hands and hiding behind my legs from the dogs. I would always ask them about their families, who were labourers of one kind or another. They explained how their parents left early in the morning to look for work and left them bowls of food, which they were not to eat until the sun became very, very hot. They loved oranges and I would steal some to give them. Grandmother was aware and would call me in to give them real food, which they wouldn't eat, but would ask me to put in plastics so they could take home. Theirs was a hunting-gathering household where the spoils of the day were all brought home to be shared at the end of the day. We would sing a ditty they had taught me on the walk to the gate.

There were others too, whose homes I would also visit, though Grandmother disapproved. I always wondered what it was about us that made Grandmother consider us superior over others. She would never explain and I had to surmise it had something to do with her deceased husband the schoolteacher and our parents, though she would scold me out of her room any time I would ask about them.

It was as if, in the absence of our parents, Grandmother wanted to reinforce some sense of us as a normal, nuclear family, with Thembi as one of the varying number of extensions normal to all households in these parts. And in truth, we were not very different from other households in our township. Many were headed by grandmothers or, depending on circumstances, by various other relatives – fathers' brothers, bitter spinster aunts, and even people unconnected by blood. These of our playmates seemed always either more brutal in the way they would demand their share of whatever spoils we acquired – for we were hunter-gatherers and scavengers also – or diffident and the last to receive their share of stolen potatoes, buried and baked under a fire, or the ligament of a sheep's tail, our reward at helping, if only by our presence, in the slaughter of the animal.

Thembi too came to have her favourite replacements for the girls from the country neighbouring ours who no longer visited – pubescent girls from down the road, who, until they were called home to light the stove and fetch water, she would teach the ways of being a woman, so that her room would sometimes come to life again.

She hugged corners. She no longer turned up the radio up as

she used to, to dance to a favourite tune. She did not participate in my brother's fraught discussions in the kitchen. She would only interject when she felt compelled to rubbish an obviously preposterous statement or to defend her compatriots from the country neighbouring ours against whatever slanderous allegation was then doing the rounds.

Thembi collected magazines and stacked them neatly on the floor beside her bed. She read them voraciously, from cover to cover and wrote in for the various specials on offer: scholarships for distant-learning courses in bookkeeping; food hampers containing tinned fish, corned beef and condensed milk; beds with fake velvet headrests in burgundy; recipe books. Weekly almost, she would send me to the shop that served as our post office to mail her applications off, invariably to the city at the centre of the country neighbouring ours, where most bright things came from.

I would occasionally return letters for her, yellow or pink envelopes with smudged writing on their faces and small skewed stamps bearing the head of an animal, a rhinoceros or the white face of the leader of the country neighbouring ours, or a lion. But none of those letters ever contained a prize. We would have known if they did; however isolated she was becoming, Thembi was still part of our family and would have let us in on her good fortune, just as she would the bad. Like the way she would when letters would arrive, telling of the passing away or ill health of someone dear to her, someone unknown to us but rendered distant or proximate to her by the degree of her distress. If she simply sighed after an accounting, we would know it was not someone particularly close. If on the other hand she hurried back to her room and locked the door and refused to open it to my knocking, we would know someone significant had been lost.

I would try to imagine the lost person. What they looked like, how they dressed, what comforts they might have brought – a tall uncle, with a car and a clearly important job as a clerk in an office in a town, to swell the home with laughter and distribute small gifts that would wash away the day's bitterness, again; another relative, a woman probably, there when someone was sick to do all the right little things to put everything back in order; or a friend to share arms and shoulders and gossip for the long walk home after school.

These letters were not frequent, but were regular enough to suggest that life was more precarious over there, in the country neighbouring ours, than it was here. They confirmed the war; not war exactly, because those affected were not victims of guns that Grandmother would sound as "qwa, qwa", but rather victims of an almost apologetic, almost accidental but unending and brutal attrition of lives.

That there was no war here was on account of the simple caprices of history. Or so a simple reading would suggest.

By the time the vanguard of the imperial ambition arrived in these parts, they had learnt a cost-benefit analysis that figured the prodigality of mosquitoes, the endlessness of the sand, the ceaseless throw of rocks on infertile scratches of earth as unworthy of too much effort. A carefully scripted report would be hurried first by horseback to the coast, then by ship to the home country and finally by suitably liveried messenger to an appropriately peripheral office for the management of the affairs of this particular part of the empire. It would intone the savagery of the natives, occasioned in large measure by the harshness of the driven, endless, burning, almost purposeless sun, by a habitat of swamps and watery recesses that harboured vipers and leeches and countless other dangerous and hitherto unknown creatures, by high reaches of huge endless mountains hanging from the sky, with nothing in them save lost animals and man eaters. The missive would end with the consideration that although not enough was known of the hinterland of this landscape, this might indeed be the home of the legendary one-eyed creature spoken of by earlier explorers; brave men in a hazardous and deathly place.

Containing not much more than a throw of huge boulders that rose to mountains on the distant horizon and a wild and restless people, this place was not worth too much exertion. It was not worth the deployment of too many troops and administrators and priests – just enough for the replication of administrative systems tested in other, meaner colonies and enough to keep the generally docile natives in their place.

But we were told of another more complex history. Told it in our schools and amongst ourselves on the streets. Told it by men who by virtue of age and lineage, or unemployment and nothing else to do, had time to tell our grave story and its dark legends. Stories, as all stories are, sparked by feats of courage and marked by fierce battles and a people's fortitude. Legends turned by the duplicity of a clan made particular by a particular history, a clan damned forever. A boy amongst us whose name was of that clan would remember a domestic chore and hurry into the light.

Stories of fratricides and bloody murder. A daughter for an alliance, though that coupling never bore a child. A prophet with a message, hurled off a cliff and torn apart by wild scavenging animals. A darkness never before seen, at noon, of locusts that devoured every growing thing and started a terrible seven-year hunger when the people turned to eating each other.

The time of cannibals.

The time also of the arrival of another medicine man – originator of songs, sayings, knowings, knowledges, who spoke of the arrival of the man through whose ears you can see the sun; the man with eyes like water, who spoke only the lies of the damned-forever clan; the man with hair like the tail of a horse.

And closer to ourselves, a time of more familiar, known individuals, who walked our streets or were driven about in cars. A short old man with a quizzical smile, forever in the same brown crimpolene suit with a fading green tie and horned-rimmed glasses sat uncomfortably on his nose. Known by everyone and greeted effusively along the increasingly busy road at the centre of our town. Deeply knowledgeable about old migrations and their outcomes, and the current one too, having spent some time in his youth in the country neighbouring ours. Could tell the origin of the meaning of every one of our names and link each to its totem. Knew every older person, so that it appeared to us that he had been raised with them all, gone to all their mission schools, been to each and ever one of their marriages, lightly thrashed each man to announce as male the sex of his new borne child, or poured water on him when it was a girl.

Another man. Emerging blinking from his house behind the central police station. A former minister, with impeccably polished brogues, a perfectly white handkerchief, a whiff of rich alcohol about him, but slightly shaking and fading nevertheless. A writer of tracts and treaties, which he would carry to the Catholic bookshop, where they would print them in a room at the back. Well travelled. Had attended important international congresses and apparently once talked down the Queen's council. Pensioned off after yet another inexplicable cabinet reshuffle. His picture alongside the pictures of other former political incumbents on a now dated poster hung in government offices that should have been taken down months ago. Hung beside a skewed poster of traditional leaders, eyes glazed with alcohol, with our confident chief of chiefs at its centre, his eyes glazed with a mighty knowledge of power. The man's tread light so as not to have to dust his shoes. His legacy, a vague ideology argued in bars as the only way forward, or derided as the outdated, roughly put-together thoughts of a privileged sycophant. Still, we would bow our heads a little when we came across him on our streets and if he stopped us to ask after one of our teachers or after a relative or a parent, we would blush that he talked to us and draw pictures in the sand with our feet.

Others too, whose position in the emerging scheme of things was marked by signs whose meanings were daily becoming more obvious to us. Their mode of transport to work – on foot or by bus, or by private car; whether they carried provisions for lunch; whether they wore ties or overalls; how loudly and effusively they spoke the language which was not of these parts, but which we competed to master, to endow us with a superiority over others less blessed than we were.

We were quick to make connections between these things and could read the dissonance on the sweating face of a man in a suit and tie and briefcase but walking home through the tired dust of the end of the day: or the lie of an aspirant, unable to manoeuvre the language of our new enlightenment; or the way a strip of the skin of a dead animal on her wrist undid the ambitions of a woman with straightened hair, a painted face and stockings that made her thighs scratch and sigh as she walked.

We too found places for ourselves amongst the types we had constructed for this town. It was easiest, but also most unkind, to do so by association with what it was our parents did and by virtue of the things that we possessed vicariously through them. But these associations defeated many of us and undid many of our private and still nascent ambitions. So we would remove ourselves from the levelling glare of public spaces and reveal ourselves to each other in quiet, trusting moments, amongst trusted equals who would not mock us too much.

For my brother and I, our parents' absence knocked against the fact of Grandmother's not inconsiderable pension to place us in an ambivalent position. We could stoop low, so to speak, and design patently achievable futures for ourselves. It was not inconceivable that having successfully completed our basic education we could, a few years down the road, become junior public servants, similar to the tenants at the back of our house, who each month queued outside the national bank to cash their pay cheques. And this was no cheap ambition because eventually they did graduate out of our yard to acquire government plots and build safe two-roomed houses for a wife and the children to come.

Indeed the fact of their occupancy at the back of our yard for which they would come to pay Grandmother at the end of each month suggested the least that my brother and I could be. It became clear the more we progressed through school that Grandmother expected us to be more than that. She would not rest, she told us, until we had both passed through our single local university that used to be a seminary for the manufacture of priests. Our parents would expect no less she insisted.

Secretly then, my brother and I would talk about the opportunities that would come to us by dint of passage through that venerable institution. Admittedly they were few, but they were still much better than other available options. Amongst our after-school friends and acquaintances, some talked of working in the country neighbouring ours as their fathers did and spoke brightly of all the things they would bring home at the end of each year; blaring battery-driven machines, unavailable here of course, for spinning records and the latest music; clothes like in magazines; tables with four chairs to uplift rooms; cars even, eventually, with number plates from the country neighbouring ours and six lights at the back; and money, for the others, because we all knew very well that nothing was ever only for ourselves.

Others talked of apprenticeships, then employment and finally self-employment fixing cars or radios, or installing electricity, or water, or making things out of wood or steel, all in fitting with the changes so evident in front of us. Men who worked for themselves did well they reckoned and could even come to own buses that ply the mountains and take home those who had chosen, incorrectly it was implied, the option of migration.

A small bunch amongst us would inevitably drift out of the circle of such discussions. We were after all gathered together because we needed the numbers for a game of football and lived in the same neighbourhood and were the same age and attended the same school, even if some amongst us may have repeated a class or two for poor performance. It became evident that our coming together did not presage equal opportunity for us all.

Whether these boys, invariable afflicted by sniffles and sores on their knees that never seemed to heal, were excluded through some form of self identification, or by the way we, the more self-assured others would laugh at their foolish and obviously unattainable images of their future selves, did not matter in the end. We simply constructed clans of ourselves. Not warring clans for the moment, though later, as the consequences of their existence became as tight as money, they would assume a new hostility that occasionally erupted into outright war. Each clan, and there can't have been more than three or four, acquired its own language, its own nebulous codes of entry and exit, its own rules for the conduct of relations with the others, its own understanding of its place.

Our best option, mine and my brother's, was to attempt to enter into the university and from there, to advance into whatever became available by way of employment in the numerous government departments sprouting visibly in front of our eyes. New buildings and offices to house foreigners and their retinue. Strange tall buildings with circular windows and bright painted colours competing with the sun. Large steel containers out of which men in overalls or in bare chest when it was hot, would carry out more steel, long blue pipes for water, small engines that would buzz like mosquitoes, countless bags of maize or flour or beans. Well-guarded houses to which these foreigners retired at the end of each day, with bright green gardens and small white-haired children who would show us their toys from behind fences and scream for the maid when we threw stones at them.

Cars we had never seen before. High cars, Land Rovers and Jeeps with big wheels but not as big as the wheels of working lorries or buses. With names and flags and letters across their sides. With government number plates or special, different coloured plates, the codes of which we tried but never succeeded in cracking. With white people inside them, and people from our own country also, at the front to drive or to explain and open the way, or in their open backs, bent and holding their hats against the rushing wind.

And stolen and come together like escapees from our homes on a Saturday night, to find a line of cars in the centre of our town, parked against a red curtained window that leaked laughter and a mix of aromas that made our eyes wide and looking at each other in imagining. Or further into town, to a place where the ground rumbled to music that sometimes played on our radios and other music that we did not know. We took turns to peep inside through a hole where the black paint had flaked off a window.

I saw a man I knew, an older boy really, from our village, who worked, dancing with a white woman with long hair that hung to her buttocks. He was holding her close across her waist and she was arched backwards, her belly pressed in towards him, her short skirt lifted at the back so that I could make out her taut white thighs, shadows at the back of her knees and the pink tendons of her ankles. The music stopped and they came apart. He smiled and adjusted himself and holding her hand, disappeared into the depths of the place. Behind me, my brother insisted it was his turn. But then the watchman saw us huddled by the window and came shouting towards us to go away, my brother and I and our four or five companions from our township. We bolted into the darkness across the road and took turns throwing stones at him until we tired at our poor success and made for home. We peered into shop windows and joked about and laughed as we walked along the deserted main road of our town. Later, a threat of light scarring the darkness of the far horizon, we jogged in time to a song to bring together our coming home.

That was our opportunity then. To be like the older boy from our village who worked and had his own car, and had his shirts ironed and his white socks starched for dancing with white women in discotheques on Saturday nights. He beat his girlfriend who washed his socks and sometimes we would hear her crying.

Not to beat girls, but to have access to them and to money and to sit behind curtains and have men made dark and glistening by the brightness of their white shirts serve us sizzling food and to laugh between a bite of this, a savour of that, a quaff of the other. To move out of our township one day, into flat 18 or 21 on the highest floor of an upstairs-downstairs block of flats just behind the main thoroughfare at the centre of our bustling town. Not to have to walk or take a bus back to the township at the close of business each day, but to amble about the shops with a newspaper under the arm and to stop in at a pub for a drink and connivance.

The young man never gave us money in the township. He would, however, throw coins at us in town, if he were with a girl, all pulled together and precariously balanced on high shoes and giggling between a set of perfectly white teeth. Or if he was with a white man or women he worked with and our grey legs were not too speckled with piss. In the township, at best, he would like Abuti Jefti all ashen and sulky in his house under the trees, send us to buy him beer and let us keep the change. Or if he had someone in, not his girlfriend whom he sometimes hit, but another woman, fresh and newly discovered and bright in measure of his resources, he would send us on long treks to far-flung taverns to find whatever beverage for ladies was then the fashion.

We learnt all of these things. And things also from the slightly older others who had preceded us at school, or who were related to us, or who were from our township. We learnt many things also from people we did not know but whom we came to know by their position and place in the unfolding patterns of things.

Chiefs and politicians walked with their heads up and to the side as if to sniff the air for poison and intrigue. By midday already, teachers with scuffed shoes with their so much walking about dusty classrooms, their shirttails hung like skirts across their buttocks, their once crisp collars a muddy paste of sweat.

Young nuns did not want to see and crossed the road to avoid their fallen sister, mad now, her habit black from days, months, years in the sun, but steadfast still in her knowledge of faith. We imagined their bodies.

Soldiers carried their guns like walking sticks or draped them over their shoulders and hung their arms over them. It was only much later that they were to savour their capacity to break flesh. Soldiers then were simply men in uniform with guns and not particularly useful at anything, what with the way they had ran away.

Others wore the blue uniform of the worker and boots, hard hats or balaclavas in winter and in between digging at a road, sat about rolling tobacco or long pungent dagga cigarettes in brown paper. Or accosted girls with vaseline legs and sensual swinging buttocks, or domestic workers in pink pinafores, who would chain the dog and let them in for a quick fuck in the rooms at the back of the yard, before the madam returned.

And below all of them, a world of countless, other often barely visible people skulking about the periphery of things. Visible only in affront to the now acquired, now generalised ambition of this place. Stumbled down from the mountains, animals lost to a drought, crops to a frost, a son's promises to the unknown caprices of the country neighbouring ours. Shoulders draped by a blanket eaten by hunger. Stick in hand in memory of cattle herding in the mountains, and to fight off city toughs. Huddled with other men in front of a hut of stone and thatch at the periphery of our town for a bucket of sorghum beer to pass around, to pass to the itinerant come strumming a constructed instrument of wood and stolen wire, singing of contrition, of a man's murder in a black hole, of revenge, of when we were heroes.

Bearded one who is feared by all the people.
Feared by the children and their mothers!

Here, in this low flat place,
There is no pasture for the cattle to roam.
They are fattened in pens.

My bovine,
Daily at the westward slant of the sun,
Used to low in loud voice,
Lowed until their voices reached the place of council.

Stop the sun in the sky.

Turn it back on itself.

Make redundant this dance we dance,

We broken, previously tall men,

Who used to take off our blankets at the approach of an enemy.

Now we are only the sweat that falls off the brow of the earth. The dirty issue of its exertion. Absolved only if we could nourish the soil that our women till.

But they do not see us. Neither do they, mothers of our children, hear our singing. They see us only fading in their dreams.

"I could be your welcome," she said, sitting at the stoep of her falling down house.

"I have many things I could give you. Beer, a plate of food for your belly. A place to sleep for the night, or for a few nights. If you promise to return, if not with a fortune of maize flour and spinach and other things to fill these empty vessels, empty since the father died, then at least with promises. So that the lies we tell ourselves, that we tell these little frightened ones who follow their father's shadow about, don't make such a mockery of us."

This man could come into this house. We could pretend it was his house. That everything was arranged, as it should be. That these two were his, these children tripping at my legs.

Please, please dear God. He must not hit them when they reach up to him. What do they understand of who he is or why he is here? They were so quick to learn the sound of his boots when he returns to the house out of the dark. They have learnt to measure his luck on the streets by the way he sits on his stool at the side of room. They know when to go to him to sit on his lap and laugh at his breath that scratches their faces. They can guess when he might conjure something out of the folds of his blanket to entertain them; a cow sculpted out of clay whilst he waited out there, with the other men, his labour on offer for a little pay; or a marble that glistened at the corner of his always downward-cast, searching eyes; or two shrivelled sweets, more paper than anything else, given to him because they didn't have coins at the shop for change for his tobacco.

They were also quick to learn when to make themselves small, when to disappear under the table or to find insects to make games of in the shadows of the room, or when to go behind the curtain to sleep.

They know the smell of him when he takes off his shirt to lie beside me. They huddle and shiver together beyond the curtain when he rages in me, impotent from too much beer. My older child, a boy with his father's eyes, is never in the house when we wake up in the morning.

If we are blessed, these rituals I have done will keep him here. I have woken up early in the morning before the sun is up and slaughtered a white chicken where my forebears lie. I have talked to them and heard them shuffling about the space above my ears.

They have peopled my dreams. And oh, if only they could soften the firmness of this life. If only they could make me forget how the future used to look. I asked them to bury my absent husband and to give me this man in his place.

Eight

THEMBI STOOD UP to the call of one of the priests and made her way to the front of the tent to speak of my brother in his still slightly humming coffin. I had not read the programme for the service, printed on a glossy, gold-embossed brochure that two of the boys of the t-shirts had handed out as the mourners had entered the tent. I had caught a glimpse of my brother's picture on its front and remembered that a funeral programme delineated the milestones of a life; the deceased's date and place of birth, his or her education, his employment, his marriage and offspring and his significant achievements. The programme also listed the proceedings of the day, who was to speak when, though I also remembered that speakers never kept to their allotted time and rambled on and on, as if the duration of their talking would speak the depth of their relationship with the deceased.

I had not taken a programme as I entered the tent. To have done so would have implied that I, my brother's only directly living relative, had had nothing to do with its shaping, or that I had not been party to decisions to put one speaker before another, to chose this individual rather than another to speak on behalf of his colleagues, his drinking friends, his golfing friends, his neighbours.

I had arrived too late here to have anything to do with the arrangement of things. And even if I had arrived on time, I was too long a stranger to these parts, too ignorant of what had become of my brother's life to be of any help. I did not know whom his friends were, who was the sufficiently senior bureaucrat at his place of employment to speak on behalf of his working world.

I could have come here a week ago. I could have come soon after I received Thembi's breathless telephone call telling me my brother had died. But I hadn't and had lied to Thembi and by association, to all those others who had no sense of my life and the lives of others like myself, over there, overseas. I had not told her that I needed time to put together the money to buy the ticket to fly me home. Instead I had said I was occupied with something urgent that would not allow me to immediately break away.

I had had no choice but to lie, for after all, who was I to shatter one of the central myths of life in the Diaspora; that our existence at the centre of the world was an existence amongst wealth and opulence and bright lights and opportunity; that despite our increasingly infrequent letters, our lives continued to be about thrift and saving and education and connecting with people who would expand all our possibilities. We were in truth, nothing but cold, lost men out there.

I knew many people who had been over there far longer than I had. Old people, some of who could understand my name. They would pour me drinks and introduce me to their lovers to whom they would explain the meaning of my name, "he who pays, he who bears recompense". "For what?" their women would ask, those sweet English women with tinted hair and blue veins when they lifted their knees too high on their bar stools. Who would look me about to measure my otherness, to confirm the reason for their current, and many years now, company. Call me "Lovey" and wager to forecast my fortune, my assimilation in this place. Call their pale daughters over when I did not pout and instead lightly smacked my lips against their scented, angled cheeks; their firmer though still assless daughters, in strange-heeled shoes and black, fake-leather jackets and purple paint across their eyes for colour. Called them away from their boyfriends in tight jeans and even tighter scowls whose motorbike helmets had worked as weapons in skirmishes of the urban, working-class kind. I would smile at them, then put my hand across my mouth. The streets out there, beyond the comfort of the smoke and odour of this and other drinking holes, with its men who could be my uncles, were then still unfamiliar.

156

Most of these men, these newly acquired uncles of mine, had never been home. Not once. Had left on the back of a clan's savings, grudgingly given; on the blessings of a sheep fattened and slaughtered and burnt whilst songs were sung around a fire; on the tears of a girl with the seed of a child in her belly, huddled in some outlying hut, against an aunt who would hide the secret, and the girl, because he would be back before the birth of the child; on a tide of song and ululation and too many cousins at the airport, come to mark their claim against an inevitable bounty.

Most of these men had never returned home. Not even to a brother's funeral or a mother's. They had never returned because what could they have said? Once past the suspicious immigration officer, past the vaguely remembered faces of former acquaintances who were now state security, past other tattered and broken men scavenging at the edge of the right of admission, past the hustling taxi drivers, the tourist guides in their florid shirts, what could they have declared? Savings? Education? Connections?

There would be something about the way their clothes hung on them, the way their shoes grimaced as they made their way through the always crowds that would belie their putative success. There would be something about the way they concealed the transaction of pounds or franks or dollars into local denomination, something about the way they hid the dirty notes, dirtied by their frequent exchange or their keeping in the sweating bosoms of matriarchs at the market, that would tell the truth of their exile. Mother, if it were not she who had passed away, would wonder what sin it was that kept them from looking her in the eye.

There was a woman who lived above me. A simple woman really. Almost a peasant woman. Of little education and a fast commitment to the bible. With whom I could leave my keys, though she disapproved, if some girl I happened to be fucking or a temporarily homeless brother needed access to my rooms. She would sometimes cook for me and we would reminisce about our siblings and the ways of the sun at home, over her steaming pots of fufu and groundnut stew. She worked three jobs, except on Sundays when she would wear her pastel-pink dress and matching hat with lace and make to the revivalist church at the local community centre, where they sung in tongues. She would come back amazingly restored for the next week of three jobs a day, washing dishes and cleaning offices and escorting a grey old woman whose husband had once conquered Africa, to the shops or to a neighbour's for tea.

She met a man from her country, from her clan, who soon spent nights with her, though I did not approve. He did not approve of me either and the meals I had come to share with her came to an abrupt end. I arrived home one day, a little brighter than usual after a few beers with a band of displaced friends, to find her wailing and hysterical on the floor in the centre of her unusually dishevelled room. I lifted by her armpits and was briefly shocked by the heat and smell of the sweat of her body and dropped her. I sat her on her bed and used damp cloths, pats on her back and eventually hot tea to calm her. She finally composed herself enough to relate how the man had informed her he had acquired an American passport, false for sure, but sufficient; how he talked of going over there, across the waters, because there was more hope there, because nothing seemed to have worked for him over here; how he had searched her room and hit her and found and taken her money, all the money she had saved over seven years of three jobs a week, bound in a tight cloth in a bag and hidden at the back of her cupboard; all the money she had been saving to open a little shop or a place to make dresses, to save the family, next year, at home.

I did not know what to do. I went to the community centre where her church was, to run away from such a pain, to look for help. Matrons came back with me and remained with her for the rest of the night. Early the next morning, they took her away. Later, other people came to collect her things. They wouldn't tell me where they had taken her. I never went back to the community centre. I never saw her again.

There was a bandy-legged Arab, with whom I became fast

friends, who wore a faded green beret and soldiers' boots. A first-born son. A musician. He played handheld drums and tried to teach me a little. I would follow him to musical gatherings in halls and warehouses where, always unobtrusively and to the side of the stage, amongst strange constellations of music people gathered under a brief expansive moment of funding by the local council, he would play his drums. I don't think he ever got paid, because he would never buy me drinks afterwards. Offered me hashish, but never a drink. Against his religious beliefs he would say, in between sucking at a joint. Must have played something worthwhile because they always let him in. But they never put a microphone above his drums. Perhaps his music was to be sensed rather than heard.

I only found out he was married to a local woman the day I left to come to Puso's funeral. He accompanied me to the airport. "Anybody who is going home is special," he said. "They can open the doors for the rest of us to go home."

He told me then of his wife whom I had never known and of his sickly child who was always in hospital for the treatment of some rare disease. "If I had this child at home, he would not be alive," he said. As I passed into the airport departure lounge, he shouted at me above the line of people with their smells of soap and aftershave, with their sensible clothes and manageable luggage, "Come back with a little soil of Africa." I looked at the only other black man in the line, who looked at me and laughed.

As if a little soil, however contained, could carry ghosts back. As if anything I were to carry – a cloth, food smuggled in plastics, a stone from a secret place, a re-remembered song, a photograph of a landscape against a setting sun – as if anything I were to carry could trip the spirits across the deep waters, the mountains, the rivers, the deserts or the arbitrary lines, for each according to his own, that were the barriers between this place and the places called home.

The profit of someone travelled back from the place called home was rich. A man returned with a little skill to fashion drums of wood and plastic in place of the skin of a slaughtered animal, and with knowledge of the real sway of the ritual dance, was a rich man. One such man booked a space at the local community hall, a dour place of hard concrete, graffitied walls and a smell of urine. He plied the guilt of a sister recently moved out to a good job and a better neighbourhood for funds for a meal to be shared by those to be gathered. He printed bright yellow flyers and enlisted the indignant energy of a posse of angry young men for their door-to-door distribution. He personally shepherded some of the elderly out of their cold and miserable council flats and walked them to the hall. Once everyone was assembled, he asked one of the elders to open with a prayer, in the language of their common place of origin, then, robes flying behind him, for a gathering such as this required him to be appropriately liveried, he walked to where a small group of youth were seated behind the drums he had constructed and led them in song. The drumming over, he delivered his message, come directly from home, about the old ones and the young ones, lost and broken by oppression, but willing and ready to fight still. Awaiting old clothes, books for the children at school, prayers, and money too, for which he furnished his banking details. Called for organisation, expressed first as a return to the old practices, to which someone rose and sang and danced and rushed to the stage to play a drum, but drunk and dishevelled, wavered and sat down.

In time, young children and other youth under the tutelage of variously skilled old people from the place called home came to commune twice a week at the community hall. They learnt the drum and to dance and chant boys' songs of circumcision, girls amongst them even and boys with the girls also, when it was their turn. Someone remembered the urgency of segregation and they giggled and rushed to separate, if adjoining, rooms and accepted walls as mountains, lights as the seasons, smells as the different odours of the mud that would separate them at home. They learnt to prepare special foods for special occasions, even if they sometimes had to imagine fish as long as legs, bright fresh fruit, pungent spices in place of the meagre fair that was available. Well practiced, they gathered once every few months at the dressed-up hall. The whole community and its friends. The men to one side and the women to the other or turning large spoons in steaming pots in the kitchen at the back. And the man with the first reconstruction of the drum, at the front, in even brighter robes, brought here by a lively woman friend of his, who possessed an anthropological interest in the place he was from, a personal interest in his charms, his amulets, his arms, his assets.

Ancestors for the Diaspora.

These and other instances like them were the scarce moments of our connection. Instances like the time a haggle of us descended one rare hot afternoon, on the house of a women with long black hair that extended to her waist, who collected drums and refugees and little artefacts hung beside pictures she had taken in unnamed deserts, on barren mountains tops, or at the coast of a spice island where boats with white sails chased the wind. In the muggy heat of her small, enclosed back yard, we smoked a pungent hashish and then reached for her many drums scattered about and for hours sat and played away our displacement. At some point two drunken Irishmen arrived out of nowhere, one with a guitar and the other with a mouth organ and proceeded to join us, their songs about the ale, their war, their itinerancy that, strangely, settled comfortably on top of the babble of our drums. We drummed for hours with no let up. And for all those hours, no one said a word, or got up to relieve himself or to refresh himself with a drink from the house or to pause to stretch his aching hands.

It was dark when we finished and the lights on the streets made them another land. We hugged the woman and each other and bade the Irishmen well and each quietly disappeared into the gloom of the streets, each to our separate lives.

There were no ancestors the day they took away another good acquaintance. A rude man sent down from one of their great universities for burning it down. Mad long before he arrived here, but here to sell madness as invention. Brilliant inventions of word and rhyme. Spoken as if in tongues but always with perfect meaning. Meaning which I only ever understood late at night, leant against a soaking bar, he and I, and against whichever of his disciples were assembled to facilitate our indulgences, our drunken eloquence. Evicted first from the pub and then from the after-hours drinking spot in a basement when he insulted a man who brandished a knife, then from his rooms with their scattered manuscripts and spilt bottles, and then finally from the streets themselves, screaming and swearing and railing against the rain and the wind, so that he passed the rest of his life a gibbering idiot in a sanatorium in the country.

No ancestors there, but haunting all the moments between every sound, between every shade of refracted light, here in this tent. Implicated in each and every of Thembi's words that were floated across the air to me like wishing. Flat words to explain the space my brother had occupied in her life since my departure so many years ago. Dry, ordinary words that could have been spoken by the fidgeting boy or any one of the matrons from Grandmother's burial society or one of the youths in the t-shirts extolling thrift and virtue. Words strung together to make tales of Puso's life. How he had always run ahead. How in running before the rest of us, he had achieved as much as he had. How in running, it might seem that he failed to remember his connection to this home.

But Thembi spoke of how Puso had often visited. Bringing things for them. How Puso would mark her daughter from the other children by handing her the more fragile things to carry into the house and how she in turn would lead their retinue in a little dance and skip to the house, as all children do to small delights. How they would sometimes sit in the kitchen and laugh kindly at half-remembered stories of all those who had peopled it. How he had brought there the woman that was to become his wife. Explained her place of origin. Suggested what was to be her given name. Implored Thembi who was keen to demonstrate her mastery of the new lingua franca, the language of the foreigners and people come with money to raise and then resettle the dust in the name of progress, to speak in the vernacular, so that his new wife could learn it. And when the children arrived, first the girl and then the boy, how he had also brought them from his house to this house and sat with them in his arms under the stoep under a glowing moon or took them naked into the rain to stop them from becoming thieves.

Thembi was silent for a moment and stared at the ground as if to bore at the centre of that which she was telling us. She lifted her eyes and cast them over Puso's family, over her own daughter and then over me. We recoiled collectively, as if together stung by the barbs of the history her words had conjured. Without another word, she stumbled from the front of the tent to sit down beside us. Her face glistened with a smear of tears.

She had not talked about how my brother had lost his life, although as a member of the family and on account of my ignorance of the details of his passing, she was supposed to. Perhaps the facts of the way he had died were for her too visceral to shape into a sequence of discrete acts that, strung together, would describe how a once-living body was now broken and still.

None of the others who came after Thembi described how Puso had lost his life. They talked instead, in between prayers and stood-up-for hymns, only of the achievements of his years – things I did not know about him and that he had done during my seven years away from this place. Successes all of them, so that second son that I was, they rebuked what I was, though for now, only I of the people gathered here, knew what I had become. And in talking about him, they described for me, what had become of this place. How like in countless other places like it on this continent, it had provided professional and social opportunities for a select few.

Chances for further education and travel, all of which my brother had taken up. His sojourns away from this place had always been planned, itineried, funded. And he had always returned to advance that which he was to be in the emerging scheme of things.

I imagined my brother's office at a suitably located corner of a building at the centre of our town, with a large desk against a large window that looked onto the mess of the streets below and above it, his certificates hung perfectly straight in gold frames. I could also imagine the pictures on his desk, of my brother receiving awards or laughing and hugging white people and Indians or rare Chinese in front of modern buildings of glass and steel, to boast of his travels to the capitals of enlightenment and progress, at the centre of the world. I could imagine all of this and much more, because even before I had left, I had entered many offices such as his must have been, to use a remembered connection to Grandmother or even her husband before her to secure the scholarship that had taken me away.

My brother had stolen opportunity made possible by a growing and chuckling wealth to choose and discard, one by one, possible candidates to one day bear his children. Bright young women sent down from the mountains to get a basic education and to be married by someone such as he. Women now thoroughly cleansed of the smell of goats and the smoke of dung fires off their clothes. More knowledgeable now and with a slick expertise at licking their fingers to page through magazines, or at listening to their slightly older sisters, to learn which creams would best scrape away the dark tones of their sun-burnt, bequeathed skin, what tears to leak to turn him, what promises to embed in their sighs when they opened their thighs to him.

My brother had written to inform me he had installed electricity and running water in the kitchen of our home. Thembi would be fine now, he had continued, as if in contrition for saying next that he was moving out of our home. He talked of the inconvenience of its distance from the centre of town and all its opportunities, how he sometimes had to bring people home with him who complained about the condition of the roads. He needed to get out he argued, to enable Thembi who would never afford her own equivalent place, to do all the things she wanted without having to demure to the fact of his titled occupancy of the house.

He had first moved to a room at the back of a foreign colleague's house. Later, he moved into a block of flats and boasted he was one of the first of the locals to be allowed in. It was a small place with a bedroom, a bathroom and a living room and kitchen. But the fact of his tenancy in a clearly exclusive block made the rooms larger than they were. As proud and gracious as he obviously was, he was nevertheless disquieted at being told by someone above or below to lower the noise of an afternoon of beers with friends on his balcony.

Another letter informed me how he had acquired a car through a sealed bid tendered to his place of employment. He had hinted at meetings in a bar with the official responsible for the bid and underhand activities in acquiring it. He had then justified it by saying that he would otherwise never have got the car, what with the resources available to his expatriate colleagues and others of higher seniority at his place of employment. We need to stand together, he continued, if we are to wrench away access and control from those in charge of things.

I remember laughing at his newfound nationalism, assuming that the we he referred to was the scrambled together we that made up the indigenous people of our country. He seemed to have learnt, if with a crude and self-interested intent, the basics of the language I spoke with my scattered brothers in the bars we had claimed as places of safety, over there, overseas. Other rare letters had in time come to employ much of this language, so that for me over there, it appeared as if we were sharing the learnings of a particular moment of history. His letters came to talk of self-determination, if in a narrow, bureaucratic and still self-interested sense, and how we, that same republican we that he had used to distinguish himself from his foreign colleagues, needed to be in charge of our future. They talked of origin as I did, and sought to make a long, unbroken line of our history and to identify the point that marked a great and unnatural turning. They implied an inevitable re-turning once we had captured and named that point.

My brother sent me pictures of himself. Not pictures that he might have mounted in his office, but little snaps taken at the periphery of his working life. Come home after an acrimonious night of pointless argumentation with friends, I discovered at the entrance of my flat, a letter thrown between my boots and stolen umbrellas. I immediately recognised it as my brother's and picked it up and rushed to pour myself a saviour of a drink, to wash away the rancour of the night and to open me to his stories and all the memories they would carry. I sat down in a favourite chair and stared at the face on the stamp on the letter, a face I did not know. The thought struck me that I should have had the letter with me earlier that night. I could have shown it to my friends to prove my point about change and its meaning on the surface, or rather its meaninglessness, as I had really been trying to argue. I should have had two letters actually, the one now in my hand and another from a few months before, with a different face on a different stamp. They would have understood my point – or maybe not. We had not been talking for reason that night. We had rather talked to scream, knowing we would all afterwards dismiss our memories of it, knowing all of us, the places in our hearts from which our screaming had come.

I took a sip of my drink and opened the envelope. There was no letter inside. Four photographs slid onto my lap.

The first was of my brother outside what I assumed was his flat. He was standing at the bottom of a flight of stairs that could only have been of a building somewhere at the centre of town. He had an oxblood briefcase in one hand and his suit jacket draped across the hand of his other arm. The top button of his white shirt was undone and his tie, a bright red affair, hung skew against his shirt. One of his shoelaces was undone and the other shoe was scuffled at the toes. I remembered then the dust that could not be avoided even by a migration to town.

My brother's hair was well groomed as always. He wore a handsome smile, but above his mouth, his eyes were as still as stones. I stared into the face on the picture. I didn't know to choose between the apparent mischief in his smile and the silence of his eyes to read what it was he was saying to me. Or indeed, if his was to point to an ironic disjuncture between the form and content implicit in the tension between his smile and his eyes, his dishevelled exterior and an apparently calm interior.

I turned the photo over. On it was written the words "After work on a Friday" as if to suggest that despite his success, there was also space for my brother to loosen himself as he had loosened his tie, from the strictures of the world he had come to inhabit.

The next photograph was of Thembi in a hospital bed with her newborn child in her arms. An earlier letter had informed me of the birth. The child was like any child of a few hours old, squint and wrinkled like a chicken rescued from the water, or a rat. There was nothing in the flat head of the child, or her nose or her slits for eyes that was like my memory of her mother.

Thembi's face was turned down towards the child, so that beyond the outlines of a faintly embarrassed smile, I could not read her expression. She was wearing a pale blue bed-gown and a headscarf that had slipped down her forehead. On the table beside her were bottles and containers that I assumed were for nursing and feeding her child. My brother must have taken them to her.

At first glance, I was a little taken aback by the side view of the white woman in the short skirt and tight red blouse in the third photograph. She was sitting in a swing for children made of rope and half of a car tire. She was leaning backwards against the forward motion of the swing. Her hair was swept behind her to reveal an adamant forehead, as was her dress that revealed taut thighs and stiff legs, thrust forward to cut through the rush of the air. Her eyes were locked wide open and I thought I could make out a tail of a tear against her cheek, rushed out by her forward motion. I could see the blue veins of her wrists and the struggling pink and white of her wrists clenched as tightly as if to save her life.

It was a perfect picture. Below and behind the swinging woman was a blur of green grass and leaves. Little spots of yellow colour suggested flowers in between the leaves. There were two points of darkness in the picture. In the unfocused distance of the image, a figure stood, motionless and watching the scene of this woman, this grown white woman, playing in a swing for children. Above him, a ceiling of pale blue light hinted at the time of day. To the rear and bottom of the print and partly intersecting the blurry image of the woman was the shadow of the person taking the picture. It was the shadow of my brother and for a moment I stared at it, to get another view of him, to superimpose the shadow onto the complete image I had of him in the other picture, to fuse the meaning of that image with this.

It was the day after the first picture, I thought. The day after the Friday. I got up to replenish my drink. Late on Saturday afternoon perhaps, at the tail end of a day well spent. Perhaps earlier, they had made love and then ran out of the house to clear themselves of the guilty funk of their coupling. They might have held hands or thrown stones to see whose could reach the furthest, or stopped to laugh at the invention of small children playing house at the edge of the park, or at kick-the-can at its less hidden centre.

Or perhaps they had had a planned day. The woman might have suggested a trip out of town. To enjoy nature as foreigners were always fond of doing in our country. They might have taken pictures with her camera and then stopped for refreshments at the hotel where rooms could be rented by the hour. Maybe they took a room. Not because it offered a rare opportunity, but because the heat of the afternoon in the car and the anticipation inevitable of two new lovers with a stolen moment was a strong aphrodisiac. My brother would have baulked at the disapproval of the haughty receptionist. "She knows who I am," he might have whispered. But the sight of his lover's white flesh as she burst out of her clothes and the urgency of her bites would have undone his reticence. Finished and wanting to get away from the sordid sheets of theirs and the countless couplings of countless anonymous others they would have rushed them straight home. They wouldn't have stopped at a park. They would have driven straight home and done things to straighten themselves up, like repairing the mess of the house or turning on the television to allow the world to berate them a little.

My brother must have sent the last photograph in error. It was of a group of about thirty men and women, obviously labourers, standing in the middle of a road of dirt. They had picks and shovels and other implements in their hands. They were facing in all directions, as if oblivious to the camera. A few of them were sitting on embankments of sand at the edges of the road. In the distance of the photograph, a few others stood in front of two official looking vehicles, sloped against the gradient of the landscape. They were clearly at the top of a mountain.

The men and women were in heavy coats and blankets. The light was the weak and indiscriminate light of winter.

I looked amongst the faces I could make out on the picture to see if there was anyone I could recognise. Thembi I thought, though I knew she could never have fallen as far as to become someone to work at digging roads in exchange for parcels of food at the end of the day. Or an old neighbour or a schoolmate, fallen on hard times. Or my brother, a manager of these and similar other things like it, sitting in one of the cars in the photograph's distance. I surmised the photograph was work-related and sent to me in error.

I threw the pictures to the table beside me. This was my brother's life then. Work and a ritual of drinks with friends on Friday to mark its success. Thembi and her child, so that despite of or because of the success of the first picture, a distinct connectedness to the place we had come from remained intact. I could only guess at how much my brother had been affirmed by bringing necessary gifts to Thembi, soap and little clothes, at this signal moment of her life. And then his intimate life, with the woman on the swing, which became a life of negotiated and wide possibilities.

And what, by comparison, of my life and its equivalents? Made up of little more than small pretences, small truces against a relentless hostility. Pretence at understanding a piece of art at a gallery, to bed the woman who had invited me. A lying carouse through the lies I had constructed of savage animals and even more savage neighbours to provoke sympathy and assuage her lust for something terrifyingly other than this that I was, that she knew. A momentary truce when, sitting with her knees across from me in a train hurtling under the ground, a bold black girl would fall into the snare of my eyes, and follow me out into the dim light at the stop where I alighted, and accept the ruse of a splash of water on the wet streets to jump and fall against me and tell me her name. And then to arms again when she recoiled at hearing my African name, so that my hope for a little connection, my hopes for a few brief moments of hot pleasure, for a little community beyond the community of my wayward friends, were lost.

Too much Africa for this my sister. Neither her mother nor her friends would accept a rain-drenched, homeless dog such as I, though her light skin tones and almost blue eyes proclaimed her more mongrel than I.

Too much Africa for bus conductors, who would let me stay on past the stop where I should have alighted. Sikhs inevitably, whose turbans and hair bound around their faces would never advance their assimilation, or tall singing men from the islands whose jealousy that I was a refugee or a student reconnected them to their wisdom and reminded them of things like origin, things like the sun, like Garvey, like their now frozen, now eroded, now bitter once-upon-a-time.

Too much Africa for those few places that would employ me in between my studies so that I could augment my stipend, such as the place where I modelled for a woman with long grey hair and silver rings who taught middle-aged matrons to paint, who shouted gin-soaked insults at me each time I moved. Or the restaurant where they rushed me to the safe back to wash dishes, with a man from India and another, bitter, paler one, a refugee from a war, who spat into each plate before he took it out.

Too much even for the place I had been sent to study. Poor methodology they told me. A dislocated discourse. A confusion of purpose, though in between the spaces they left me, I stole moments to read and write and talk and dream of possibilities that lay somewhere in between my brother's life and the life that I lived then.

The only picture I ever sent back to my brother was a randomly found thing that had slipped out of a book at a friend's place. There had been no other photographs to send back, because my life then was too unscripted, too unconscious, too startled for capture. And, unlike the pictures my brother had sent me, bar the one with the people standing in the road, they did not, not any one of the few I had, point to the rear or forward horizons of my then current state. They did not suggest the point of convergence of this poorly constructed life of study and a traipsing about the streets in search of god knows what. They did not put a frame to the endless dialogues with fellow exiles that were restarted always unrepaired each time we met again. They did not shade this life of rare nights of shrill reprieve. They did not propose a carefully crafted design of the future, or maps to guide my passage at times of hazard, or even suggest a loosening of whatever held me from seeking recourse in other dangerously close places, such as the sanatorium where they held my one friend, or the other desperate, hidden, illegal spaces where so many others turned the days at the bottom of this blustering, unforgiving world. They left me simply bound to this place I was in, with a poor memory of the light behind me and a cheap imagination of the light still to come.

That was the imagination I had then of Puso's life, shadowed and refracted now by the auras of the people around me in the tent, with the gleam of their sweat as the sun broke through the clouds and the tent, once again, billowed as if taking a breath.

The gathered stood again to the priest's sidemen clapping their bibles and sang a hymn about making us fishers of men that had been one of grandmother's favourites. Flagrant bribery I thought, of dubious reward. Fish a man and get what? Scattered memories of times spent together in joy and happiness? Not possible. Happiness is instant and visceral and instinct cannot conjure it up as pieces of memory. Anger? I can gather bits of anger from the ground around me, and scoop them into bags for my shoulders and walk away, their weight a reminder forever. I can invoke tears by staring at a piece of pain. I know the colours of desolation. They are the colours of the things I see when I am broken apart; the ground at my feet; the distance for seeing inwards. I see colours between my fingers when I rub them against each other.

A reward. Twice walked into the tent. I recognised him immediately. He was wearing a navy-blue coat with shining gold buttons, an expensive striped t-shirt, grey slacks and dusty black shoes. With him was a woman with gold-rimmed glasses that were too big for her face and equally bright baubles on her chests and her arms. They hesitated at the front of the tent and looked about for a place to sit. Someone behind me must have beckoned to them for they looked just beyond my ear, nodded briefly and then made their way to the row behind. Two young people made space for them and walked to the back of the tent.

The hymn came to an end and the congregation sat down. I looked to Thembi to see if she too had seen him. Her head was twisted towards the row behind us. She turned to the front and for a brief moment I caught a smile of recognition on her face.

Twice again, after so many years. Disappeared into the night all those years ago and gone to some country far beyond even the borders of the county neighbouring ours. And not a single missive from him from wherever he had disappeared, all those years. Not a single murmur or rumour to say what had become of him. Gone with the others from the country neighbouring ours, on a night when guns had rent the silence of the sky, to become a more exact refugee, or a fighter, known by another name, or a dead person, flung into a mass pit in the red earth of some beleaguered country.

Thembi might have communicated with him through the years. Or if she hadn't, perhaps the people who had come to her rooms had whispered his whereabouts. Maybe the letters she had received had hinted where it was the tall boy with the broken teeth, who repeated everything twice, had gone. She must have known where to find him, for only she could have told him of Puso's death. Or perhaps Twice had heard the programme on our national radio where each night, a man read out notices of the recently deceased and arrangements for their interment to the gloomy sounds of a church organ. Twice had never been one to do that kind of thing, unless of course he had changed and become someone different from the Twice I had known. Lost from his siblings and lost in another country, he would have known none amongst the dead whose names were intoned against the drone of the organ. Death, he used to tell me, was for us all. A weeping for the dead was distraction from the real world, he had said. His world was harsh and real then, despite his urgent telling of other, better, future states, so that I had whimpered and shrunk the meaning of mine with all its then promises.

I could not see Twice and the woman sitting behind me. I could smell them though – a broad scent that infiltrated the odours of those sitting around me. I wanted to rush him outside to look at him and talk to him. I wanted this service to end. Enough of the priest and his sidemen and their choreography at the front of the tent to stand us for another hymn and sit us for more half-lies about Puso's life. Twice was here now and his presence was beginning to make sense of my coming home. Twice would close the circle. He would soften the hard stumbling about the years. He would secure the distances and shut-up the sounds of an inner pain whose origins I could not account for. He would find a place for Thembi. Thembi my half-sister. Thembi the girl-woman, who in unknowingly baring her nakedness to me, had kindled the shadow of my first lust and revealed to me my first crude glimmer of hope for real connection beyond the prescriptions of blood. Twice I knew, would put Thembi in a place between us. He would name her granted, given, bequeathed by a time before, by a history, if only a history started one cold night when men had come from the country neighbouring ours and shuffled her sobbing frame into Grandmother's warm kitchen. Twice would raise Thembi's arms and drape them across me and tell her to tell me to let go and cry. He would be a father, at a little distance from the moment. A hardening, self-contained figure, looking away into the distance perhaps, to measure as men do, the egress of the day, the sum of its success, even if today's success was only Thembi and I flung together. Twice would place himself a little away from me. He would not be a brother. My brother was in a box of wood in front of us, though in our language we could and did anoint others brother, who were not of the same blood, by their comfort, their resilience, by their fortitude at all times. Twice would be something stood stalwart like a sentry at the extremes of all that I could truly care for. He would close the circle around me and let few inside, Puso and Grandmother and Thembi and her child and in time, gradually, softly, Puso's wife and his children. He would not be my brother. I would not anoint him brother. Not yet. Not until he had told me where he had been and what had happened to him. Not until my senses had thrilled at his accounting of the places and people and the events that had been his world. And even through this accounting, I would not anoint him until he had shifted Thembi a little and placed me at the centre of the circle of his world. But no. If through that accounting, he could only find a place for me at some diagonal, bottom corner, I would still, hard pressed though I would be, anoint him, because even there, in those corners, certain memories are kept.

Nine

IT WAS DONE now. All done. The service had ended and we had made our way up the road, past the leaning shops, to the graveyard. No one had crouched to the ground as our procession passed as they used to do in the old days. Indeed it was not a still time by the grave because on the back of a deceitful wind, the singing of three neighbouring funeral gatherings had competed with ours, interspersed by the sounds of a nearby business-as-usual shebeen.

We nevertheless put Puso in the ground and stood, Miriam and her children and Thembi and her daughter and I, at the edge of the hole in the ground. One by one we all threw handfuls of earth onto his coffin. After us, a queue of men formed, who reached one by one for shovels and spades to fill the hole. I saw Twice somewhere along its length.

No one crouched down either as we made our way back home in little communions. Briefly, people might have held their breaths or a conversation, but that was all.

It was all done then. Except to wash away the odour of death in buckets of water at the entrance of the house and eat the meal prepared yesterday by the women at the pots. And then, finally to walk about the yard, to meet this or the other relative, this or the other of Puso's friends and colleagues, until accused by their eyes, I had made to the front room where Puso's body had lain. The room was full of old people all bent under blankets and dim behind thick glasses and cataracts and claiming their privilege of hardy chairs instead of the frail benches outside; of food on proper plates instead of on the hired plastic plates still with the congealed fat of the last burial; of the front of house with its fading photographs of Grandmother and her husband, its roof, a poor shelter against the rough elements outside and perhaps against time, gathered too soon, soon come to claim them. I bowed my head to greet them and escaped to the kitchen and then to the room I had once shared with Puso that was now Thembi's daughter's. I could not stay there either and ran away again, into the sun at the back of the house. Thembi's daughter's small things, her black school dress and angry white shirt hung like the proud flag of achievement against a wall, her shoes lined up like soldiers, her sewn-together doll staring at me from the bottom of the bunk I had shared with Puso – all these things shouted at me as if I were on consecrated ground, as if I were violating a sacred sanctuary, and I stumbled out into the sun.

Outside, a squat of men sat on benches and crates against the outbuildings at the back of the yard. I went over and found a place amongst them. Behind the outbuildings, the pine trees stood taller than I remembered but as cool as they had ever been. The sand at our feet was perfectly fine. Pine trees are jealous and do not let too much happen beneath them. They will, however, allow men to plot or to steal single moments of solitude, away from the sun.

The men were my brother's friends and colleagues. At the edges of their circle were others from our village hanging about to share the beer that was being passed around. Someone handed me a bottle, prefacing the act with a murmured statement about how well we had worked, how well the funeral had gone. Another told a brief joke and that was all right, because now was the time for anecdotes to reconnect us to the real world, to wash away our distemper, to help us laugh a little. The priest's heavy work was done. The work of putting one into the earth was done. The yarn would return us to our everyday language; let us reclaim our bodies so that we could loosen the muscles of our buttocks and let our pants hang as usual.

The men gossiped lightly. I sat uncomfortably amongst them. I did not understand their jokes or their references to names and places and people and events, but smiled nevertheless.

The beer was almost finished. I called a boy rummaging around the fires of coal that barely glowed in the glare of the light and gave him money for more beer, a small act to introduce myself, to establish myself amongst these men.

Twice appeared around the corner of the house. He saw our huddle under the trees and made towards us, his face tightened by the company of women and children and old people at the front of the house, I thought. It loosened a little as he saw me. I got up to go to him. I could not look into his face. He reached up his arms and held me for a moment and I was enveloped by the rich odour of his clothes, out of place in this yard with its smoke, its odour of rubbish thrown in a hole in the corner and the flat, sweet smell of the pine trees carried to us by a sudden gust of wind.

I eased myself from his arms, a little shocked at the strength of his embrace. He was an older Twice, still thin like a rope but with the growing weight of impending middle age. He hid his teeth that used to fall out of his mouth and cause him to stutter, out of self-consciousness, I thought. Across his cheek, from his ear lobe to his chin was a dark welt that must have been an injury. He saw me staring at it and smiled. His teeth spilt out of his mouth like so many captives and rushed against each other and I smiled in return, certain he would still speak twice.

I became conscious of the men with the beer looking at us and turned to lead him to them. We would drink beer I thought, as an act to mark this moment, amongst other men, who might at other times have been our friends, our colleagues, or the husbands of our sisters.

The boy sent for beer came through the break in the now grown hedge through which Twice and I used to make our way to Abuti Jefti's house. A man took the bottles from him and proceeded to open them with his teeth. Twice grimaced involuntarily and I grinned at the thought of his teeth rushing back into his mouth in fear.

He reached for one of the bottles and tipped it, spilling a spit of froth onto the ground. It was an act we had both learned at Abuti Jefti's, a libation to the ancestors. The men murmured in approval and some of them tipped their bottles to the ground too.

We were joined then, Twice and I, to this band of men come together to bury my brother. I introduced him and he went around shaking their hands and repeating their names. A long friend I said, who had also known Puso. We sat down and sucked at our bottles. The stories came again and we laughed, Twice and I, without really knowing why. In between, we stole looks at each other as if to stalk each other's history. Neither of us said anything. We were some part of this community of men but not sufficiently to participate in the banter at hand.

His beer finished and without a warning, Twice stood up. "I want, I want Molefe to take me somewhere. I want to see, to see Abuti Jefti. Does, does, does" not twice but three times, "does he still live over there?" he asked no one in particular, pointing to the back of the yard.

"Yes he does," said a man from our village crouched on his hutches and playing with an empty bottle on the sand.

I rushed a brief thank you to the men before we made our way, with Twice walking ahead of me through the gap in the hedge.

"Let me fetch the children," I said to Twice. "Puso's and Thembi's. Wait for me here."

I found them hanging about the stoep of the house, Puso's children, Palesa and Tsepo, and Thandeka, Thembi's daughter. They didn't resist as I gathered them in my arms. "Let's go for a walk," I said.

"We have to ask our mother," Tsepo said, talking on his sister's behalf and easing himself out of my embrace. "I have to ask my mother," interjected Thandeka, to be the same as her friends. They rushed inside the house.

At the front of the house, work was already beginning on dismantling the tent. The youths in the t-shirts were carrying the chairs out and lining them against the drive that led to the front gate. Men from the village were pulling out the stakes that held the tent to the ground. Other men and women, who by their apparel were Puso's friends and colleagues, stood in little gangs at the edges of the work and stepped aside to let pass women from our township carrying plates and empty bowls. And, in between them, children twisted and ran about.

Though it didn't seem so, there was an order to the work at hand. There was an unspoken assignment of tasks, as tasks had been assigned in preparation for the funeral. Men with resources, with vans, reversed them up the drive, so that the chairs could be loaded on them and the tent, once it had been folded. The vans would also carry away the hired plates and pots and knives and forks. The van-owners' wives oversaw the cleaning up, taking particular care of the plates of china and the knives and forks and spoons that all had to be returned.

The men and women from our township, generally less well resourced than those come from outside, gave their labour. It was they who were gathered to lower the tent, whilst their wives washed the pots and plates and stole and hid little packets of food left behind.

Inside the gloom of the house the old people sat behind their blankets and thick glasses and spat phlegm into bits of cloth. Theirs was simply to bless the proceedings by their presence.

The children tripped out of the house. A moment later, Miriam emerged. She looked worn and tired. Her sleeves were rolled up and I surmised she too had been working somewhere around this house.

She didn't look me in the eyes. "Where are you taking the children?" she asked.

"We're just going for a walk. To an old friend. His house is at the back."

"You won't be long, will you?" she asked, looking at me, as if I might take them away forever.

I assured her we would not. "Just to get some air," I said.

Just then a gust of wind blew across the yard and bowled over a man holding up a corner of the tent. We all chuckled as he fell.

"Plenty of air here," she said. I sniggered again and stepped off the stoep. The children followed, still laughing at the man making a joke of himself in getting up. The other men shouted at him, "Get up old fool. You're drunk. Let's finish this work here."

We went to the back of the yard, past the fires and to the men still drinking beer and motioned Twice to follow us. "Are we going to Abuti Jefti's house?" Thandeka asked, leading us to the gap in the hedge.

I was a little surprised she knew him, then remembered that despite its rapid growth over the years and despite the electricity and running water and the antennas hung like flag poles on the roofs of most houses now, this was still a small village where everybody knew each other.

"Mother does not allow me to visit him," she mumbled, her hand held across her mouth and her eyes widened as if talking of the village bogeyman. Perhaps Abuti Jefti was now the village bogeyman, an irascible old man who threw stones and threatened to bewitch the children when they entered his garden to steal peaches.

Thandeka whispered into the ears of the other two. They turned towards me, their hands also clasped against their mouths.

"My thoughts exactly," I said to myself, but made my way along the path. The children followed at a cautious distance.

We bent low to get through the gap, but not low enough, for on the other side, I had to reach for Twice's head to dust leaves off it. His hair was permed and I stole my hand into my pocket to rub away the grease on it. He did not notice this.

"Not, not much has changed has it?" he asked as we continued on our way. Tall leaves of maize scratched around us and some small animal scurried between the vegetables growing in the yard, between the orange pumpkins and the cabbages with their huge ears and the other plants that I could not immediately recognise. Probably carrots and potatoes, I thought as my mind took me back to Grandmother's instructions those many years ago to weed her fertile garden or to bring in a cabbage for the evening meal. I remembered too that, sheltered from the dust at the back or side of every house in this township, there were gardens with rich soils and trees to give shade at midday and in some of them, neat, hand-dug irrigation channels for the flow of water. And amidst them trees that blossomed in white or pink each spring and if well pruned, sprouted juicy yellow peaches which all too often, were simply left to fall to the ground, so abundant were they. Or vines like houses, perfect for stealing a radio into to waste away a hot Saturday afternoon, though their fruit was never sweet.

We burst out of the garden into the clearing of Abuti Jefti's house. It was much as I remembered it. To the side of the yard was the tree we used to sit under to listen to his stories. A scrawny black dog lying beside the tree lifted its head, coughed an indifferent bark and then dropped its head to its paws. At the centre of the yard, a few pitch-black chickens scratched at the ground.

The door to the house was open. I knocked tentatively and a woman emerged. It was the same fussy woman who used to castigate Abuti Jefti for his profligacy, who would sometimes chase Twice and me away. On Thandeka's cue, the children rushed and clung to me. It was not Abuti Jefti who was the bogey; it was this woman, dark and bent and the image of a woman who might very well be a witch.

"Who do you want here?" She had a cloth in one hand and held the other in a fist against her hip.

"Is, is Abuti Jefti here? We are from the funeral, funeral next door. I am Twice," he continued, "and, and this, this is Molefe. We have, have, have just buried his brother."

The woman motioned us into the dark of the house. She was wearing a faded brown seshoeshoe and on her head was a carelessly tied headscarf. The hair at her nape was completely grey. She left us in the front room from where we could hear her saying to Abuti Jefti that he had visitors.

The room was much as I remembered it. The bookshelf was taller and held many more books than I remembered. Dusty records lay piled against the shelves. On the ground were twisted wooden carvings of twisted bodies with grotesque faces and arms bound in loops of chains. Against the walls were hung mud-coloured and dull kente wall hangings, interspersed by fading posters in black and white of African writers and politicians, various dark men in military kepis and buboes and other lighter men, from the North of the continent, with shining black hair and headscarves. Some of the faces had been disfigured with a thick black pen, the probable outcomes of Abuti Jefti's rage, or perhaps a more considered reflection that these faces could not hang above him in his room. On a table below the faces was a pile of student scripts, some similarly marked by an angry pen. Abuti Jefti had remained a teacher all these years.

I peeked at the script on top of the pile. At the top, in barely legible writing was written, "What would you do if you were Prime Minister for a day?" I was about to lift up a script when Abuti Jefti burst into the room.

"What do you want with those papers?" he demanded, rushing to take the script from my hand. He hadn't looked at us. "They're not very good anyway. I should fail them all, stupid kids," he continued. Then he stopped, the pile of homework in his hands and looked at us as if he was noticing us for the first time.

"Ah. The boy from next door. And you. Twice. I wondered if either of you would come around. I didn't know if you saw me." He bent down to squeeze the papers into a bag under the table.

He straightened and looked about us, Twice and I and the kids hanging back at the door to the room.

"Come, let's go outside. Its too small in here," he said pointing about the room almost apologetically.

We squeezed ourselves out of the room into the light of Abuti Jefti's back yard. He called back to the woman in the house, "these are my friends. These are my friends, Twice, the boy who ran away and the boy from next door," he hesitated, squinting at me to remember my name.

"I am Molefe," I said. He had forgotten my name. He dropped his arm, which was pointed at me.

"Yes, Molefe, 'Lefe. You went away. I was at the funeral,"

he continued. "Didn't you see me? I saw you. You were sitting at the front with your brother's wife, yes? The white woman. And with this girl's mother," he said pointing at Thandeka.

Thandeka put her hands to her mouth and twisted her legs around each other in that amazing way that only children can do. A small village indeed, if Abuti Jefti knew Thandeka was Thembi's daughter, despite that she had probably never come into this yard, except perhaps to steal fruit from the garden. I didn't think Abuti Jefti ever ventured into our yard.

"Come, let's sit down and talk. You children," he reached into the pocket of his trousers, "run along and get you fathers here some beer."

More beer; any excuse for beer; the heat, the cold, the coming together of friends, their parting; even the simple act of coming home. Beer for an occasion such as the birth of a child, or a death, such as my brother's, when people first heard he had died and had come together to hear how it had happened and what was to be done. And different types of beer, as everywhere. Cheap beer for those with shallow pockets, brewed for income by women in smoky huts with tall, variously coloured flags to announce their distinctive, individually named fare: Morara of the grape; Hoposo; Pineapple – thickened with brown bread and sugar; the potent Thothotho – brewed with toxic additives – the acid from a car battery, or turpentine or an emulsifier, or whatever other chemical was at hand; Takonyesa – enough to make you shit yourself; Skipa se ntekane – thrash you so that you can't take off your skipper to go to sleep; Dintja di'nchebile – would make you paranoid to the point that you think dogs are looking at you. And countless other brands, advertised by word-of-mouth or through the demonstrated effect of ribald merriment around a hut. And beer produced by state monopoly and promoted on billboards at the taxi rank, fronted by hard-working men in vests and bulging muscles at the end of the day, or by men like my brother, in bright red ties and suits and with laughing women with long, flowing hair, in a place of tall buildings and the lights of many cars.

The best job you could ever get in a country such as ours, whether as a labourer, or technician or manager, is at the brewery. Demand is guaranteed and supply is never to fail, so that even at a time of drought, water is made available for the huge stainless steel vats that bubble at the centre of the pristine and well-guarded factory.

But then, people drink beer everywhere, if they can. They drink it in large quantity in the place from where I have come, in a ritualised, publicly managed way, though alcohol was always available if you knew where to get it. They must have drunk it in the places where Twice has been, though he is still to tell me of their rituals there, their customs and salutes, the songs they sang when they were exalted.

Twice and I sat down on the bench as we had always done, before he had gone away. Abuti Jefti stood above us. "My boys are back. I knew you would be back. The two of you. And I missed you. I had few friends after you left."

Abuti Jefti's woman came out of the house and watching us from the corner of her eye, made to draw water at the tap in the yard.

"Hardly anyone, though your auntie here never left me. She is quiet now, but you will see, she'll soon become the woman you remember."

Abuti Jefti was clearly convinced our memories of this woman were indelible. I remembered her of course, though she had been a vague and barely visible figure those times I had narrowed my eyes to visualise this place and this man who had given me my first beer and who had sat me down to tell me stories I could not have heard anywhere else. If Abuti Jefti thought we remembered her, then he had remembered us, Twice and myself. For him, memory, like affection or endearment, or even their opposite, was reciprocal. If I see you, you see me. If in the garden on a blazing afternoon, I think back to you, to our times together, to the stories we told each other, surely somewhere, sometime, you must think of me.

And she did become the woman we remembered. The children were back, each with a beer in their hands.

"You've started again, haven't you," she shouted at him from across the yard. "Beer again, with these friends of yours, though we don't have any money."

I wondered then if she remembered us or if we were just more of his friends come to waste their meagre resources under the tree. But Abuti Jefti had said that Twice and I were the only ones who had come to see him. He ignored the woman as he always had. She disappeared into the shadows of the house.

"The only reason you are back, the both of you, is for the funeral. It must have been good where you were." He pointed at me. "You went to school didn't you? So, tell me, what did you learn over there? What did they teach you?"

I was startled. I thought Abuti Jefti would ask me when I had arrived and if I was staying next door. I thought he would offer conventional words of sympathy – how young my brother was; what a waste his death was; but how we are all in the queue for dying, so that there was nothing for it but to take sympathy and move on.

"Tell us then. Tell us, what did you do?" he continued impatiently, between wiping the froth of the beer from his lips.

I started to tell him about the institution I had attended, a venerable place he would have heard about. I started telling him where it was located and about other famous institutions with which it shared its street, as if to locate it and by extension, locate myself within that esteemed space. I continued to tell him about my professors, repeating the names of those famous on account of their not infrequent, expert council on world radio, beamed from the place where I had been.

Abuti Jefti did not respond. He wasn't interested. He wanted to hear other stories that would describe what had become of me. He wanted to know if I was still the same person who had left seven years ago. But what was I seven years ago? Who was I, seven years ago, beyond an upstart a few years out of short pants? Then, my knowledge was limited to my experiences of this village, this town and the poor roads that led to other, even more isolated villages in this country. Everything else I knew was second-hand, borrowed from patches of conversation between wiser others, or from lessons at school, or books that even then had become good friends, or from the radio that used to screech at us from the windowsill in Grandmother's kitchen. I had a pitiable memory of myself and could not now reconstruct it to isolate those things about myself that might have held meaning for Abuti Jefti.

Despite his stammer, Twice had been the articulate one. I had been the one to run off to get more beer or to disappear into the house to turn a record, whilst they, Abuti Jefti and Twice, twisted the meaning of words and the world at each other. I had been the one Abuti Jefti would damn for being from this place of his, of their – his and Twice's – exile. I had been the dumb one. I had never had answers to his questions, nor had I ever been able to spur him on, to rouse him to sit upright and explain again, with more clarity, a point about a chain of events or about an imagined future.

So, I would be the dumb one again, so that we could carry on where we had left off. I would let Twice re-double and lead our new discussion. I would interject sometimes, to locate my life within the genealogy of the events of his inevitably harsher, more certainly defined life. But I would wait for appropriate cues and tender my silence for his telling of the bitter places he had been, the torn-down people he had known, or a more sanguine rendition of the years that had passed.

"Where I was, the natives were not like that," to which we would laugh at conjured images of tribesmen in the place of the low sun where he had been. Or "How did you survive? It must have been difficult," to make him our hero again.

I was always still the leg – most deeply sunken into the embers of a fire – of the black, three-legged-pot of the type they had used to prepare the food for Puso's funeral.

"I got this scar the day I left here." To bring us to the beginning. "I, I was here for about a, a, a week after I last saw you," he continued. "I, I couldn't see you. It was too dangerous. I did pass the house a few, times, times, times, though." He teeth danced to his stutter.

"After, after the raid. We, we all ran about like wounded dogs. We didn't know where to go. I, I went at night to the places we used to meet to smoke, smoke, behind, the school. I surprised the others there and they hit me and hurt me with a stone. They broke my jaw."

They had all been frightened for their lives and had hit out against everything they didn't know.

"I wanted, I wanted to come back here," he continued, looking at me. "But, but I didn't want you to get in trouble. They, they were going to all the places we stayed to see if any of us had remained behind."

"So where did you go boy?" asked Abuti Jefti.

The children were trying to invent a game of the weakly, yelping dog. It ran behind them then lost the point and made out of the yard, with them following after it. The woman reappeared from the house with a stool in her arm and sat down beside us.

Twice stuttered his story. He told us of much travelling about, by aeroplane to cold, cold countries, where from the air, the throw of countless lakes glistening in between dark forests against a silver sun, intimated the end of the world. He told us about his poor diet of bread, potatoes, fish, pork and a harsh opaque liquor that flowed like oil and burnt like fire, but served to warm him until he was blind and comatose against the cold – a cold that splintered your bones and froze your marrow, he said. He had trained as an engineer, but also in guns and surveillance, he explained.

He told us of long dusty trips on the backs of trucks into the rural hearts of hot, swampy countries at the centre of this continent. Later, he had spent time at a single cabin at a beach in a tropical country and together with a woman he was with, he had learnt of the bounty of the sea. I knew they had made love in all the months they had stayed there like two castaways.

"What happened to her?" I asked.

"I don't know," he replied. He looked at the ground and was silent for a moment. "Something better to drink, yes?" He reached into his pocket for money and calling the children sent them off to get us more.

He described the efficiency of fishing in ponds with hand grenades and what the flesh of hippo tasted like. He laughed as he described how a wild boar, "a pig with bull bars" he said, had chased him one day, on and on until one of the others ran beside it and shot it.

He was slow and double stuttered when he told us how one amongst them had gone mad and started shooting in the air, then put the gun to his head and killed himself. His body was thrown into a pit and left to be eaten by wild animals, to serve as an example to all the others. The man must have been some kind of friend.

He told us of others who had died and their names even, though these were their names for the war. He told how men had come at night and caught them by surprise and killed many of them. He had survived because he was in the toilet, in the pit latrine at the end of the camp at the time of the attack.

"Did they also call you Twice?" I asked, curious to know how he had named himself.

"No. And, and, no one calls me Twice anymore." He was telling us to call him by his real name. He had outgrown the name we had given him those years ago, which had been useful then for his purposes as a refugee.

"What is your real name then?" I asked, realising for the first time that I had never asked him before.

Abuti Jefti laughed. "Who is she and what is she to you?" he hummed the words of a song. "Look what these times have done to us. We all have seventeen names and forget how to call each other. But it's alright because we are all here again." He stood up. "There were times when I wanted to talk about you, to find out about you. And I only knew you as Twice, the boy with the bad teeth," he laughed again. "Thembi couldn't tell me anything. We would meet sometimes and talk. She did tell me about you though," he continued pointing down at me.

He turned towards Twice. "So what is your real name then, or is that still a secret?"

He laughed as he made his way to the house to get glasses for the vodka and ice the children had brought from the shop. "Bloody drink. It's too hot here for this stuff. Pure poison, I tell you. You'll stop drinking this stuff soon enough. The war is over my boy. You can tell us your name now."

Twice poured the remains of his beer on the ground. He lifted his fresh glass and sucked at the liquor and ice. "What does my name matter? Call, call me as you always have."

Twice never told us his real name. Neither did he ever tell us his nom de guerre. His eyes had shifted from side to side and he had sought to turn the talking by asking me to recount the places I had been to. It was as if he was frightened of who he had become, as if he wanted to keep the deeper meaning of his years in the bush secret from us. His existence had after all, been nothing but flat stones skipped across a hold of turbulent waters. He had offered us only the bare outlines of his life since he had left this country, but they were enough to suggest more profound truths, more robust moments of fear and salvation.

Twice had not traipsed around the world. He had been thrown about it. He had been hurled from one hidden corner to another, in un-straight lines. He had been cut by the sharpness of his flight. He had different names now. Three names; the first, a given name of then low import, but now crucially important if we – he, Thembi, Abuti Jefti and I and countless others I was yet to meet – were to finally, truly arrive at home at the end of this war; his second, a name we had given him on account of his stutter and stuck to him it seemed, forever; and his third, perhaps a similarly elusive name, or more likely, to keep him hidden, a name to draw him as someone dangerous, a clever one who approaches his enemies from the side, who eats their bloody hearts and shits in their dead, open mouths.

Was I to be afraid of him, this man come back from the wars? Was I to walk carefully about him and to make sure never to come up behind him? Was I to always announce my entry in his space by knocking at a door, or by clearing my throat against the air in lieu of a hard surface? Was it for me to always defer to him, to follow and not lead him into a room, to agree to his plan for the moment, to view his view of things seen and heard and felt? And even if his name for the war had been an ordinary name to make him other from who he was, was I to defer to him because he had been in the wars and seen horrors his mumblings here under the trees could not shape or describe? Did horror empower him beyond its primal lessons and leave me simply to wonder in astonishment and marvelling at the survival of it?

He wouldn't tell us his names, at least not then. I knew I would be disappointed by his real name. It would be a common name, of the type given to their sons by women like I had seen in the photograph he had shown me years ago. His name would probably be the direct translation into English, to render it pronounceable – to paint him from black to white – of a name in the vernacular chosen to mark a signal occurrence at the time of his birth: a riot, or death, because death is common and doesn't require much imagination, or the vaguely understood doings of a celebrated individual, a statesman or sportsman or an adventurer, whose name and picture had graced newspapers during the heady eighth or ninth month of his mother's pregnancy. As if the boy in his mother's stomach could ever one day circle the earth in a Sputnik or an Apollo, or discover a fall of water, or more modestly, open an institution of learning for those previously without.

In not telling us his names, it was as if Twice was frightened we would need to re-learn him, to re-know him as someone other than the person we had known. It was as if he was sanctifying this place, this village and the present company and our time together those years ago, as if the intervening years had been an accident and that the normal and correct course was the course we had then been on and now might continue.

He didn't tell us how he had come back to his home in the country neighbouring ours at the end of the war. Perhaps he had found no one there that he knew. Perhaps they were all dead or moved away by poverty or the state, or by marriage.

Possibly someone had known him, an old man come blinking out of his house with a newspaper in his hand, or a madman standing at the edge of the enquiry into the whereabouts of the family that used to occupy the house.

'The neighbours might have said, "There was a girl, an Ausie. She was the last one of the family here. She left to go somewhere one day. Yes, with her daughter. She had a daughter."

And then perhaps a brief dispute amongst the neighbours as to whether the girl had one or two children. "The child was as old as this one here," another might have intoned, twisting a crying child off her back. "She doesn't cry all the time," she might have continued, by way of apology.

Another neighbour might have added, "She wasn't married though. She left the people now in the house to look after her things. She never came back. You should ask them," a weighted them, "where she went."

The only one in the house, a girl with breasts sprouting through a worn t-shirt, who kept her eyes to the ground; a good girl who would never tell a lie, unable to say what had become of Twice's sister, who promised to tell that the brother of the woman who used to live here had come. He would come again, she would tell them.

And other people in the other places who had known him but saw little opportunity in knowing him once again. Or who traipsed behind him, promising everything, the best places to go for a drink, the cosy dotage of marriage-passed women who would be more than happy to cook for someone such as he, hot curries in exchange for fumbled moments of comfort, or a car if he needed one, a not too expensive, legal one.

Twice would probably have gone also to their informal places of re-encampment, the places where they called him by his war name, where he and his comrades drank away their history and schemed their futures, some more loudly, more effusively, and more financially liquid than others. He would, despite songs of despair amongst many of them at a reality that compromised their images of the future, have found many things. He had after all, come here with some of the tangible attributes of his so-far success; the well-groomed woman he had left behind in the house separated from us by a well-tended garden, the large car that had brought him here, the odour of talc still lingering on his face.

"We, we, we will remake this place." Twice was talking about his country, the country neighbouring ours. "We are at our own, own year zero. Everything is possible. Not everything exactly, but most, most things, now that this thing is done and we are free, free, free men at last."

Abuti Jefti laughed. "Year zero: Almost a good term. But I wouldn't use it myself. It's got a bit of stink to it." He wrinkled his nose as if to highlight the point. "And anyway, there is nothing zero about the present, because things will continue as they have always done. Yes, changes here and there, but otherwise, everything remains the same. And anyway, we've had many year zeros before."

He continued, "I for one won't be leaving here or changing my name," he giggled, "though I do hope to come and see you in the country neighbouring ours to see how you will do."

"No Abuti Jefti," Twice rejoined. "This is a year, year, year zero for most of us. Things will not continue as they were. You can remain here and as you, you say, keep your name, but for us, everything is possible. I have not told you the half of what happened to us out there. But you know why, why it happened and why, why, why therefore everything is possible. Otherwise these scars on my face and the scars I couldn't show you would be for nothing. Whatever you, you, you may think, we know what we want and how to get it. It's all actually very simple and it won't come about by our simply, simply sitting and talking in places like, like, like this."

He had pointed about the yard. Abuti Jefti winced and clenched his mouth.

"No offence Abuti Jefti. I don't mean this, this yard specifically. Only other yards or places like this where all that has happened is a bitter talking and harking back to a past. It's, it's, it's easy to hurl insult and we shouldn't stop from doing so. But our people deserve more. I deserve more."

"Look at 'Lefe here," he pointed at me. "Come back because his brother died. Look at the clothes on the bugger," he continued. They stared at me, Twice and Abuti Jefti, and the children, who sensing an intensity beyond anything their games could conjure, had gravitated close to us.

"I, I, I used to wear worse clothes than these. Donated things. Shoes, shoes, you wouldn't know which was, was, was the left one, which, which was the right. But, but now look at my clothes." He lifted the sleeve of his jacket that he had draped across his knees to show us a label, which would normally have been removed, or so I thought.

"This shirt cost me..." I couldn't do the conversion, but knew it had cost a lot of money. That was the point after all.

His hand was firmly tugging at his shirt. "Just as our people deserve more, I, I also deserve better. You see unlike you 'Lefe, I had no choices, no, no chances. I could have remained in my country and lived, lived a short brutal life like everyone else I knew. Where are they now? I, I, I couldn't find them there. Those that I did are bums, drunk, drunk or homeless fools or just stupid thugs who think their shitty, shitty stolen cars, their, their added-on houses, their menial, menial jobs, their girlfriends who cheat, cheat on them anyway, are what it's all about. They're all dying anyway. AIDS. Many of us have it. Many of us from the war. I've, I've seen men, falling apart and shitting in their beds, too weak to even cry that they are dying. It gets women more easily though. Some were my friends, friends, but I was never sorry for them. Cheating death is what it's, it's about. Until death gets you. I've been too, too, too close to death not, not to know that."

He sucked at his glass to replenish himself. "I knew death even before, before I went to fight. Look, I, I was never shot, or caught, caught or tortured. But my friends were. I can sing you songs we sung for, for those who died."

He started singing. A low repeating song, in a language from the country neighbouring ours, whose meaning I would have made even if he had not told us. He got up and first started swaying, then lifted his feet and gently stomped them to the ground to the rhythm of his song. He sang for us and danced and was for that time, transferred from where we were to the places he was telling us of, to the people he had known, some dead, some simply returned and disappeared into the dangerous rush of homecoming, some on television even, standing in disciplined lines like boys in a choir. Self-conscious and aware that we were judging him by his dance, he had curbed its inherent exuberance. He had intimated how with others, feet must have crashed harder into the ground in a stalwart rhythm, voices must have been raised louder, more urgently, as if to stamp out the life of a devil resident somewhere between the ground and the sky. With others, his singing and dancing must have served as an alter for communion, for breaking bread and drinking blood, for shielding death from the living and putting those passed away amongst them to forever rest.

One of the children began to dance beside him. He stopped suddenly, and looking at the dust of his dance, wiped his brow and sat down.

"We will remake this place," he said, breathing heavily from the exertion. "We, my comrades and I will build this country for ourselves and our people. We, we will not let anything get in our way, though, though we are not stupid and know when to advance, when, when to retreat. And in the end," he was silent for a moment and stared into the ground, "in, in the end, we will be free. And, and proud," as if as an afterthought.

In dancing, Twice had revealed himself more than he had in telling us of the places he had been. He had intimated at a militia in community by its purpose, by its losses, its many years waiting listlessly in the shade for the order to take freedom, which encompassed all their reasons for being there. The tempered precision of his dance undid his stutter and described the places he had been like photographs. His dance revealed all the things he had learnt out there, in the bush and in all the other places he had been, and demonstrated the depth of his certainty with which he would draft a way to mould the future, like the simple moulding of clay to make little cattle as we used to do when we were young.

I was distraught. Privately.

Twice's confessional was enslaved. It had the ardency of the aggrieved and the conviction of men who possessed only hope. It was imprisoned by itself. It left no hope for dialogue. It allowed for no other view. It dismissed my outlook – to the extent I had revealed it – the outcomes of my pitiful, self-indulgent experiences, my ambivalence, my uncertainty, my isolation here, despite the comfort of the breeze and my warmed marrow. It shrugged off the comfort of our gathering and the power of my brother's death that had brought us here. Twice had come here from a war.

Abuti Jefti had his hand over his mouth. His eyes trawled the ground.

"You know, the children where I teach make themselves into little gangs," said Abuti Jefti, breaking the momentary silence. "The boys separate themselves from the girls and the older ones from the younger ones. It's normal. It's normal for people stuck together for whatever reason to make gangs and to make songs and ways of dressing and other rituals to make themselves different from others."

He continued, "There is a group of boys at school who wear one sock up and one down and I am forever after them to lift them. There's also an after-school habit of another group to wear their ties on their backs."

I didn't understanding what his had to do with Twice.

"The point is, and please don't get me wrong, we all have rituals and can all dance when called to. For me, that's not enough. After all, how many times have men in uniform marched from one place to another, to meet other men and kill each other? It has no end. For me, that is not enough. All that does is to make endless year zeros. I mean, how many places have you been Twice, where the streets have dates – July this or September that Street – all after some year zero? I have been to a few. Most were built as big avenues, but now they're lined with corrugated-iron shacks with raw sewage spilling out of them and jammed with horrible traffic, donkeys and dead dogs.

He laughed. "At least that's better than the streets named after our dead leaders. You can imagine them turning in the graves at the thought of their legacies. After all, after a few years, only the old people remember who they are. The rest know these streets as places where you can get mugged or stuck in traffic for hours."

I didn't get his point.

"The point is," he continued, "men will be fighters and will go to places like the places you have been and fight and die for God knows what. And for a while things will be different and the victors will enjoy the spoils of victory. They'll write new laws, make speeches, open buildings, new roads into the interior," he laughed again, "and for a while most people will be happy.

"But," he continued, and I could see him as a schoolteacher prancing about at the front of his class, "that is not enough. There must be a better idea. There must be something to explain how we are to prevent all these endless year zeros; what it is we must do; what must be done. Otherwise it's all a waste of time."

"Look, it's not as if I want to say all you did was a whole heap of rubbish. It's not as if I am saying what you did, Twice, was a waste of time. I don't understand where you have been, so I can't judge it. If I do, please forgive me." He took a sip from his glass. "But the point is, wars have been fought on this continent. Many, many wars and many more will be fought in the future. And all that has happened, all that will happen is that for some people, for some time, things will be better."

"I am looking for something more lasting than that. Even though I have not done anything except teach my students, listen to my music and sit here with my woman, I don't see why I shouldn't be allowed to want something else." He turned to me suddenly. "You 'Lefe, you are the one who went to school. What have you learnt? What can you tell us? What's the latest theory to do away with the oppressor? Is there anything else for us to be than boy scouts in new uniforms?" he said laughing again.

Twice had been turning his head and shifting his legs as Abuti Jefti talked. He got up and went to lean against a tree. His mouth was tightly clenched and I knew that he was furious.

I had a headache. I was drunk I realised, and ready to do something else. Yet I wanted more, or something else, to push us off the edge of this difficult point where we had arrived. I wanted something to gently push us into a soft darkness, so that we could find each other in a less crude, less brutal way.

It was as if we had been fools all along. I, ensconced in that safe place where I had gone to study, remembered being apologetic about, or seeking to explain why it was what we were. We, defined as the widest assemblage of the past, current, future, wayward lineage of this thing called Africa. This Africa to which I had returned, embraced by a still yard with a gently blowing breeze and a setting sun, warming hearts, bone, marrow.

We had been bequeathed and had inherited a wide definition of this place – its geography and its music; its blinding colours and its diasporas; its despots and teleports to take one from here to there at the cough of an old lady and a wisp of smoke; its appeasement and coastlines and brutality; red eyes and children with shining, vaseline smeared legs; storms and never travelled beyond this village people; justice and falls of water; its poetry and tanks paraded on independence day; a man asleep under a tree; its pre-history – as if history could ever be before itself; its stadiums full of people to watch men in harsh colours chase a ball; its wars that fled people like Twice; its only yesterday put-together shanties and first ladies and blackouts; its thunderstorms; its victories and ear-to-the-ground wisdom; its pungent sexuality and massacres. And more. And more.

Apologetic for all of this and proud as well. Seeking causation; what sin committed where, by whom had led us to this point? "They do not understand," I would say to a friend from the continent at the end of a bitter interaction with a group of natives to our then temporarily adopted land. And we could and will never find cause. To do so would be like scratching at the final centre of the universe for the first light.

"We must define ourselves for ourselves," my friends had said, "and stop looking to them to see ourselves; stop using them as a mirror to view ourselves and view ourselves by ourselves, against ourselves, since we have been defined. Massacres, yes, and wisdom and teleports and drought, and their ensuing therefores. Define ourselves for ourselves. We are our own destiny."

We, ourselves, however encumbered, however named.

Twice's reading of "we" was patently different from the one I had become accustomed to. It was a less diasporic, a more enclosed, a more exclusive fellowship of we. It had posted invisible yet evident sentinels at its edges to let in a few and keep out, define out the rest on account of a perspective learnt by rote, the lessons of a time spent together, a paranoia that would not allow a seeking at the unknown.

Twice could name the beginning of things. He could conjure a storm in some easterly place as the cause of a fall of rock in the south. The wind blew and a bird's egg fell to the ground close by us. The dog swallowed it up and chomped its jaws. A girl was raped. "The price of oil will go up," he would conclude with a perfect confidence.

My brother has died and here I was, thrown seven years back to continue where I, where we, separately and together had left off. Except now, Abuti Jefti lives waiting to die, Twice is the inheritor and I have no comfort.

"And your brother?" Twice asked to get us away from ourselves.

Abuti Jefti lifted his finger to me, "Your brother is with your ancestors now. Where we will all go."

Twice spluttered and held his hand in front of his mouth.

"Ancestors? What ancestors? You see, these are the things that hold us back. When they're alive, they abuse each other, murder, swear, cheat. They beat, beat, beat their children and steal. They're as evil a bunch as we are. And yet, yet, as soon as they die, we make them ancestors and want them to mediate on our behalf."

He continued, "No offence, but I wouldn't want any of my relatives, my father or mother or any one else to stand in for me, to talk on my behalf. What is it about death that it can suddenly change a bunch of fools into something else, despite, despite their lives?

"And how do we talk, talk, talk to them? And if we can, are they there, thousands, thousands of them kneeling before God and pleading on our behalf?" He snickered. "They're anyway probably busy enough pleading for themselves to have, have any time for us, the bastards."

I imagined what he was describing. Thousands of the dead, dressed in orange, or naked and kneeling before a white man with a white beard at the centre of a white light, wailing and pleading, whilst the white man scratched his beard in the boredom of eternity.

"There would be nothing to it then," he continued, "than to make libation from time to time and then everything would be alright." He tipped his bottle and spilt some beer to the ground.

We were silent for a moment as we watched it colour the sand. Abuti Jefti suddenly got up. He unzipped his fly and walked away from us.

"No. Piss, piss won't do it Abuti Jefti. Pissing is for marking turf." He laughed and got up to join Abuti Jefti at the back of the house.

Spill some beer to the ground. Drink my dead brother. Drink

this spirit for me. Not this manufactured, quality controlled, advertised, distributed spirit, this alcohol with nothing of me except that I have drunk of it. Drink a more genuine beer made of fire to boil water, of a harvested sorghum, yeast and sugar bought in little sachets from the trading store, and time to test the mettle of all our purpose. A white flag hung outside a dirty spill of huts calls neighbours and itinerants. A plastic to hold the profit, between her expansive bosoms, between the heaving, sweating breasts of the woman with a flag outside her huts. A plastic to hold the profit.

Ten

I SHOULDN'T WRESTLE so much. These binds on my wrists.

We're going up a hill. The road is steep but smooth. It can only be the road to the north. All the other tarmac roads go south, except the few in town and one or two others.

Blood in my mouth from when they took me. I should swallow, shouldn't spit. They must think I'm unconscious. Jump when they stop. It's a good thing it's night. They won't see me if I run, or throw myself off a cliff. I would be all right off a cliff. I'd roll for a while, then something would catch me and then I'd get away. I could do so now if I could get to the door.

Miriam will wonder why I haven't called. I normally call the kids every day to ask them about their day. I'm supposed to take them out tomorrow. I've never failed to do so. My side of the bargain. Then she leaves me alone. Most of the time, except when they're ill or unhappy. Find all the house crying or contagious with fever.

Who are these people? I don't have enemies who would do this to me. I am not a political man. I don't have businesses anyone would want to destroy.

It could only be Jonas. He could do something like this. I shouldn't have blown his story. Should have left things to continue as usual. Made myself a hero for nothing.

All for nothing. Got nothing out of it and Jonas wasn't fired or anything. Moved sideways. He gets in the way all the time now. Covers himself by saying he has nothing against me, that in different divisions as we are, all he is doing is looking after the interests of the organisation. Makes himself as unfairly treated, though everyone can see through him.

The truck is still going uphill. This must be the road to the north.

Downhill now. There should be a village coming up, if this

is the road to the north. What's it called? It has a police station at the edge of the road.

Get up now. Push my legs. Get my elbow to the handle. Push. Shout. At the top of my voice.

God, I sound pitiful.

A hard pain at the back of my head. I am almost unconscious. They have hit me with a gun. I sway like a bag at the bottom of truck.

I must breathe, just breathe, make the pain go away, steady myself.

We must have gone past the village now. The truck is going uphill again.

It must be the same guy who hit me in the face. I thought he was also just leaving the pub. Approached and greeted me. Thought he wanted a lift or light for his cigarette or something. Hit me suddenly hard in the face. The next thing, I'm in this bloody truck. Sounds like a Land Rover. Maybe they are army people, though other people have Land Rovers.

Sometimes Miriam almost makes the kids sick on purpose. To get me to the house. Or she makes up all those stories she is so good at telling about how my daughter lies, or how my son has been truant from school.

I can see when she is about to clench her face and fall into a blubber of spit and tears. Does it in front of the children. The whole point, I suppose, so that they can see her crying and blame me. Never does it when we are alone. They crowd around her and say, "Don't cry mummy," and I feel like a shit. Then they clam up and look at me with tears in their eyes. I should simply stop going, but then she'd have that over me. I should get someone else to bring them over when it's my turn. Safer that way, though I wonder who I'd ask.

They could be army people sent by Jonas. He could do something like this. And paid enough, army people would do anything, the bloody uncouth animals. You'd think that with all their training, army people wouldn't do something like this. But they're the worst. Bunch of mercenaries who would do anything for a little money. Jonas can't be paying them very much for whatever it is they're doing. Doesn't have that much.

Tried to get me fired. Wanted my job. I can understand why. I get much more than he does. But he didn't understand I don't get my money from the government anymore. With the privatisation I'm paid through foreign funding. Without the minister's approval, who would anyway need the foreigners' consent, there was no way I was going to get fired. And they wouldn't want that would they? The foreigners I mean. I was married to one of them after all.

When I raise my head, I can see outside. It's a beautiful night.

The man above and beside me is leaning forward to talk to the two in the front. Something about petrol.

Maybe they'll stop soon. I should be prepared.

I wonder what Molefe would say. 'Lefe my brother, on the other side of the world.

I should write, or call at least. Find out when he's coming home. Every time I ever went overseas I tried to route my flights to spend my time where he was, but strangely never could.

He doesn't write much. Must be having a good time of it. He'll come soon though. His scholarships long expired as that bloody Jonas is always ready to remind me. Told me they wouldn't extend it, would stop whatever stipend they were still sending him. The money isn't theirs to start and stop as they wish. It's foreign money. This place is run by foreign money. And anyway, 'Lefe won his scholarship fair and square. Look, it didn't hurt that I was able to put in a word for him. But he got it and was accepted to study and that's it.

The car is stopping. The driver's hooting.

There are cows on the road. I can hear their cowbells and smell their sweat. Maybe a herd boy will come. It is the northern road. There are many cattle posts along it. Many herd boys. Maybe one of them will come to move his cows. I should push the door and jump.

What are they going to do with me? All the way out here? What do they want with me? Hope it is Jonas behind all of this. It'll be something important to tell Miriam. I won't immediately spill everything out when she asks about my swollen lip. I'll make as if it's nothing, downplay it, make as if things like this happen here all the time, that she shouldn't get distressed. I know she'll insist I tell her everything. She'll want to put ointment on my lips and lean hard against me I know, hoping I would get aroused and want to make up and repair things between us. I'll lean back a little. Not so much that she could ever claim I had done so, but enough to raise her hopes. That way she'll do what I want her to do. If I ask her and I will, once I know these are Jonas people, she will talk to her people, who would talk to the minister. I don't know how far I would want her to push things. Maybe just enough to get him fired.

Lift my elbows behind my back. Turn a little. Get my hands to the handle. Pull. Pull again. Push the door.

The wind in my face. The musky smell of the cows.

The door is open. Jump now. Jump and run. Run for my life. A herd of cows will save my life.

Fall in between them. I get up and struggle through them. My hands bound behind me make it difficult to stand upright. I have to run up the mountain. The cliff drop is on the other side of the truck. The cows break apart and lift their heads. I bound for the scrub.

It hurts to run. The stones and thorns catch and throw me.

It is a beautiful night. I can see the moon hanging like a spilt bowl in the sky. There's a belt of countless stars from this horizon to the other.

Small animals scurry away at my feet. Behind me, the men are shouting to get through the herd of cows that have saved my life. They have made a kraal around the men and lowered their horns to let me get away.

I wonder what Molefe would think. He'd surely laugh at the absurdity of all of this. He'd laugh at how someone's cows had saved me from men intent on killing me. I know now that they want to kill me. If they didn't, they wouldn't have brought me all the way out here. 'Lefe would cackle in disbelief.

They're coming after me. They're getting closer.

Miriam would leave this place and go to her country. Maybe she'd meet 'Lefe. They'd probably get along and sit there and talk about me. Her side of the story.

I must write. Let him know how things really are here. How close I am to being where I want to be. Making something of myself, a name for myself in this country. I'll call him to come back so that he can join me. Plenty of opportunities for someone like him, especially with me as his brother. We can't let these others, Jonas and his type, take over. It'll be just like when we were young. 'Lefe and I, we never let anyone take over or tell us what to do.

I shouldn't have gone this way. I should have run the other way, across the road, down the cliff. They wouldn't have got me. The cows would have blocked them.

One of the men is upon me. I stop and wait for him to get close, then turn and fall on my back and lift my legs to trip him. He buckles over then gets up quickly and comes for me again. He throws himself against my chest. The other two arrive out of the darkness and put their knees to my chest. They swear at me and punch me and lift me by the shoulders. They drag me to the car.

Fresh blood again, in my mouth. At the edge of the road, the cows that almost saved me stand about and blink their large eyes.

They throw me in the back and this time, two of them sit above and on either side of me and kick at me and laugh and swear at me again. I do not know their voices.

Things weren't always easy. All right, all right, look, I never went without work. I never really had to scrimp or borrow to keep things going. But how many times did I have to bow to fools or obey some instruction from an ignorant superior, only in the job because of some family connection? How many times did I have to listen to my wife's friends, her friends from her country, when she invited them over for drinks? I hated the way they would wear rough jeans as if to hide their wealth. Obscene. As if poor people could ever come here from overseas. I hated the way she'd parade me like some exotic acquisition. Clever bunch, they were, all full of simple answers. They'd tell me to read this or that, or talk to one of their others. As if what is at stake, how things are here, how they should be is simple and just like in some other corrupt country where they claimed they "turned things around". And they'd talk slower when they addressed me, use simple words as if I was a moron or something. Miriam would try and lead me, help me to find words to answer, as if I needed her help. In the end, most times, I'd find an excuse to get away from them for a moment. I'd go to the kitchen to fetch something, or go to the children or to the garden to smoke.

The truck is moving faster now. They're excited and pass a bottle of alcohol amongst them. They're laughing and swearing. I wish I knew what is going to happen to me.

Maybe they've made a mistake and should have taken someone else. After all, it was dark in the car park when they took me. I'll sort things out as soon as we stop. I'll tell them who I am. I'll tell them that I'm not of their world of thieves and gangsters, though I'll be sure not to call them as much. I'll reassure them that though they've got the wrong man, I won't take things further.

Yes. Yes. I'll tell them I have a wife and children. I'll even tell them where I live so that they'll believe me. No, they are rough, rural people unfamiliar with the suburbs. I'll tell them about our old house in the township where I grew up with Molefe and Thandeka and Grandmother, remind them of its squat shebeens, its dusty streets, the bus stops along the main road along its centre and where they would alight to get to our house. I'll tell them that from our house, you can hear the Chief's dogs barking.

God. I hated they way they were so good at telling stories of other places and comparing them with things happenings here. As if to say what had happened in other places was sure to be repeated here. I hated their little acts of heroism, like the one woman who took in a child, only for the while she was here, she told us. I challenged her and asked what would happen to the child once she left. Or the way another one of them had organised theatre groups and such, to 'promote local culture' as she put it, though everybody knew she was only really after the young boys with their tight stomachs and eager smiles. And Miriam also, mother of my children. I detested the way she'd make me put my knife and fork together after I'd eaten, or make me put my hand in front of my mouth when I dug at my teeth with a match. Not a good example for the children she'd say, as if to say, she and not I were to be the example for the children.

The car stops. They open the doors and pull me out.

In front of us are three rude huts huddled like widows. A little way off are the rough stones of a cattle kraal. If the first cows didn't save me, maybe these will now.

They hurl me inside the first hut, slam the rude door and fasten it with a chain. They make for one of the other huts, leaving a sudden still silence behind them.

Of course things were good at the beginning. There had been something about Miriam's eagerness, the way she seemed to know exactly what she wanted, the way I was only one part of what she wanted, that used to excite me. Unlike the local girls, Miriam didn't need me for money or self-improvement. As soon as I had acquired my first car, local girls always wanted me to drive them home at weekends so that their parents would see me and invite me in for tea and scones. Or they'd ask me to drive them along the main road of our capital city busy with those who could shop, young civil servants and teachers, on Saturday mornings, and wave to the strangely numerous colleagues they suddenly seemed to have.

When we first met, Miriam had taken a long time to tell me about her family. She didn't ever say much about them. A few weeks before our wedding, an embarrassed affair with few of my relatives and none of hers, she told me her family did not approve. She had seemed excited and not disappointed at all by the fact. I had had the sense that as a black man from this part of the world, I was something of catch. It had something to do with the way she and her friends always spoke about how they were different from others from their countries and that how by marrying me, Miriam was proving her difference to the world.

Early in the morning, that's when they'll come for me. Isn't that what usually happens with these things? They'll come before the sun is up, before the boys have taken the cows to pasture.

Must get away. Before the sun comes. These ropes around my wrists, maybe I can cut them by scraping them against a sharp edge. I must find something. A stone, the lid of a pot, anything.

They've chained the doors.

No matter. First things first. First to loosen my hands. Then to find a way out. I could go through the thatch. They didn't search me. I have a lighter in my pocket. Burn myself out of here. But, no, they'd quickly smelling the burning thatch and drag me out or stop me getting out. That would be something, burning myself to death in this stupid hut.

I could shout, but there would be no point to that either. Whatever it is they want, whoever they are, they wouldn't let me go. Though a voice carries easily across these mountains, no one would hear me, or if they did, no one would come. Or else they would have put something against my mouth.

I'm thirsty. Wish they'd given me water or something to drink. And untied me to let me drink.

No matter. No matter. Once I'm out of here, I'll get something on the way home. I will hide out until a government or other vehicle passes by. Get the driver to stop somewhere, get a cold beer and make a quick call to say I'm all right. Apologise to Miriam for not coming for the kids. Talk to a friend to find out who these people are, what this has all been about.

A sound outside. Someone has opened a door. Be quiet. Be still. Must be one of them going to blind a lizard.

No, they're all outside. They're going to the other hut, opening the door, talking to someone inside.

How many men? Three? Four? They're coming here.

Close my eyes. Push saliva into my cheeks. Make as if I'm unconscious. Whatever it is they want, they'll want me awake and responsive to their demands, their questions.

I'll tell them I don't know anything. Who took the money, who spilt the beans, whatever they want to know. Tell them this is no way to do things. They don't have to act like a bunch of barbarians to sort out what can only be a small problem, if there is a problem at all. I'm not such a big man after all. I know many things, yes, but there are also many things that I do not know.

They'll understand and set me free. They'll probably even apologise and offer me food, before whoever is in charge, the person from the other hut, orders them to take me back home, back to my car.

They're at the door, unravelling the chain. On my elbows. No, lie back. Just in case this is something I still have to understand.

Be still my brother, be still.

Eleven

MY BROTHER'S SON follows his mother about their house. To the kitchen, to the bedroom, to some other rooms and back to the front where we sit, Twice and his wife, Thembi, Miriam's neighbour Ipuseng and I. The other children are outside scolding each other at a game on the stoep. Miriam finds reasons to exit and re-enter the room.

Her friend Ipuseng talks easily to us, about the frustrations of her job as if we are long acquaintances. She asks Twice's wife about herself, who answers hurriedly in a fluent, accented voice. Twice must have been attracted to her by her ease at conversation. She glances at him frequently for approval.

Miriam re-enters the room and sits down. She cracks her knuckles. "When are you leaving then?" she asks. "I thought you would stay a few more days." The right thing to say.

"No. I have to be back at work tomorrow," Twice says.

"We are trying to set up our place," his wife says. "It's not big or anything, but things are so expensive. I mean, we both work, but Twice's job doesn't pay very much and we have debts, what with the car, the new place and things. We had to dip into my small savings for money to come here."

She continues quickly, "I know how difficult it will be for you to pack everything away to leave. But what can you do? Twice also had to come home after such a long time away, and with his line of work," she giggles, "it hasn't been easy."

Twice turns to his wife with a frown. He says something to her in their language, which I make out to be a reprimand. We sit about in an uneasy silence.

"I've decided we're not going after all," Miriam says suddenly said, as if a decision just arrived at. "Though the children would get used to things at home, they would hate it at first and why should I put them through that?"

A person's home is always where they are born, I thought.

"For the past seven years, this place has been my home," she continued as if refuting me, "and I don't see why anything should change."

A silence hangs in the air and we stare at our shoes.

As if to break the weight of the silence, she continues, "I'm lucky 'Lefe is here. You'll get Puso's things for me, won't you?" she says, her emboldened eyes turned towards me. "I don't think I'll be able to go over there and I don't know if anybody there will bring his things back," she says bitterly.

"How do things work here? What should I do, or is it up to that woman to bring his things? I want his things," she ends, almost hysterically.

She was declaring her claim to Puso and to the purpose of her life here, despite everything that had, happened. "You will go, won't you 'Lefe?"

"Yes, I'll go," I answered. "I'll go with Ipuseng."

Ipuseng and I would go. We'd fetch and throw his things in the spare room, his shirts and ties and underwear on the bed, his shoes on the floor, his bills, letters and postcards, work papers, photo albums, pens, briefcases into plastic bags.

That done, we'd select what to discard, what to keep, and in doing so, know a little more of his private, less visible life. His thoughts scrawled hurriedly across writing pads, his friends bunched together in old black and white photographs, his tendency to hoard tiepins and badges, rubber bands, paper clips, playing cards of naked women, stopped watches. His books, old textbooks and more recent how-to management manuals and professional magazines. His old records, which I would laugh to look at, remembering how he might have danced to them.

But what value to give to his officiously underlined notes, to his photographs populated by unknown men and women, to his pins and cheap cufflinks? His rumpled clothes to a charity, yes, though his good shirts and suits, they would stay until it was decided what to do with them.

Miriam would have to decide, although all anguished, she would probably take herself away and tell us to get rid of them. Ipuseng and I would conspire and keep some of them. We would surreptitiously stack his records with the others in the front room of the house and hide his photos and other things in plastics at the top of a cupboard. Miriam would come around, we would reckon, get beyond her grief and recall their value, if not for their pragmatic day-to-day use, then as sentinels to her memory of him. Their interrupted life.

Puso's death, much more than that. Much more than an inconvenient interruption of the rhythms of their lives. Even though for some time now they hadn't lived as a family, there must have been expectations that things would one day be repaired and continue as they had. They would surely have had in mind a return to daily patterns, washing and feeding the children in the morning and dropping them off at school, the occasional lunch together at a restaurant in town, evening meals, the soft weekend pleasures of friends around a braai in the garden, more ribald later, once the sun had gone down.

And their other more intimate connections, interrupted by Puso's serious indiscretion, but saved and packed away for their continuance, once he had returned; the rituals of going to bed, of reaching to each other, of naming, in their secret, unspoken language, their sometimes angry, sometimes remembered, but more often disconnected, functional coupling. Their memories of earlier more urgent times, sparked by a person collided into on the streets, or perhaps a song on the radio; their mutual recognition of the language of their bodies, their frowns and sighs against the weight of the days; their banter, in between the children, during lighter, shared moments.

I could imagine what their life had been. There was enough evidence around me to suggest it. I began to understand then that Puso had revolted against the pledges he had made to Miriam and the children. The costs of his promises to be constant and unwavering, to be engaged and engaging and by so doing, to be content, had become unbearable. His immersion into the world had been uncomplicated and of easy reward. He had a good job, money and the status accompanying it, opportunities for occasional travel overseas and through his wife, connections to an alternative network of people. At home, his shirts were perfectly ironed. His meals were brought to him by one of a succession of replaceable domestics, whose names he never remembered. His house was comfortable, artfully furnished and well on the way to being fully paid up. When he returned home from work, his children would rush to him and dance around his car and ask what he had brought for them.

Yet all of this had become insufficient. He glowed to his children's delight at his homecoming, though with less enthusiasm than when they were infants. They tended to hang back a little now and to be less demanding of his attention. His wife's gossip about her colleagues or about her new work assignments didn't describe anything beyond themselves. He remained polite to her friends, who brought little to interest him, and would walk out after a few pleasantries. Even his own work, except for his management of its onward and upward mobility, didn't offer any new challenges. On the streets and in those places where he would meet with friends and colleagues after work, everything was repetitive and unchanging. Even the country's politics, a game of crude contestation over limited spoils, now came to bore him. Whereas before, whom he sided with determined his chances, now, as a disengaged, externally contracted technocrat, he was free of the unscripted patronage arrangements that made success possible.

Perhaps that was why Puso had taken a mistress. His infidelity had been almost accidental. He had offered a lift to a young woman late one night, who had invited him into her two rooms and then, quick to assess potential financial benefit, had offered herself, her open thighs gleaming in the yellow light of a paraffin lamp. Briefly washed, then home to a dark and sleeping house he had let himself in, whispered a quick excuse to Miriam and quietly whistled himself to sleep.

He had found it easy after that. At first, he returned to the woman with the two rooms with his wallet presciently loaded with bills, not for the sex, he had told himself, but to help with her rent due in a few days. But she had soon stopped exciting him. He wanted something more diverse, more fraught with tension and risk. He learnt that young woman students, finished with their evening studying for tests or exams, found it easy to ask for lifts of him, after which they would almost inevitably invite him into their rooms. Those who lived in little hired rooms were easier. They did not have to negotiate the watchman at the university campus to allow his car in. In any case, he didn't want his car to be seen too often on the campus. Too many people knew his number plates and would wonder why someone neither a parent of a student or engaged in academic work of any kind was so often there. He felt safer too, not having to turn his face away from some student who might know him, walking down the fluorescent-lit passages of their dormitories.

Then he had met the woman he was to move in with before he died. She had taunted him, called him an old man after young girls, buying his way to their favours. She had turned down all his advances, his suggestions of dinner, or afternoon drives to isolated lodges in the countryside. He had offered her small gifts, perfumes purchased on overseas trips, little blouses from the one or two boutiques in town, sealed envelopes of cash delivered to her office, to help with the bills at the end of the month.

A few months into his advances, she had suddenly called his office, desperate for a lift to her village, where her mother apparently lay supine in a state clinic. He had concocted a quick story for Miriam and with nothing other than money and the clothes on his back, he had collected her from her rooms at the outskirts of the town.

They were tense in the car. She had been distant. For much of the journey, her head was turned to look out of the window. She had responded briefly to his questions about her mother and declined offers of refreshment. Occasionally, when he was quiet or whistled to himself, she would speak, as if she had suddenly remembered the favour he was rendering.

Briefly, her face would light up as she talked about her home, the school she had first attended and then the convent where she had studied for her higher education. She would become almost inaudible as she described her sick mother, and her brother in the country neighbouring ours, to whom she would need to get an urgent message.

The countryside had been a refreshing break from the dust and dirt of the city. A late summer afternoon, the ochre burn of the sun bronzed the soil and deepened the green of the trees and grass at the side of the road. Men and women stood in casual clutches in front of the village shops and children ran about. Higher up, against the mountains that bordered the horizons, shepherds brought their sheep and cattle to kraal.

Puso had been surprised at the new houses and developments along the road. He hadn't been on the road in many months. Almost all the larger villages now boasted a police station, a bar splashed in the bright yellow and red colours of the leading brand of beer and a funeral parlour with stretched cars as hearses parked in front.

There was also considerably more traffic than he remembered. Police and army vehicles, taxis, buses and dilapidated sideways cars now raced dangerously along the narrow road. And as if to signal its treachery, half-decomposed dogs lay splattered along it at intervals to mark the beginning of each village.

The hospital, once they arrived, had been an unsettling place. A watchman at the gate had made a great noise that Puso should park his car at the relatively distant bays indicated for visitors, despite the many empty spaces by the entrance. "Typical white-man-says small mindedness of a petty official," he had fumed.

The waiting area smelt of a malodorous soup of disinfectant, medicine and body odour. The fading pale green walls and shining linoleum floors of the corridors echoed to the brisk tread of nurses and orderlies and the less confident walk of patients and their visitors. With no one at what served as the reception to direct them, they had cautiously entered the first ward they came across and had reeled back at the sight of heads of many AIDS patients lying in rows as if in a mass grave. Half the favour to transport the woman carried out, Puso had abandoned her and escaped to the bar of the single hotel in the town.

A few hours later, she came to him. They had a quiet meal in the restaurant, empty except for a few expatriates and their retinue. The woman told him her mother's condition would improve. She gently nodded her head when he informed her he had booked a room for them. It overlooked a sumptuously kept garden with a gurgling water feature with a pissing cherub as a centrepiece. Her ablutions done, the woman had asked him to turn off the light so she could undress. They had made love tentatively and when they were done, she turned her back to him. Much later, her soft sobbing awakened and then lulled him to sleep again.

Over the next month, they made three journeys to the hospital. In between, Puso would see her in the evenings after work and having eaten, they would talk briefly and then quietly make love. She would always cling to him afterwards as if to use his body as a shield against what he assumed to be her fear at the impending death of her mother.

He did not go to her mother's funeral, but made what he felt was a sizeable contribution towards its costs with money conveniently paid to him as back pay for leave accrued.

Her mourning period over, their trysts had continued as before. He began to spend nights at her place. Their coupling done, he found it increasingly difficult to break out of her soft, clinging arms or to turn his back to her moist, wide-open eyes, to dress and walk out into the cold, or the rain, or the accusations of the brilliant stars and make for his house.

Miriam at first accepted his excuses about work trips to outlying towns, but one day, frustrated at having to construct yet another lie, he had blurted out the truth and gathering a few clothes into a bag, he had rushed past her flailing tears into the night. A few days later, his wife at work and the children at school, he had stolen into the house to collect a few more belongings. Their domestic had turned her back to him and shrugged to his threats that he would turf her out if she did not stop being rude. "I am still the father of this house. I still pay your wages," though they both knew that his wife could as well afford them, "and I will be damned if a domestic will treat me like this in my own house." The tea she brought him was cold and overly sweetened.

Miriam had been wretched and tearful at their few meetings at home or at the back of half-empty restaurants in town. On each of these occasions he kept himself resolute and used the ruse of lighting a cigarette or going to the toilet to get away every time her quiet wailing became unbearable. At home, the children hung back from him and refused to take the little bribes he proffered. They refused to go with him when he came to collect them on Saturday afternoons.

He had hired an apartment for himself and the woman, the same upstairs flat he had occupied when he had first moved into town and he had mused at the possibility that a circle was closing, though what circle he couldn't imagine. He had bought modest furniture to compliment her meagre collection of second-hand chairs and cupboards and stocked the fridge with hams and yoghurts, cheeses and cold beers. He had given her money to purchase curtains, bedclothes, pots and pans and the other infrastructure of a home. At first, he had been dismayed by her choices. She had brought home garish coloured curtains and faux gold tissue boxes and lamp stands. She had sulked and refused to make love to him. He was polite about her next acquisition, a table of green glass with the wrinkled grey legs of a hippopotamus. They would be happy nevertheless, he thought.

In all the time since he had moved out of the house, Puso had never made any overtures to formalise his separation from his wife. He had simply discarded her and her children, though incompletely, because he did drop in, most often unannounced, to find the front room still and perfectly composed, the children held back despite the gifts in his hands and Miriam choking on her tears and her anger. He continued to pay the school fees, and his debits for the house remained unchanged. He had tried to explain to the children, but their large, uncomprehending eyes had rendered him dumb. He would take them out sometimes, to the park, to the single movie house at the centre of the town where he would ply them with chocolates and sticky drinks. He would take them to their friends' homes, where their parents didn't ask too many questions. But the way they would walk back to the house and the strained smiles on their tear-thrashed faces had been too much to bear. By the time he died, he had not seen them for over a month.

Despite that, despite his hunger for his children and for a truce with Miriam, he could not come to leave the woman, even though a few months into moving in with her, the soft shadows of the flesh behind her knees did not rouse him as it used to. His lust for her was dissipating. On her part, she was deeply inward looking when she woke, as if fermenting the tears that she would later offer him. But her tears failed to rouse him as they used to. Her mother now some time dead, he couldn't understand what she meant by her tears, nor could he be impassioned any longer by the power over her they had once given him. He was irritable in her presence. He mumbled in response to her stories and forgot her errands or the things she asked him to bring from the shops. At home and hidden behind a newspaper, he would pretend he didn't see the food she brought him. When she implored him to eat, he would shout at her that it was cold. He refused her money to buy yet another porcelain figurine to add to her collection. She would sulk. He would run out of the house.

Yet he could not come to leave her. He was kept by a mounting obstinacy to prove himself to himself, and to Miriam and all the limits to his chances she had come to represent. He needed proof of the rightness of his decision to leave Miriam and if such proof wasn't extant, then his was simply to wait for it. To have packed his bags and returned would have been with his tail between his legs. It would have rubbished his claims against all the opportunities that he felt were his to assail and conquer. To have gone back would have confirmed what he considered Miriam's and her friends' self-seeking vision for this place. He would have had to humble himself before them and listen once again to their stories of their success in redefining purposes, for that is what they had come here to do. He would have had to smash his own vision of what had been bequeathed and owed to him. He had remained with the woman, and in a strange way, finally saved himself from himself by dying.

Miriam, then, had buried a memory. She had buried the father of her children and a husband she no longer knew. She had put to earth bones like rediscovered bones exhumed from a pit and recognisable only by a wisp of cloth hanging from a muddied femur. She had had the dubious satisfaction that comes in confirming, "These are the remains of the loved one who was taken and was lost," but had been confronted with a doubting silence to the question, "Was he was thinking of me, did he remember us?"

Twice got up from his chair and motioned for his wife to do the same.

"We had better be on our way. I imagine the border will be a mess, what with the time of month." I remembered arriving in this town and the choke of migrant labourers at the border.

"We, we, we'll come back. See what we can do to help," Twice's wife interjected. She also stuttered sometimes, but I guessed consciously to empathise with her husband.

I couldn't imagine what they could do to help. I couldn't see her as a best friend to Miriam. And I suspected, that for Twice, his outward sympathy hid an inner, almost gleeful accusation that Miriam had brought this on herself.

"Yes, we'll be back," Twice said looking at me, as if implying he would be back for Thembi and me and for time with Abuti Jefti in his yard and not for this pale woman in whose house we were gathered.

I wondered if I would ever see him again or if events would conspire once again to disperse us. I would go to seek him out in the country neighbouring ours and would hope for board and lodgings whilst I made my way about. He was, after all, obligated to me. But perhaps I wouldn't find him and perhaps he wouldn't return and that maybe would be better. Too much and we would deface our memories of each other.

As we walked to their car, Twice apologised about his wife as if indicted by the way she was. He stuttered about the job he was returning to and enjoined me to pass his greetings to Abuti Jefti and to come sometime to the country neighbouring us, laughing and saying, "Then you'll see, see, see what we will do," in memory of our talk in Abuti Jefti's yard.

One departure so soon after my return. I would go to the country neighbouring ours, for a visit, to see what they, Twice and his comrades, would make of the place. I would go for no other reason than that I wanted to be at a singular, vital point of history. I wanted to see the conscious remaking of a history and if chance allowed, participate in its remaking.

I was of age. I was able and free and unencumbered. I had no debts, or if I did, I could simply ignore whatever summons might make their way from over there to this place, to the shop, no doubt upgraded now, where we used to receive our mail, the shop where I had stolen the letter to Adelina informing her of a death, so many years ago.

I would go to turn into substance all the things that we, my friends and I, on scholarship or in exile, stranded and inconsequential in the fog of Europe, had talked about. I would go to jump into a rent in the fabric of history, into a crevasse that promised to break the hopelessness of an unending landscape of distress. I would stand as in a raging river with other men and arm in arm, feel the exhilaration of passing a covenant, hidden for centuries, across to the other side, to its rightful place. I would stand with other men, with a fashioned song to further the labour of building a monument to the places we were from, the places we would go.

Perhaps like so many others before me, I would go and become a migrant and send remittances back for Thembi and her child. I could also, like so many others, be swallowed up by the rough imperatives of an eked out life over there and simply disappear.

I would go also to escape the limits of this place, with Twice and his influence ahead of me to open opportunities for me. I would go to hear the stories that I was sure must always come at the end of a war. To be among people who were old friends or strangers and others emerged into the light, and come together to placate the past and invent a future. Perhaps I would learn from Twice and join arms with the others to do the little I could to remake that place, which would be to remake this place, separated, the two, only by a river, by the intensity of a war and little else.

I had only been a few days here in this place that is my home. Yet I knew already that I could survive here. I could work, reconnect to old friends and spend some time with Ipuseng. She seemed eager.

But I couldn't flourish in a place like this. My time of history had come. I was back from Europe and thrust into the light and dust of this place. I could keep on my shoulders the damp weight of Europe. I could carry its complacency, its finicky sensibilities, its spurious attention to detail enabled by a small sky, the angst of an introspection that only served to contain the oppression of order.

Or I could be arrogant, though that would quickly make me into someone like Abuti Jefti and trap me in an unmoving, unchanging, backward slanted, bitter outlook.

It would be all right for a while to walk about the streets. I would wear a hat low over my face to hide away from eyes squinted to recognise me. I would rediscover old, barely held together public taxis and quickly learn which to avoid for their music. Some blare the American country and western music so resonant of rural life, a woman's unfaithfulness the occasion for a punishing drought, or its discovery announcing a blanket of locusts that devastate a promising harvest. Some taxis shout the more optimistic if martial music of the migrant. Others play the new popular music that shocks the matrons in their scarves with their allusions to things that shouldn't be discussed in public. I would, returning to our township at the end of a pay-day Friday, quietly laugh at the debate between hurriedly drunk men and women of one of a number of rapidly growing messianic religious orders, about Jesus and his blood, or the trousers and short-skirt fashion of young girls prancing at the edges of the road. "They are asking for it," the men would say, pointing at such a one, her gleaming legs, her dancing buttocks, to which the women would agree, arguing for God's absolution as the only way.

It would also be all right to silently slip into a bar and sit besides publicly talking men and women and try to piece together the names and occurrences of current scandals. The girls who work the bars hide themselves and could be anybody's girlfriend, yet reveal themselves through their bloodshot eyes, their roughly painted, broken fingernails and scuffed shoes. Custodians of such places as they are, they would ask, "Who are you stranger?" and huddle up to me to get me to buy them a drink or caress my thigh to entice me.

Thembi away at work and her child at school, I could sit in the quiet of the yard at the front of our house and relearn the mountains on the far horizon and the way they change coats as the sun crosses the sky. Or listen to the sounds of animals – the scrawny black-feathered chickens foraging at my feet or the penned-in cows mooing to be milked. I could watch the white and mottled pigeons flying in formation from the roof of the shop that serves as our post office and remember how pigeons are a signal of prosperity.

I could make a fast friend of Abuti Jefti and walk through his fertile, whistling garden to drink beer at the end of the day and tell him about my years away. I knew I would go sometimes to the graveyard to read the names engraved across the falling down wooden crosses of the not so well off and the carved tombstones of the more affluent. I would imagine who they were, these grandparents and fathers and mothers born and dead a long time ago and their more recently deceased children, born in September 1968 or January 1970 and wonder if they were victim to the tubercular disease, here called a something in the chest, that was ravaging these parts. I would pass my brother's grave sideways.

And at night, I knew Thembi would shriek in delight at my stories about white men digging roads, or the lies I would make up about how their daughters always had time for me. The radio would be playing as it always had and Thembi and her daughter would show me the latest dance and laugh at my poor imitation.

I could travel deep into the mountains and, for a while, immerse myself in re-learning the bind of subsistence: planting, harvesting, the downward migration of cattle from the highest slopes as a bitter wind marks the onset of winter, rituals all, to mark the beginning and end of seasons and find there a stick-fighting companionship amongst exuberant, dancing men home for a while from the mines.

It could also be all right to find work. With my tenure in Europe, I could earn good pay with one of the foreign organisations so abundant in poor countries such as this. But their Frenchmen and Canadians and Americans and token other Africans would incense me by their knowing more about this place than I.

And all of these would be temporary diversions only. My brother's death had forced me here and in doing so had obliged me to more fundamentally reckon with my future. The children standing beside me, their broken mother inside and Twice too, with his wife and their well-defined future, required more of me than to simply observe. Observation I had done in Europe.

The engaged thing to do would be to avail myself to Miriam and her children, to divert them from themselves a little. I would help in every way I knew how, though Miriam would probably not want me to. She would not want me to so that I would not see her struggling at her now irrevocably confirmed status as a single parent. My helping would only confirm the reality of her life. It would make me an accomplice to Puso's dying and to all the things he did before he died; all the things he did that had left her on her own, that had left her crying bitterly at some deep point in the night. Helping her would be as if I were hurrying her anguish away, as if I was washing away my complicity in the tight knot of her bitter, wrung pain.

I would nevertheless come frequently to this house. I would approach Miriam sideways and ask her eyes what I should be. A brother? A weeping wall to throw stones at? Indebted and always crossing the street away from her, always sitting mute in a darkened room to her rapping on the door, always rushing to an urgent errand away from her questions, Puso's things, what of this country let him lie, why always electricity blackouts and why couldn't I, why wouldn't I do something about it?

And in time, despite Miriam, rituals would emerge and coalesce for the person I was to be in her house. As they would for the person I would become in the house on the other side of this town, where for a while at least, I would live with Thembi and her child and once again call it my home. I would become a bridge between the inherited first and more recently acquired second parts of the family they were to me. And though inherited, I would choose them both and come to walk the earth less alone, and make of them, without expectation, whatever would be. Because now, anything else would be too hard to bear.

Coming home has made me weary of myself. It has forced me to reckon with the fundamental differences yet copious similarities between Europe and this unforgiving place here in Africa. I am tired of the small, eyes-closed, finger-rubbing, contained consciousness that is my world that does not let me be free. I have had too much of myself. I have too often repeated possibilities to myself, too often chased myself around like a dog its tail. I am worn out. I want to move to things outside myself, sudden things, things behind my back, above me, planned things even, but without fear. I want to yearn without rancour for simple things. I want the comfort of everyday people, the consolation of days passed without too much despair, the succour of cool, sour milk and bread.

This place without too much ambition, yet desirous of every possibility, could finally make that possible, could finally free me from myself. It could make a friend of me, hold me, spur me a little, turn me as in a dance weeping people dance, then spark the elements to tickle me so that I can finally laugh a conclusion for the present and for other moments to come. Make a wet sapling of me, so that I would not break, but bend to every, to any, conspiracy, even though nothing is conspired. Things, time, the turn of the earth and the sun against it, the rush of deities and dead things through the air, nothing sits in council to plot against me, whilst they also do, to pit yesterday's outcome against current ambition, to make an intrigue of a company of men, to curdle and spill milk, to rush me to myself and to even more bitter memory of myself.

Who am I to be then? The real world. Cold Europe shouts at me from behind my back and though I have to try, I cannot ignore it. I will write to my friends over there to tell them of the end of the war and approaching possibilities; though, what could they understand of the end of wars, insulated and isolated from such things as they are?

Illiteracy is a sad matter;
Your letter is read by someone at the chimney.
You know what? He laughs in front of the letter owner.
He remarks, "As for your news, I understand it sir;
They report starvation,
Lack of clothing, corn worms in the fields over there."
Gentlemen, the hawk of the Maboloka cliff,
It prevents the little chicks (children) from foraging;
It swoops on them continually.

For this place, I make a rod to conduct lightning. It is proud and dallies with danger. Doesn't ask too many questions and would leave me alone. Would also remember me and would, I know, after I have prayed and lain on the ground and lifted things to my mouth to taste them, forgive me. It doesn't explain itself, or force itself, yet is very jealous. It points Puso's death at me, as a finger. Commands me to know Thembi and her child and orbit around them. For Puso's children, as for Miriam, it demands that I must be something they can approach, sideways at first and as if without intention.

Demands that I, too, should hold my eyes away and make as if I do not see them approach, so that they are not frightened by a thing in my eye, until they are upon me and snuggled under my armpits.

Twice? Twice will remain the question he always was. I will go to him though I am not convinced he will be an answer or be able to answer things for me. But then perhaps that is what he was always meant to be and for that I am grateful. Others, Abuti Jefti, Ipuseng, the woman with the staring black knees, old friends I needed to rediscover and know again? They would be rewards, though I wouldn't know if by accident or design.

And then? Nothing left except hope and prayer as action, as genuflection, as opening myself to whatever would come, so that finally I can walk amongst men, to be of them, asking nothing of them but bread, water, their time and company and the little comforts that anybody else would ask for, so that I can live this life I have been bequeathed.

Twelve

AN ALCHEMIST, an African man who lives in this world and in others, would tell you that salt is more potent than sweet root. That once drunk, the soup of a certain boiled leaf can thin the air so that dreams of dying are rushed to the front of the head. Mud almost as dense as stone and found at hidden quarries is layered with the etchings of time and can, once fired, reveal memory. It is given to cure insomniacs and liars, though unlike other things, it has no blood. Other herbs loosen the bowels and force out things put there by rivals, or provide relief from menstrual pains. Animals are dangerous. They contain poisons. But poison extracts poison and thus heals. The man would lay you down and put a creature on your back that will leave scratches that will forever flinch at being touched. Animals also conjure up beings, because every being lives with some crudely domesticated living thing that scurries about the edge of the way they see and serves to herald their coming or to scrape and brush away the evidence of their presence, once they are disappeared into the dark.

An ancestor entered a trance and saw his hidden companion. It is marked as scars across the forehead and cheeks of his sons and their sons and their sons, to the point of war and a great hunger at the calling of the totem. Blood courses through all things.

But for everyone, his own thing – smaller, always, than anything a clan would die for, yet persistent and crawling at the edge of a fire or under a favourite resting stone, or in the sky behind a rain cloud. A thing of dreams, so that a young child come across it for the first time, a night animal even, in the brazen light of day, would hurry to someone trusted to ask its name. Then make a song for it of words no one would understand, then fainter and fainter into the years, the words blurred by the language of men, the clamour of living, to the point of forgetting. Until it comes to you, suddenly and always and only at the point of your undoing.

If you were to ask the man of many worlds of the fires of a human life – heart, liver, kidney, bile – fear would light his eyes and he would turn away. He would turn back to explain, eventually, because a known thing cannot be hidden.

Wash in another man's blood and then take water, stone and sand to scrub the evidence of it off you, so that you can walk again amongst other men. And once amongst them, walk persuaded that because they look you longer in the eye, bend a little deeper when they make your company, canvass eagerly for your needs even when you have not asked, everything is assured. But fail to notice they are sniffing at you, testing your colour, measuring the space you occupy, even if they are not aware of what is they do.

You could, in the same way, seek to put away the evidence of other, less salacious deeds, but their intention, come alone and undiluted by softer, tested palliatives would find you fallen and dusty in the middle of the road though your feet are firm, your thighs robust; find you wailing against a public wall, and finally only just able to get away; find you unable to lift yourself from your bed, all alone and no one to call; find you with a thumping heart, bile scratching your throat, your stomach heaving and your brow furrowed at just going about your day and always, people always falling away from you.

The African man would remind you that despite these things, the sun can be returned. To a moment before the deed, so that it is burnt away and caused to never have occurred. The sun can put light to the shadows even of the cause of the deed, a rage, a tumbling as if down a steep slope, a beating desire that would have no satisfaction, so that even its roots are braised.

Magic it takes.

Not the magic acquired by men who would steal the fire of another's life, nor even the magic of other flowed blood, offered as a promise of another son to return and drunk by men and women in a line, one after the other. Blood is too common a thing, too familiar a thing for magic.

Reality is unknowable and beyond control. Music makes magic, chanting, dancing. Drums capture time so that it loses itself and twists before after and later before now. Drums also invite spirits. Dance makes for participation, dispels thought, bewitches feeling, and creates clear spaces. Chanting trances. To answer to these words spoken in a dream, "I am cold. I am thirsty. Share some tobacco with me," left all alone, the ancestor, demanding his due.

What would be the world with the sun returned? Would I find our parents at last and Puso beside them? Would they triangulate me, the three of them and put me at the centre? Or are there distances behind the membrane of death, Puso close by and our parents at an endless, still speeding distance to the original place of light? What could they do for me? Could they take away these aches in my bones, could they cure this pneumonia of my soul? Could they fan me cool air, pour me water, soften the ground beneath me, gently breathe into my mouth so that I can live again?

I want to see the world again, as if for the first time. Coming home has done that to me. It has made me wish for easy, simple things that would save my life. It has made me want to forget everything I know and learn everything again for the first time, to thrill again to everything like a child would; to lift things, stare at them to know them, put them to my mouth to taste them, throw them to the ground to hear the sound they make when they fall. I want to feel the heat of the sun and follow the warmth of the juices inside me. I want to lie on the ground and spread my body to the curve of the earth and feel it hurtle through space. To hear the sound of little crawling animals scratching through the grass. To listen to the wind wave the trees and spatter little specks of dust against surfaces. And far above, to see clouds as they shape and reshape themselves.

Thirteen

Tongue first. Fingers. A bloody, salty numbness in my
mouth. Cough. Swallow blood, my head in the vice of their
hands.

It is dawn now and on the far horizon is a hint of the first
promise of the sun. White specks of sheep make their way up
a mountain. In the valley below is a river with huts above it,
leaning as if to fall into it. Trails of smoke billow from beside
them.

A hand grabs my head in a grip of elbows. My arms are held
fast behind me. The man in front of me wields a knife, a
folding knife that men carry in their pockets and open to peel
a fruit, to slaughter a sheep, or to use in defence. It drips of
my blood. He raises it to my naked chest and stabs. It sinks
in, to the hilt. Blood courses down my stomach as if someone
else's. There is no pain except as he turns the blade to open my
chest. My eyes pulse. I feel to fall.

The man's eyes are bloodshot. His blood, and mine reflected
in them. A sliver of saliva hangs from his beard. He turns to
one of the other men and says something. Another man
standing hesitantly to the side approaches and lifts my head
by the throat. The first man leans into the blade and tears it
through the blood, to my stomach. A gas respires.

They drop my head. It slumps forward against my chest. A
hose of pink intestine hangs out of the rip in my stomach,
grey-green, slippery pink intestines.

I hear a whistle in the growing light and the chime of a
cowbell. Somewhere behind me, someone is with cows, taking
them out to pasture as every day. So near, but they can't see
me or hear the words of the men as they advise each other, or
hear my soundless screams against my dying. I am at the
perfectly sensate point between life and death. My prescience
is vital, my memory deliberate.

The man drops the knife and squeezes his hands into my chest. He reaches for my heart, a writhing, squirming thing, in a well of blood. He grasps it, then cuts at it. I see it raised and dripping above me as I fall.

More cowbells now but growing fainter as they make their way to a distant pasture. And further away, a truck belching its way up the road, up the road only a throw away from these huts. This day as any other day.

The losing light is an ochre-dulled darkness. The colour of old blood. Sound, a dissipating breath. Falling, round, a blown-off a tree leaf. Collapsing to the dirt, turned to clay and yielding further, to moss, then something softer still, so that I am finally the same as the earth.

At the bottom of the valley below me, men with horses and blankets turned a stone and returned the sun. But that was 'Lefe's dream and I do not belong in it.

Other Fiction Titles by Jacana

Ice in the Lungs - Gerald Kraak
Bitches' Brew - Fred Khumalo
Silent Minaret - Ishtiyaq Shukri
Song of the Atman - Ronnie Govender
Uselessly - Aryan Kaganof
Kitchen Casualties - Willemien de Villiers
The Dreamcloth - Joanne Fedler
In Tangier We Killed the Blue Parrot - Barbara Adair